COLD FURY

A COLD HARBOR NOVEL - BOOK THREE

SUSAN SLEEMAN

EDGE OF YOUR SEAT BOOKS, INC.

Published by Edge of Your Seat Books, Inc.

Contact the publisher at contact@edgeofyourseatbooks.com

Copyright © 2018 by Susan Sleeman

Cover copyright © 2018 by Susan Sleeman

1

"A killer's on the loose, and Maggie will be dead by then!" Jackson Lockhart didn't bother hiding his irritation as he looked up from the video to find his Blackwell Tactical teammates watching him instead of the footage.

The recording of the college lecture hall continued to run in the background, but Jackson had played it like a hundred times, and he was more interested in his team's take on the video. Or maybe their take on his outburst. That was more likely the reason for the skeptical looks.

"We have to think about our client's best interest here." Company owner Gage Blackwell planted his hands on the long conference room table. "No matter what you uncovered in this video, Martin hired us to find his son's killer, not to protect Maggie Turner."

"So, what you're saying is we leave Maggie to fend off this killer by herself?" Jackson's heart beat hard at the thought of the woman he once loved in danger. "How can you even think that when the video clearly shows her bumping into the killer? Now that this video is public, he has to know she can ID him. He'll want to take her out before she can. And you want to let her work that out on her own?"

Jackson took a breath and met his boss's gaze. "Unbelievable, Gage. Just unbelievable."

Gage came to his feet and stretched to his full height. Six two like Jackson, his boss glowered at him. As a former Navy SEAL, his intensity was always over the top, and the guy was downright intimidating, but Jackson wouldn't back down. Couldn't back down when it came to keeping Maggie safe.

"If you'd just listen," Gage said, his tone low and intense. "You'd know I didn't say that. I'd no more leave this woman to die than I would my own wife. All I'm saying is it's going to be tricky to find Scott's killer and protect Maggie at the same time. There's bound to be a conflict in your priorities."

Jackson sighed out his relief. Priorities. Right. That was Scott Dawson until an hour ago. He was strangled on his college campus in the last month, and his father Martin hired Blackwell Tactical to find the killer. The murder occurred in a lecture hall where Maggie taught anthropology. And now, the video showing she bumped into the killer on her way out of that classroom had become public. The camera didn't catch the killer's face, but Maggie looked him in the eye, and he could be gunning for her.

Jackson couldn't—wouldn't—leave her unprotected. Sure, they'd broken up six years ago under difficult circumstances. So what? He would always care for her, and she had to be his priority right now. Trouble was, his team was also counting on him to take charge on the job they were hired to do.

He would balance both aspects. He had no choice.

He drew back his shoulders, making sure he conveyed confidence. "You can count on me to do what Martin needs and protect Maggie at the same time. Won't be the first time

I've walked a tightrope on one of our investigations. I'll manage just fine."

"But it will be the first time you've done it when you're emotionally connected to one of the players." Cooper Ashcroft's dark brown, almost black eyes locked on Jackson, giving him a moment's pause. "And trust me. Gage and I both know how hard that's gonna be for you."

The pair shared a knowing look. Both men recently headed up investigations involving a woman in danger. Everything turned out just fine. Gage had since married Hannah, and Coop was engaged to Kiera.

Not that their situations related to Jackson's circumstances at all. This was different. Totally different. He and Maggie might've once been in love, but there was no way he'd wind up engaged or married to her. Even interested in her again. Not with the tragedy they'd suffered together. No way.

Like he said. He could handle it. "So, I have the green light to offer protection services to Maggie?"

"You're good to go." Gage ran a hand over dark hair, not as deep as Jackson's coloring, and Jackson preferred a shorter military cut. "But don't let your personal connection take over and make me sorry I'm not sending one of your teammates instead."

"Anyone have a problem with this plan?" Jackson surveyed the team, starting with Eryn Calloway who shook her head sending her jet-black ponytail swinging.

The only woman on the team, she was once a cyber security professional and agent with the FBI. She might only be five seven or so, but she was as fierce as the men. Still, it was obvious she was touched by his desire to warn Maggie.

He moved his focus one seat over to Riley Glenn.

"I'm good." He leaned back and placed his hands behind his head. His surfer blond hair and reddish beard gave him a more laid-back look than you'd expect from a former sniper for the Portland Police Bureau, but Jackson had worked alongside Riley long enough that it wasn't hard to imagine him perched behind a sniper rifle, target locked in.

"You wouldn't be my first choice, but let's see how it plays out," Alex Hamilton weighed in. As a former Recon Marine, he likely thought he could do a better job scouting out the situation at the college.

Shoot, everyone on the team probably thought the same thing. They all frequently believed they were the best person for the job. Jackson honestly didn't know how Gage kept their egos in check, but he did.

"Just don't screw it up," Coop added.

Jackson rolled his eyes but didn't respond.

"We're a go, then," Gage said. "Report in on a regular basis, and whatever you do, be mindful of Martin Dawson in every action."

Jackson nodded, his thoughts already going to the logistics of getting from Cold Harbor to Maggie's place in Ashland in the shortest possible time. "I'll need the helo. Who's gonna take me?"

He waited for Gage to veto the resource due to fuel cost, but Gage didn't say a word. He would do everything necessary to protect the innocent, and Jackson was just being touchy because this involved Maggie. He shouldn't have even questioned Gage's motivations.

Jackson glanced from Coop to Riley, both pilots, but Riley only recently received his license.

"I'm always glad for more air time." Riley lowered his arms and snapped his chair forward. "Plus, I have a buddy from the police force in Medford whose dad owns a nearby logging company. I'm sure he'll let us put down at their helipad and lend us a vehicle to make the short drive to Ashland."

"Then let's get after it." Jackson headed for the door and assumed Riley would follow.

Outside, he paused to wait for Riley to join him in the unusually steamy evening for the end of June. The ocean breeze whisked inland from the Pacific, cooling everything in its path, thankfully keeping the temps bearable today.

Riley lifted his hand to a gust of wind. "Gonna be a bumpy ride."

Jackson nodded, but he didn't care. He would take a helo up in a tornado if it got him to Maggie before the killer figured out she knew about him and came looking for her.

Jackson strode to the utility vehicle and climbed behind the wheel, his knee aching in protest as he folded his leg to settle inside. He'd taken a bullet to his right leg in his last skirmish as a Green Beret and was given the choice of riding a desk or leaving the army. Yeah, right, like he was desk-rider material. No way. He wouldn't choose desk duty any more than the rest of his teammates would. They'd all suffered on-the-job injuries. Some in the service. Some in law enforcement. All losing their chosen professions as a result. The loss united them all in a way nothing else could.

Jackson got the vehicle headed down a winding road lined with soaring pine trees, thankfulness for Gage's rescue from that desk job always at the top of his mind. After a serious injury to his arm, Gage was forced to leave the SEALs and had the brilliant idea to start Blackwell Tactical. The team was devoted to training law enforcement officers, investigating any manner of situations, and providing private protection services for people in distress.

Near the compound's property line, Riley pressed a

remote mounted on the visor to turn on in-ground lights circling the concrete helipad. The helo sat in the middle of the pad, a boot on each rotor tip strapping the helo down to an aluminum securing point sunk into the concrete.

Jackson shoved the gearshift into park and left the keys so one of his teammates could retrieve the vehicle while he was gone. He was jonesing to get into the air and get to Maggie before the killer did, but a preflight check was necessary to be sure they were safe. Wouldn't help Maggie in the least if they crashed along the way.

Still, Jackson could help speed things along. "Want me to remove the tie-down boots while you start the checklist?"

Riley nodded and got out of the vehicle. "Just be sure you don't manhandle the rotors."

"Me, manhandle something?" Jackson laughed.

His teammate knew him well. Shoot, all the guys on the team often used more force than necessary to get a job done. Eryn was the only one with any finesse.

Jackson strode to the first ring and squatted, his knee aching. The humid ocean air often made it hurt, but he'd do about anything to stay on this team, and that included enduring a little pain from living on the southern Oregon coast.

He released the first strap and stood to take off the boot and push the rotor up. He tried to imagine the moment he would walk into Maggie's life again. Maybe her home or even her summer school classroom. He saw her standing at the lecture podium, looking to the door and seeing him. Her face creasing in the same agony as the day they'd parted ways.

Pain gripped him like a charley horse that wouldn't release its hold. It'd been some time since this particular ache had taken him down, but even years later it felt the same. He could force the memories away, reason them away, work so hard there was no place for them to surface, but the pain still pushed its way up in unguarded moments and left him reeling.

Did Maggie feel the same way, or had the passing of time healed her wounds?

He had no way of knowing. Meant he couldn't tell her he was coming. She could refuse to see him, and he wouldn't be able to help her. Actually, odds were good that she would send him packing. After the tragedy that tore them apart, they'd agreed never to see each other again.

In the many years since that day, he kept his promise no matter how difficult it had been.

Surely, she would understand why he was breaking their agreement now and be willing to talk to him. Right?

Devastation stretched out in front of Maggie, and her tears weren't far from the surface. Stately homes now lay in smoldering ruins of rubble and ash in the once-majestic Oregon hillside. Gray skies hung above, dark and ominous like the ash that still drifted in from nearby fires.

She sighed. Rain was coming. That was good for the Middle Fork Fire still burning with a hazy glow in the distance. Not good for the recovery effort, but Maggie wouldn't let that stop her. Couldn't let it stop her. Families depended on her to identify their missing loved ones. She would work in rain, sleet, snow, hail, or you-name-it if she could bring them closure.

She shook her head at the utter and totally preventable destruction caused by teens setting off firecrackers in the Willamette National Forest. High winds took care of the rest, blowing the Middle Fork Fire into the Summit subdivision during early morning hours just a few short days ago. Firecrackers were illegal in the area, and even if they weren't, the teens must have known the spring was drier than normal, already putting forest fire season in full swing.

"Dr. Turner," a female voice came from behind.

Maggie dragged her focus from the disturbing scene and faced the young woman holding a microphone. Maggie was five nine and the woman stood taller, her bleached-blond hair styled to perfection. She introduced herself as Felicia Nutley, but Maggie needed no introduction. She recognized her as an up-and-coming local television reporter.

"How can I help you, Ms. Nutley?" Maggie asked.

"I was hoping you'd give me a minute for an interview."

"I don't know..." Maggie looked back at the search and rescue team hard at work gingerly sifting through the rubble. The sun was already drooping low in the sky, leaving her only three hours or so of daylight to complete her work. "The others are depending on me."

"It'll only take a minute," Felicia said. "Our small community is so devastated by the loss of life. I know the public will be relieved to hear that a forensic anthropologist has been called in to help with victim identity."

Would they? The fire burned extremely hot and fast, and the crew was no longer finding bodies, only bone fragments. The team poured debris by the shovelful through fine grates and sifted. They discarded anything that fell through into piles near the foundation of cordoned-off houses and carefully examined what remained.

Wouldn't it creep out the viewing public to learn the crew was only finding fragments? They probably wouldn't want to discover what her job actually was, taking over after the team finished the initial work. She was trained to distinguish a fragment of bone from rock or burnt clay, and it was her job to scrutinize any pieces remaining after the sifting. Still, maybe it would be a good idea to let folks know that she and the team were doing everything they could to recover the missing homeowners. She could leave out details of how that was happening.

Maggie faced the reporter. "I'll give you two minutes, but then I really need to get to work."

"Thank you." Felicia smiled and signaled for her cameraman to join them. "Just relax and look at Zeke when you talk."

Zeke, a scruffy-looking stocky guy, joined them and turned Maggie by the arm. "Light's better facing this way."

She nodded and took a long breath. She'd been digging through ruins for nearly twelve hours and must look a mess. Maybe just a quick hand through her hair to straighten it. No. No, she wasn't going to primp.

Felicia quickly fired questions at Maggie, and she answered them as succinctly as possible. At the two-minute mark, she excused herself to step behind the barricades and work her way over the ash-strewn street. Brick mailboxes and retaining walls stood at the sidewalk like sentries to former homes. Clay flowerpots once filled with blooming plants sat near metal patio furniture—the only reminders of the lifestyle in the vibrant neighborhood just a few days prior. Now the only colors amidst the gray ash were red flags, planted by dog handlers to mark where the dogs found human remains, and the brightly colored clothing of the search and rescue workers.

Tears pressed against Maggie's eyes again. So much destruction. Total and complete. And fifteen lives lost. Two men still missing.

Oh, God, why? she asked but really didn't expect an

answer. She'd been asking a similar question for six years without an explanation and didn't think she would get one now either.

She let her nails bite into her palms to stem her tears and continued down the street toward dog handler Parker Amburg, his dog Quasimodo on a leash. The black lab was covered in ash, but still seemed eager to work. Not Parker. No, this job was taking a toll on him. Thin, about five foot nine, his tan face held large splotches of ash, and his shoulders sagged.

He stopped in front of her with a resigned sigh. "We have another one."

"Another one, what?"

"Victim." His well-duh look told of his frustration. "In the shed out back of 5040. I just confirmed it."

5040? She shot a look down the street to a house three down from where she'd been working all day. "That can't be. No one was reported missing at 5040. The entire family is safe and secure on vacation in Florida."

"Well, I'm telling you, there's a victim there. Quasi doesn't make mistakes."

"He must have." She frowned. "Only two people were reported missing in the entire neighborhood. This would be number three."

"Like I said. Quasi doesn't make mistakes, and he was confirming a hit by another dog." Parker scrubbed a hand over a jaw covered in stubble. "I marked the location with flags. You do what you want with it."

"I'm sorry, Parker," she said sincerely. "I don't mean to call your expertise into question. Of course, I'll check it out. And I'll do it right now."

He nodded and turned toward the makeshift parking area for workers. Maggie doubted he was done for the day, but since Quasimodo just lighted on a victim, he would rotate out for another dog. This same dance had been going on from sunup until sundown for days now while they checked every home in the large neighborhood, not just the ones whose owners were reported missing.

She continued her course, the first few drops of rain hitting her face. By the time she reached 5040, a steady drizzle was falling. She was glad to see that the crew had already erected a canopy with light over the location to preserve the remains. She stopped to settle a particulate respirator over her mouth and nose and stepped off the road.

She worked her way through the rubble, her boots sure and solid when the ground underneath shifted. Passing by the house, a spiral staircase climbed eerily toward the dark sky. She would never forget the sights and smells of this recovery. Bad dreams haunted her for days now, but she wouldn't let that scare her off when desperate families needed her help.

She slogged through the debris to the back of the property, where ashen trees stood forlornly looking over the remains of what was once a storage shed. Near the red flags planted by Parker, she set her bag on the ground and snapped pictures of the area for documentation, taking long shots first and moving on to close-ups.

She stowed her phone and set to work, carefully excavating rubble. She found bases for a rake and shovels, the steel impervious to the hot fire, but their wooden handles were gone. Before long, she found her first bone, a femur. Hoping that she might have found an intact skeleton, she continued, carefully picking up and discarding debris from atop the bones. The work was painstakingly slow, but hours later, she reached the upper body covered with a large steel wheelbarrow, and she lifted it off.

Experts told her that this fire burned close to twenty-two hundred degrees, taking most everything in its path. But the melting point of carbon steel was over twenty-six hundred degrees, which is why metal structures remained intact.

As she settled the wheelbarrow out of her way, the sun disappeared below the horizon. Didn't matter. No way she'd quit before learning more about this body. But she needed to turn on the overhead light to continue working.

She stood and stretched up to click on the bulb. She took a moment to give her leg muscles a chance to recover from squatting and let her gaze roam the quiet site. Her fellow workers had all taken off. Not unusual. She worked late most nights by herself just to keep up with the demand for her skills. And standing there wasn't going to get it done.

She squatted again to brush away more debris, revealing a narrow, heart-shaped pelvis that told her she was looking at the remains of a male. One of the missing men? Neither of them lived at this address, but it was possible this guy came over here to get a hose or some other tool to try to stop the fire from spreading.

Eager to find leads on his identity, she moved up to the skull. The head was turned to the side, and she spotted a circular hole in the parietal bone in the rear. The wound beveled in, one of the most obvious responses of cranial bone to ballistics.

This man had been shot.

"No way." She sat back on her heels and stared.

Murdered. Someone murdered him. That was obvious by the location of the wound. He couldn't have shot himself in the back of the head.

She examined the front of the skull but didn't find an

exit wound. The slug was most likely still in the skull. Would make sense if the wound was caused by a handgun and small-caliber bullet. She quickly measured the entrance wound. Yeah. Small caliber. Most likely a handgun.

She glanced around, looking for the weapon, but found none. She wanted to do more. To look for the actual slug. But this was a crime scene now, and the medical examiner and county sheriff needed to take over.

Heart hammering, she hurried down the street toward the recovery truck lit by a hastily rigged streetlight so she could make the call and get additional equipment. She passed a burned-out car with melted aluminum rims running in rivulets down the street, the metal now solidified. Past the other homes, their foundations dark with eerie shadows.

At the truck, she pushed up the respirator and snapped off her latex gloves to dig out her phone.

"Nate," she said after the sheriff answered. "Dr. Turner here. I'm at Summit, and I found something you'll want to check out."

"What's that?"

She leaned against the truck and described her findings. "The circular hole along with the beveling in the skull is clear evidence of a gunshot wound. This man was murdered."

"Oh, man." He sighed out a long breath. "You're sure."

"Yes. The wound is a classic bullet wound, and he was shot in the back of the skull."

"Which is unlikely for a self-inflicted wound unless the guy rigged something up to hold the gun and pull the trigger."

"Right," she said, her mind racing to make sense of this

scene. "And odds are good that he didn't do that. Much easier to shoot himself in the mouth or temple."

"I'll get on the horn with the ME and get her out there. If you need to take off, I'll dispatch a deputy to protect the scene."

"I'm not going anywhere until we figure out if this guy is one of our missing men." She shook her head. "Imagine that. A murder in the middle of this terrible tragedy."

"You think you've seen everything in this job and then..." His voice fell off, but he didn't have to say more. After years of working forensic anthropology investigations, Maggie got it.

"Okay," Nate said. "I'm about thirty minutes out."

"I'll wait for you at the shed." She disconnected and stowed her phone. This was such a crazy turn of events, and it was likely going to be a long night. She should grab a bottle of water and protein bar from the cab before getting the equipment.

She rounded the truck and came up short.

A man stood in the dark, the moon barely outlining him.

Her heart seized with fear, and her arms went out in an automatic defensive posture.

"Hey, sorry. Didn't mean to scare you." The guy held up his hands and stepped out of the shadows, taking away a bit of the fear factor. He had an average round face, full beard, and glasses making him appear kind of scholarly...like one of her fellow assistant professors or one of the older students on campus. In fact, he seemed familiar somehow.

"Do I know you?" she asked, trying to get a good look at his face with shadows still hiding much of it.

He shook his head. "I just got off work and wanted to check on my house. My place is one of the few that survived."

He sounded legitimate and didn't look all that threatening, but still, she wished she had a weapon of some sort or was still on the phone with Nate.

"Which house is yours?" she asked, hoping to ferret out the truth.

He jerked a thumb over his shoulder. "Big blue one on the left about a half mile down. Wife put that ginormous concrete fountain out front. Can't miss it."

Maggie remembered the house and fountain he was describing.

"It's crazy how some houses escaped damage, isn't it?" he asked.

She nodded and started to relax. The fire didn't burn as hot in some areas, leaving entire homes in the subdivision without any damage. The destruction all depended on how the fire hopped from one location to another.

"Not that I'm gonna live here anytime soon." He frowned. "Not with the destruction all around. Still, I check on the place every day. Pick up a few more things. Never know about looters."

"I've been working here for days and haven't seen anyone who wasn't here to help."

"Good to know." He tilted his head. "You're working kind of late, aren't you?"

"There's much to be done."

"You're the anthropologist, right? Saw you on the early news tonight."

She nodded and hoped he didn't gush about her volunteer work the way others were doing. She was just a regular person whose skills allowed her to be of assistance in this dire time.

"Well, on behalf of myself and neighbors, thank you."

He smiled and erased all worry from her mind. "I'll let you get back to work."

She nodded. "Nice talking to you."

He took off down the street, and she headed for the cab to grab her water and bar, glancing over her shoulder along the way to make sure he kept going. He strolled down the middle of the barren street, the only safe place to walk at night—the best place even in broad daylight. She chugged some water, stowed the bottle and bar in her apron pocket, then went to the back of the truck. She unlocked it and climbed in.

The victim's teeth, though ashen gray—meaning they were extremely fragile—were intact and could be compared to dental x-rays of the missing men as a quick method of confirming his identity. She would use a handheld x-ray device for that. With only fragments left to recover, no one used it for days, and she suspected it was buried in one of the bins on the truck's shelves. She worked her way down the right side, pulling out containers, digging through each one until she reached the front of the vehicle.

She found the device in a lower bin. Finally. She pulled it out, and carefully set it on the floor. She stood to stretch, her lower back stiff from bending over ruins.

An arm came around her neck, jerking her back against a hard body.

She screamed.

Once. Twice. Loudly.

Then he cut off her air supply. Totally. Completely.

She strained to speak. Couldn't emit even a peep. Tried again. Failed.

She only had a minute—maybe less—to get free before blackness settled in.

Hurry! Hurry!

She clawed at the arm in long frantic gashes. His long sleeves prevented her from ripping into his skin. She reached up. Clutched a fistful of hair. Yanked hard. Pulling. Tearing.

The man grunted but didn't release her.

"I'm not going away for murder," he said, his tone like a hissing snake.

What in the world?

He tightened his hold.

She tried to suck in air. Couldn't gain a breath. Not even a sip of oxygen.

The darkness came, obscuring her vision. Beckoning her. She blinked hard. Blinked again but couldn't fight the shadows descending over her eyes.

2

The screams tore through Jackson's body.

Maggie. He was too late, and she was in trouble.

He bolted from Vince's battered old pickup and charged into the subdivision. He could use help. One of his teammates. Why did he insist on Riley remaining at Maggie's place in case she came home?

Stow it. He couldn't do anything about that now.

He raced toward a large truck parked under a streetlight. Probably a truck used to store recovery supplies. He hoped to find Maggie there—unharmed. He ran full out and rounded the back of the vehicle. The door was open. A man stood, his back to Jackson, struggling with a woman. Was it Maggie?

"Let her go!" Jackson charged toward the door.

The man spun, releasing the woman. She crumpled to the floor, gasping for breath.

Jackson climbed onto the wide bumper.

The man bolted, barreling into Jackson and knocking him off. He hit the road hard. His head slammed into the concrete, and his breath whooshed out. The man landed on top of him.

Wooziness had Jackson blinking hard. He reached up to restrain the man, but the attacker scrambled to his feet and took off. Jackson tried to turn. To get a good look at the fleeing suspect, but his equilibrium was off, and he couldn't focus.

He pushed up on his elbow. The entire area whirled before him, and he couldn't move without everything spinning wildly.

Some protector he was.

Get up, man. Get up.

Seriously, he needed to dig deeper. Draw on reserves he knew he possessed.

He gulped in air and forced himself to sit up. He saw the woman still laying in a heap in the truck. He glanced in the direction where the man had taken off, but the guy was long gone. Jackson could try to go after him, but the woman might need immediate medical attention, and Jackson had first aid training from his army days.

He got to his feet and stumbled the few steps to the truck like a town drunk. The woman lifted her head. Their gazes connected.

"Maggie," he said her name, one that he never thought he'd utter in her presence again. His throat clogged with emotions.

"Jackson." His name rasped out, and she clutched her throat. "Is that you?"

"Yeah."

"That man. He tried to kill me."

"I know," he said. "That's why I'm here."

"What?" She screeched, finding her voice, her gaze

darting around the area. She was heading toward shock or was already in shock.

He needed to calm her down. He climbed into the truck, nearly losing his balance but making it upright, and offered his hand. He expected her to refuse, but she pressed her fingers into his. The touch of her skin sent a bolt of heat straight to his heart.

He was suddenly back in college. Back at the hospital. Back with her on that last day when they'd made their promise, and he fled from her life...from their loss...like a coward. Now here he was. His heart still as raw and broken.

Shake it off, man. Put it all back in the recesses of your mind and help Maggie. Protect her.

He gently tugged her to her feet and led her out of the truck so she could sit on the bumper. The minute their feet hit the ground, she started crying, tears running down her cheeks and making rivulets through the dust clinging to her face.

"Aw, honey, don't cry," he said, knowing if tears were flowing, she was totally destroyed inside. An incredibly strong woman, she rarely cried in the time he'd known her. Okay, fine, not so rarely after the tragedy ended their relationship. Then she couldn't seem to stop.

She turned green eyes up to his, her head tilted, leaving her ponytail hanging over her shoulder. Her full mouth quivered. The mouth he'd kissed hundreds of times and felt the same irresistible draw to kiss now. He wouldn't follow his desires, but he also wouldn't stand idly by while she broke down in front of him.

He drew her close, and she came willingly, surprising him. She settled in, fitting her body against his. Her head rested on his chest just below his chin, the fit as perfect as he remembered. Her tears turned to gut-wrenching sobs. He tightened his hold and stroked her back covered with dust and ash.

Imagine if he hadn't gotten here in time. When he and Riley had arrived at her house, her roommate told him she was working this recovery scene. If he hadn't come or even if he'd argued with Gage another minute...no, he wouldn't think about that. He was here with her, and she would be all right. Once she got over the shock of the attack.

He loosened his hold to dig out his phone and dial 911. She didn't seem to notice his movements or the call. He got that. Shock often consumed everything else, burning and devouring like the fire that almost erased this subdivision and many acres surrounding it.

He gave the operator concise details of the attack, and after receiving a promise for a deputy to report to the scene, he stowed his phone. Maggie continued to sob, though her chest heaved less. He rubbed circles on her back and laid his head on top of hers, trying to comfort her the best he knew how. Her crying eventually turned into quick little hiccups, and she planted delicate hands on his chest to push back. He wanted to continue holding her, but he let go and led her to the bumper where he sat by her side.

"A deputy's on the way," he said, breaking the ice.

She turned and peered at him as if seeing him for the first time since he arrived before looking down. Maybe with the shock she'd gone on autopilot and now she realized he was the one who came to her rescue. The one who'd held her so close.

"I'm so thankful you're here," she said, the tenor of her voice throaty and raw. "I'll never be able to thank you enough, but..." She raised her eyes to his, her gaze searching deep. "I thought we promised not to see each other again."

He expected her to say that, but it still hurt to hear. "I had no choice."

Disbelief flashed across her face. "We all have choices."

His thoughts traveled back to their breakup. "No, we don't." The words slipped out in a whisper before he even thought about them. "You of all people should know that."

She jolted back as if he'd slapped her.

"I'm sorry, Maggie. I shouldn't have said that," he said over a lump forming in his throat. "I did have a choice about coming here, but when I learned your life was in danger, I had to come."

Her face turned ashen, and she shot a look around. "You think my attacker is still here?"

"No. No," he soothed. "He's long gone, but the ongoing danger isn't."

"I don't understand." She started rubbing her fingers together, over and over as if trying to rid herself of her attacker's touch.

"You know Scott Dawson, right?"

"The murdered student." Her tone climbed into the quiet night. "How could I not? He was killed in the lecture hall I use. But what does that have to do with me?"

"The investigating sheriff ran out of leads so Scott's father hired my team to find the killer."

"The army's involved?"

"Right, you don't know. I had to leave the Berets. Tore up my leg. If I stayed, I would've been riding a desk."

"I'm sorry, Jackson," she said, and hearing her say his name drove another spike of pain into his chest. "I know how much you loved the Berets."

"I'm employed by Blackwell Tactical now." He took out his business card and handed it to her. "We work private security details, do investigative work, and train law enforcement officers. It's a great job. Maybe not quite as exciting as the Berets, but far better than any other civilian job I could have found."

"I'm glad." A half smile tipped her lips, revealing a dimple on the left side that he'd often teased with his fingertip. "But again, what does Scott's murder have to do with me?"

"We discovered during out investigation that the university recorded your lecture hall for an attendance study."

"They did what?" She gaped at him.

"They installed cameras in the front of five lecture halls to record video of the students in attendance. A computer program analyzed the images to assess the number of occupied seats."

"They never told us." She sounded mad.

"They didn't want to bias the study."

"I can't even begin to wrap my head around this. It's such a violation of rights."

"Yes, and university officials are now being investigated for that."

"And this is somehow related to Scott's murder?"

Jackson nodded. "The cameras recorded during classes or when someone came in the room and the motion-sensor lights turned on. The recording stayed on until the lights went off."

She clutched a hand to her chest, grabbing onto her shirt and twisting the fabric. "Did one of them capture Scott's murder?"

He shook his head. "That happened out of view, but it did record the killer entering the room before the light was turned off."

"Then you know the killer's identity."

"No. He wore a hoodie, and his head was down."

She tilted her head to the side and pursed her lip. "I don't understand. How is this video of value then?"

"The video caught you leaving the classroom. The killer opened the door at the same time and pushed past you. You said something to him, but he kept going, and you walked out. The murder happened shortly after that."

"I bumped into the killer? Really?" Her hand moved to cover her mouth for a moment before she dropped it to her knee. "Since I teach in this room, the police questioned me. Why didn't they ask about that?"

"Without these attendance videos, there was no reason to believe you may have seen the killer."

"Say what? The administration didn't turn the videos over to the police?"

"Right. Not that they were hiding them. They said for privacy reasons they'd all been destroyed after the study ended, but our tech person recovered copies."

She sat, staring ahead, and he could almost see thoughts traveling through her mind. "Sounds like you're hoping I can remember this guy."

"We are, but now that word has gotten around campus about the study, we're afraid the killer will realize you saw him and want to stop you from identifying him. Which is why I'm here. To protect you."

She sat quietly as if processing the news, then suddenly sat up higher. "The guy who just tried to strangle me said he wasn't going away for murder. He has to be Scott's killer."

Jackson didn't like the sound of that, but it did confirm Maggie's need for his protection. "Did you recognize his voice?"

She shook her head. "No, but I talked to a guy before I got in the truck. I thought he looked familiar, so he could've been the one who attacked me. He said he owned one of the houses not destroyed in the fire, but maybe he was Scott's killer, and he was trying to throw me off track."

"You talked to the killer?" Jackson's voice echoed through the barren neighborhood. He tried not to sound so upset, but he couldn't help it. She'd not only seen the killer face-to-face at the college but had likely just talked to him again.

Maggie sat on the ambulance bumper and stowed her phone from updating Nate on the attack so he knew what to expect when he arrived. Speaking to Nate reinforced the truth of her night. She'd been attacked. Really, attacked. How could that have happened? Just the thought of it sent a chill over her skin, and her hands were still shaking. In less than five minutes, her life not only tilted on its axis but completely spun out of control. So many things left her head reeling, she hardly knew where to start. The terrifying attack. The attendance study. Scott's death.

But Jackson? Seeing him again after all these years?

That was the hardest by far. She just couldn't process it. Worse yet, she could hardly take her eyes off him. He stood talking to the responding deputy who'd already taken her statement. Feet planted wide, he wore khaki tactical pants that he always favored and a black knit shirt that stretched tight over his broad chest. He was a powerful man with wide shoulders and a trim waist, and he never failed to turn heads when they went out in public.

He pivoted, and his grayish-blue eyes sought her out, locking on tight and not relenting. He had this way of looking at her as if nothing else existed. She always reveled in it, but right now it left her uncomfortable. She shouldn't be feeling anything for him. Nothing, period. And yet, a simple look from him made her heart beat hard.

She jerked her gaze away and focused on the strobing lights on the patrol car instead. He had this effect on her from the second they'd met. She was twenty-four at the time. He was in the army, and while on leave, he visited her college roommate's brother. They ran into each other at a party, and she fell for him on the spot. He oozed strength and confidence, and yet he was both funny and tender. Combined with eyes that were intense and at the same time comforting, she could hardly look away from him. After a whirlwind courtship, they'd gotten engaged, and she foolishly slept with him and got pregnant.

She was actually thrilled at the thought of having his child. She would've finished her master's degree by the time the baby was born and could work on her PhD part-time. But Jackson didn't have the same reaction. He didn't want to be an absent father, which as a Green Beret would be unavoidable. His dad frequently traveled for business, and Jackson didn't want to put a child through that, but he also wouldn't even consider leaving the Berets.

She wasn't about to trap him in a marriage, so she gave him a pass. Told him to go back to his unit, and she would raise the baby alone. He took off, breaking her heart in the process. He returned on his next long leave, but by that time she was eight months pregnant, and the baby was just waiting to be born.

The memory of that day came rushing back. Jackson's eyes had gone soft the moment he saw her. He pressed his hand over her belly and told her he wanted to work things out with her. Wanted to be a father in any way he could. They went out to dinner to celebrate, but on the way to the restaurant, the discussion turned back to his future deployments and it got heated. They argued. She grabbed his arm. Accidentally jerked the steering wheel in the process, and the car crashed, injuring her and killing the baby.

Their relationship couldn't recover. The gut-wrenching pain didn't allow that, and they split. Not a day went by that she didn't think of their daughter, and as a result, thought of Jackson, too.

She looked up to see him heading her way, his long-legged stride eating up the road when she wasn't ready to talk to him yet. He stared ahead, his face an unreadable mask at this distance.

Was he thinking of Alison, too? Did he think of her often and feel the same guilt? Beat himself up and wonder what God's plan was in this tragedy?

She wasn't certain of many things anymore, but she was certain God made a mistake. A baby should never die.

The thought put a lump in her throat, and she swallowed as she tried to stow her grief and panic from the attack before she started blubbering and let Jackson hold her again. She needed to think logically because logic said she should send this man packing and find someone else to help her out...although her heart said to get up and fall into his arms.

Really, Maggie? What are you thinking? One look at the guy and you want to forget all the hurt, the pain, and tumble back into his arms? Seriously?

She inhaled deeply and blew out her breath. Drew in another one and contemplated what she might say to him. He was expecting her to allow him to step in and serve as her bodyguard, but could she let that happen and still remain sane? Could she afford not to let him do it?

On the recent update with Nate, she asked about assigning a deputy to be with her full time until this killer was caught, but he didn't have the manpower for that kind of time commitment. So what choice did she have?

Jackson stopped toe-to-toe with her and stared down at her in the wash of light coming from the streetlight. She didn't like having him this close and especially not towering over her. She got up and put some distance between them. That earned her an arch of his eyebrow, but she felt better with a little breathing room.

"Everything check out okay with the medics?" he asked.

She nodded. "You really should have them look at your head, too."

"Nah, it's just as empty as it's always been." He smiled, lighting up his eyes with a sparkle.

Her heart instantly warmed, and it took all her self-control not to run back into his arms and kiss him. How was she going to spend time with him and not do something she would regret? Just how?

She started to sigh but stopped herself before drawing further study.

"Something wrong?" Concern tightened his jaw and nearly had her caving and begging him not to let her out of his sight.

She forced her mind to still, her heart to calm. "No."

His response was a clipped nod, but that concern lingered. "The deputy cleared you to leave, and we should take off."

"Hold up. I didn't agree to your proposition."

"Didn't you?"

"You know I didn't."

"Look." He stepped closer, and she had to fight the urge to back up. "I know it's going to be hard to be together. It'll bring up old wounds, but your life is in danger, and I'm not leaving you alone."

Hard to be together? That was an understatement if she ever heard one. Try impossible. "Can't someone else on your team serve as my bodyguard?"

"No!" His sharp tone drew the attention of the others. He glanced around and his hands curled into tight fists. "Sorry. I need to do this, Mags. Really need to. Maybe I'm trying to make up for not keeping the car on the road and losing Alison. Or maybe it's because you'll always mean a lot to me, but either way, please let me do this for you. Please."

She hated to see him beg, and yet, her heart was touched that watching over her was that important to him. Something she couldn't dwell on or she would fall into those arms again.

"Fine. I accept. But I won't go into hiding. I'm needed here and will keep working. You'll have to figure out how to make it safe for me to do so."

She expected him to argue, but he nodded. "I'll get a few of my teammates to join us in the morning, and we'll secure the area."

"Okay, but I'm not leaving just yet." She gestured at a county SUV coming to a stop. "The sheriff is just arriving, and I need to meet with him."

"About the attack?"

She started to shake her head but pain ripped across her throat, halting her movement. "Another body was located late this afternoon, and the skull has a bullet hole."

"Here?" He shot a quick look around.

She nodded. "In a shed at the back of a property. I was in the truck getting the portable x-ray device when I was attacked."

"Man." He ran a hand over his jaw darkened by a thick five-o'clock shadow. "That's rough."

Another understatement.

She caught sight of Nate stepping from his SUV and was eager to get back to the shed. "So you see why I have to stay?"

Jackson didn't look happy but nodded. "With the law enforcement presence here, it should be fine. Still, you've had a shock. Fatigue is going to set in soon. Promise me when it hits that you'll agree to go."

"I know my limitations. If I get tired enough to make mistakes, I'll take a break." She turned her full attention to Nate.

She couldn't help but compare him to Jackson. Nate was around six feet tall, sandy blond hair shorn military-short, and his face was tanned from the summer sun. Jackson's complexion was dark and swarthy, and his hair, though short, wasn't as close-cut as Nate's. Both men were muscular, but both men didn't send her heart beating with a look. Only Jackson could do that.

Nate joined them and rested his hand on his sidearm. "You okay, Doc?"

She nodded. "Thanks to Jackson."

She introduced him as working for Blackwell Tactical, but didn't mention that they'd once been engaged, and she definitely didn't tell Nate she and Jackson were once expectant parents.

"Blackwell, huh?" A look of respect crossed Nate's face, and he extended his hand. "I took one of your courses. You've got a first-rate class."

Pride for Jackson's skills blossomed in Maggie's heart. Seriously, how could her heart keep betraying her like this? Maybe it was the attack and tiredness. She was sure she would do a better job in the morning. She had to.

"Thought you looked familiar." Jackson released Nate's hand.

"Mind telling me why you were here tonight?" Nate asked.

Jackson explained about Scott's death. "After the attack tonight, it's looking like our theory is correct."

"Sounds like a good possibility." Nate frowned.

Maggie brought him up to speed on the man she talked to, a subconscious shiver rushing through her body as she called up her memory. "Your deputy checked out the house the man said he owned. He wasn't there, and I didn't see him leave the subdivision."

Nate's frown deepened. "You think this guy's your attacker?"

"I don't know. At the time, I believed his story about being the homeowner."

Nate nodded. "While we wait for the ME, I'll run the address through property records and bring up a driver's license for the owner."

"It's the blue house just down the road on the left."

"I'll be right back." He started down the street.

Jackson turned to her. "I should ask. Is there anyone else in your life who might want you dead?"

"You're joking, right?" She laughed.

He frowned. "Wish I was."

She couldn't believe Jackson was standing there, much less asking her who might want to kill her. "This is just crazy. I can't think of anyone who would want me dead. Well, maybe a failing student, but only in a manner of speaking."

"I think it was Scott's killer who attacked you, but we still have to perform our due diligence. I doubt it's a student, but with your part-time forensic anthropology work, you could've consulted on a case where someone might be out to get you."

"I suppose that's possible." She let the thought settle in.

He could be right and that might be the key. She would review her work files when she got to her house. The sooner they found Scott's killer, the sooner Jackson would go back home, and she wouldn't have to think about the past, including how much she once loved him.

3

Jackson gave his full attention to the crime scene analysis going on in front of him. He'd never participated in processing a crime scene, and he soaked up every detail. He never knew when it might come in handy in the future.

A photographer had showed up on the scene thirty minutes ago and immediately started snapping shots of the remains. The camera's click echoed through the still night, and the flash lit up the area like the flare from an explosion. Then the ME, Dr. Charlotte Owing, arrived. She was tall and thin with short spiky blond hair and wrinkles between her eyebrows that narrowed when she frowned. With the depth of the grooves, Jackson suspected she frowned a good bit of the time.

She squatted next to the victim and moved clockwise around him in a duck walk, evaluating the remains from all angles. She didn't speak but uttered a few hmms.

Holding his phone, Nate picked his way through the ruins and stepped right up to Maggie. He held out his phone. "I got the photo for the owner of the blue house. Doesn't look to me like the guy you described, but..."

Maggie took one look at it and shook her head. "Definitely not him. Among many differences, this guy's smile is perfect. The guy I talked to had crooked teeth."

"So the jerk lied to you," Jackson said, though it went without saying. "And he could very well be your attacker."

Nate nodded, but his focus remained on Maggie. "Did you get a clear enough look at him to meet with a sketch artist?"

"I did."

"Good," Nate said.

Jackson didn't agree. Okay, maybe it was good for the investigation to find the guy, but Maggie close enough to a killer to be able to describe him for a sketch? Jackson hated that. Still, he wouldn't say anything, as it served no point.

"I can make an appointment for an artist to meet with you first thing in the morning," Nate continued. "He could come out to your house. Would that be okay?"

Maggie nodded. "I can do it before my work here."

Dr. Owing stood and towered over the victim, but her gaze went to Maggie. "He's all yours if you want another look before we move him to the morgue."

"Thank you." Maggie stepped closer. "He displays the general burn pattern that you would expect to find for a person lying face up."

"That's good information to have," Dr. Owing said.

Maggie squatted by the body, and with gloved hands, gently turned the skull. Something moved inside. She looked up at Dr. Owing. "With no exit wound, that's likely the bullet moving in the skull."

The doctor nodded. "Since we don't have a through-and-through, we're likely looking at a smaller caliber bullet."

"The size of the entrance wound reflects that as well," Maggie said.

Nate took a step closer. "Most common handgun ammo sizes are 9mm or .38 special. As far as bullets go, I'd classify both of these as medium sizes. Would such a bullet exit the skull?"

Dr. Owing faced the sheriff. "I'd say on average they tend not to because their velocity is marginal after the first impact, but there are so many factors, making each wound different from the next."

"Maybe the slug will tell us something," Nate suggested. "But then bullets are generally made of lead and would melt at pretty low temps. Could it even have survived the heat?"

"A jacketed bullet would move the melting point much higher," Jackson weighed in. "Especially if it was jacketed in steel, but copper's more common."

"Copper's melting point is still three times that of lead, so we might get lucky on the slug," Maggie said.

Nate turned to look around the area. "This shed would have quickly flashed over. Especially with a concrete pad for a floor and nothing much combustible inside. And we can already see that the heat wasn't as intense back here as other places in the sub. All of that's in our favor."

"But it was intense enough to leave the skull calcined and porous." Maggie peered up at them. "I don't want to manipulate it any more right now. Better to do so in a controlled environment."

"I concur." Dr. Owing met Maggie's gaze. "Our little morgue doesn't have an anthropology lab, but I'm glad to have you join me at the morgue."

"Thank you." Maggie looked back at the body. "Dr. Owing, did you notice the location of the humeri, radii, and ulnas?"

"I did."

"Whatever you're referring to sounds significant," Nate said.

Maggie nodded. "Without getting into too many details, when muscles are exposed to extreme heat they tighten. This causes the fingers, wrists, and elbows to flex in a pugilistic posture."

"So a boxer's pose," Jackson clarified.

Maggie nodded. "Which means when the muscles detached, these bones should not be located under the spine."

"But his are." Nate frowned. "How could that be?"

"It's likely that his hands were bound behind his back." Maggie stood. "I'm also wondering if he was shot elsewhere and the body dumped here."

"Why's that?" Nate's interest seemed to perk up.

"He's laying perpendicular to the door and the entrance wound is on the back side of the skull. There's no way a shooter could have made this shot in here unless it was point-blank. At that close of a range, I suspect we would have a through-and-through. I have no scientific evidence to support this, of course."

"Sounds like a promising theory, though," Dr. Owing said. "Hopefully a closer look will tell us more."

Maggie nodded. "I'd like to help you prepare the body for removal so we're sure of a safe transport."

"I'm thankful for your help and expertise." Dr. Owing dug her phone from her pocket. "My assistant is waiting in the vehicle. Let me get him down here with the gurney and tools we need."

She stepped away, and Maggie continued to examine the remains while Jackson studied her. Her anthropology classes always brought out an intensity in her, and it looked like that carried through into her work.

He should look away, but he just couldn't get his fill of her. Man, he missed her. They had this rare relationship where they instantly connected on a level that many long-term relationships never reached. When they were together, he was the happiest he'd ever been in his life. Until he wasn't.

The squeaky wheels on the gurney grabbed his attention, and he was glad to redirect his thoughts. He turned to see the assistant bumping it over the ruins. Dr. Owing shone a flashlight in his path to guide him. Jackson stepped back to give him room. The short guy had a thick head of rumpled gray hair and wore a Tyvek suit like the docs.

Jackson kept an eye out for any immediate danger but continued to give considerable time to studying Maggie as she worked with the doctor and her assistant. Jackson's last day with Maggie came to mind. He would never forget it. Ever.

He'd arrived back in town after months of deployment to find her eight months pregnant. His child in her belly. He was so overcome with emotions that he nearly dropped to the floor. Instead, he pressed his hand against her stomach and felt his child move for the first time. His love for Maggie grew tenfold that day. Maybe more. And then...then...just hours later, everything came crashing down around them.

He shook his head to knock the thoughts free and bring his focus back to the job at hand. To make sure this woman stayed safe. That was all he was here to do. Not rekindle his feelings for her or lead her on. Or even remember their past. Protection was his only job, and he best remember that.

Once Dr. Owing and her assistant carefully carried the gurney to the street, Maggie yawned and stretched her arms high.

Jackson loved the way she moved so fluidly and gracefully. Her long arms overhead, her torso stretched, reminded him of how agile she was and highlighted her curvy figure. She turned and caught him watching her, her pink cheeks all he needed to tell him she was aware of his attraction and maybe felt the same way.

Stow it. Leave it in the past.

"You ready to go home now?" he asked, hoping she would agree so she could go to bed, and he could bunk on the sofa and breathe normally again without her nearby.

She nodded, and he didn't wait for her to change her mind but escorted her up to the road. They passed the truck, and the memories of arriving to find her under attack felt like a mule kick in his gut. He glanced at Maggie to see her reaction. She cringed and shuddered. The urge to take her hand was nearly overpowering for Jackson. He shoved his hands into his pocket and turned his focus ahead.

In the lot, he pointed at the rusty old Ford belonging to the father of Riley's friend. "We'll take my truck."

"I don't like leaving my vehicle out here," she said. "Isn't it safe enough if you follow me?"

"Safe? Maybe, but you're tired, and I'd rather drive you."

She sighed. "I'll be fine, Jackson."

He wanted to keep arguing, but there was no point. "We'll leave the truck and take your SUV."

She watched him for a long time, but finally nodded.

"Mind if I drive?" he asked.

She shook her head and handed him the keys. He opened her door, and she slid in. He made quick work of climbing behind the wheel, moving the driver's seat back, and getting them on the main road.

She glanced at him. "I'm having a hard time getting used to this new life you lead."

"Back atcha," he said.

"And speaking of your new life," she continued. "I need to know how much your bodyguard service will cost."

What in the world? "Seriously, Maggie? You have to know I'd never charge you."

"But your team. They need to be paid, don't they?"

"Scott's father is paying for us to locate the killer and..." He paused because he didn't know how to say this properly.

"You think I'll be bait for the killer?"

"I was trying to come up with a nicer way to say it."

"And is that really why you're here?" She sounded disappointed, maybe angry. "To find the killer?"

"I wish I could say that didn't play into my plans. But even if I wasn't hired to find Scott's killer, I'd be by your side." He glanced at her. "It hurts that you doubt my intentions."

She flinched. "Why? With the way we left things?"

"Yeah, that wasn't so great, was it?"

"No." Short, concise, one word only, then she turned to look out the window, clearly putting an end to their discussion.

He wanted to talk about the past, hash it out, so maybe it wouldn't hold this incredible power over them, but he would respect her desire not to. For tonight anyway. Tomorrow was a different story.

They drove for fifteen minutes in silence, the SUV nearly bursting from tension. Jackson could hardly believe they'd once been so good together. But they had been. Opposites in so many ways, but still a natural fit. He never loved a woman as much as he loved Maggie in those days. Hadn't since, either. Everyone he dated paled in comparison to her. He shouldn't be comparing, but he did every time he met someone, until he just gave up on the whole dating thing. Much easier that way.

He made the final turn on their route, and they climbed steeper into mountainous terrain until her home came into view. Two stories, it sat on a lot surrounded by towering pine trees. After having just left the neighborhood devastation, he couldn't help but think that surrounded by all these trees, her home would quickly go up in flames in a forest fire. Conifers were fire magnets. They burned all the way to the top because of the chemicals in the tree, basically turpentine. The small needles allowed oxygen to get between them, and the trees burned in a flare, taking ground fires up into trees and causing the fire to go out of control, spreading it at an alarming rate. He didn't like that thought. Didn't like it at all.

He pulled to a stop in the wide driveway and turned off the ignition. "I always thought you'd be living in some big metro area where your skills as a forensic anthropologist would be in greater demand."

"My dad's health failed, so I came back here to take care of him. He passed away last year, and I inherited the house. I want to have a full-time career in forensics again, but I haven't been able to bring myself to leave."

"I'm so sorry for your loss." Jackson pulled out the keys and handed them to her, careful not to touch her hand. "I only met your dad that one time at your school, but I liked him."

She gave a firm nod and got out. He joined her on the stone walkway, and together they strolled to the house and climbed wide stone stairs. While she located the right key on her ring, he looked around her property. The tall trees blocked the moon, casting dark, almost sinister shadows, stopping him from getting a good read on the place. He'd gotten a cursory view earlier, but not enough to plan a tight safety perimeter. After the team arrived in the morning, he'd take a much better look and make that plan.

He followed her inside to a soaring foyer that he'd only gotten a glimpse at when talking to her roommate Daria. Maggie turned the deadbolt behind him and dropped her keys on the hall table.

"You might not want to keep your keys in reach of the front door. Someone could break the side window and grab them."

She paused mid-step to stare at him, her gaze appraising. "You really are worried, aren't you?"

He started to reply in his usual straightforward way, but when she seemed to curl inward in an attempt to protect herself, he searched for a gentler response. "I don't want to panic you, but our top focus should be your safety right now. Everything else needs to take a backseat."

She lifted her shoulders. "As I said, I won't stop working the Summit neighborhood."

"You made that clear, and I'll go along with it as long as it's safe. If that changes, I'll have to ask you to reconsider."

"And I promise to heed your warning, but the victims come first for me."

"Above your own safety?"

She frowned. "I thought you of all people would understand that. As a Beret, you risked your life all the time for others and went overboard to make sure the people you cared about were safe."

She was right. That was his thing. Protecting the innocent, especially helpless people, but he wasn't going to let her sidetrack the discussion to him instead of her. "My service in the Berets was different."

"How?"

"I was trained to protect myself. You aren't."

She seemed to mull that over, but instead of responding, she went to the family room with floor-to-ceiling windows looking black and ominous in the night. He didn't like the exposure these windows brought but would keep that to himself until he formed a plan on how to deal with it. Another wall held a massive stone fireplace. The remaining walls were covered in slatted wood painted a fresh white, and the ceiling was made of rustic logs.

A door opened in the hallway and footsteps headed their way. Jackson suspected it was her roommate but rested his hand on his sidearm. He couldn't be too careful when it came to Maggie's life.

As expected, Daria stepped around the corner and rushed over to Maggie. Not much over five-two, Daria was on the plump side with dark curly hair. She wore gray yoga pants with a darker gray T-shirt, and her feet were bare. Her worried expression fixed on Maggie. "Are you okay?"

"I'm fine."

"Your neck. It's already purple." Daria covered her mouth with her hand and shook her head. "I can't even imagine."

"It's fine," Maggie replied almost tersely. "Really."

Daria shot a look at Jackson as if asking him to do something to help.

"Thank you for giving Riley a ride back to the chopper," he said to change the subject.

"Happy to do it," Daria replied then nibbled on her lip.

"I appreciate it, too," Maggie said drawing Daria's attention again.

"He said he'll be coming back with others in the morning, and they'll all be staying here with us." She sounded panicked by the thought.

"We haven't worked out all the details yet," Jackson said. "We don't want to be a burden."

"No, it's not that, but there are only four bedrooms." She clasped her hands together and then shook them out, only to clutch them together again.

"No worries," he said to try to stop her fidgeting. "I'll be bunking on the couch so I don't need a room, and the others won't mind sharing."

"You can have the guest room for tonight at least," Maggie said.

He shook his head. "Couch has a better view of the main access points to the house."

"Oh." She looked around the room as if finally realizing she might not be safe in her own home.

Daria started shaking. "I...this...I'm afraid."

"Perhaps you'd like to stay with a friend until all of this is over," he suggested.

She cut her gaze to Maggie. "I couldn't leave Maggie."

"Sure you can. The team will be here with me." Maggie stepped closer and took her roommate's hand. "In fact, I'd feel better if you were somewhere safer."

"Are you sure?"

"Absolutely."

"Then I'll make the arrangements." She turned and fled from the room as if Maggie's attacker was hot on her heels.

Jackson was relieved. It would be better for all of them not to let another person's safety divide their attention.

Maggie faced him. "I'm going to grab something to eat. Are you hungry?"

He was surprised she could eat after her night, but he'd missed dinner and was starving. He nodded. She wasted no time but went to the adjoining kitchen. He took one last look at those tall windows, wondering how in the world he could protect her with so much glass in the room, and trailed her into the homey kitchen. He should have said no to eating and put that much-needed space between them. But she would sleep better if she ate something, and he suspected if he'd said no, she would've headed off to bed hungry.

She was already at the sink washing her hands, and he joined her. She scooted as far away from him as possible while still able to reach the water. He felt like he had some communicable disease. Despite his desire to put space between them, the thought didn't sit well with him.

She quickly dried her hands and tugged on the stainless refrigerator door. "I made chicken salad for sandwiches last night. Does that sound okay?"

"Perfect. Can I help?"

"I remember your kitchen skills." She looked back at him. "Have you changed or are you still pretty helpless?"

"Still helpless." He grinned at her.

"That's what I figured." She quirked a smile, a welcome change from the avoidance dance at the sink. She gestured at the stools by the large island.

He took a seat while she retrieved bread and plates, thankful to have at least the island separating them.

"The bread is two days old so not as fresh as I would like." She opened the bag.

"I'm sure it will still be amazing." Cooking and baking were her hobbies, and when they dated, he rejoined his team after leave a few pounds heavier.

She sliced thick pieces of bread, loaded them with the chicken salad mixture, and cut them in perfect triangles. She handed him a plate and poured two tall glasses of iced tea. He waited for her to sit next to him, but she remained on the far side of the island. Maybe she wanted to look at him. More likely she wanted to stay as far away from him as possible.

She waved a hand at his plate. "Dig in."

He took a large bite of chicken, apples, and celery in a creamy mixture. The bread was far fresher than she led on, and his taste buds were in serious bliss. He groaned and swallowed. "I missed your cooking."

She chewed her bite, warily watching him as if not knowing what to say to that.

He set down his sandwich, his appetite now gone. "Since we're going to be together, we should probably set some ground rules."

"Like?"

"Like maybe we should talk about our past and clear the air," he said, seizing the moment instead of waiting until the morning.

"No." She shook her head hard, her ponytail slapping her face. "That's not going to happen. Not tonight or ever."

Her face creased in a stubborn expression he recognized very well. Next, she would plant her feet on the floor and declare she planned to stick with her statement.

But he could be equally as stubborn. When the time presented itself, he would once again raise the discussion of their past. She could count on that.

4

After a sleepless night, Maggie stared at the laptop Jackson had placed on her kitchen counter. He sat on a bar stool next to her. She barely finished making morning coffee when he asked her to take a look at it.

Hardly the thing she wanted to do before her first cup of coffee. She especially didn't want to watch it over and over again for the last thirty minutes when Jackson kept hitting play, but she did want Scott's killer found. Not only because his father deserved closure and the killer would be behind bars, but selfishly, it meant Jackson would return to Cold Harbor.

Jackson. What was she going to do about him while he was still here?

When she woke up and remembered he was on the couch, she peeked out just to be sure she hadn't imagined him spending the night.

He'd stood there staring out her picture window, his back to her. He wore a T-shirt that stretched across his wide shoulders, and without a belt, his pants hung low on his hips. He turned to look at her, issued a sleepy good morning, and ran a lazy gaze over her. Her heart started galloping like a champion racehorse, and she mumbled good morning before ducking behind the door to catch her breath.

She knew she shouldn't be responding to him. Shouldn't be interested in him. And yet, before bed last night, she'd looked up Cold Harbor on the Internet and learned that it was located on the southern Oregon coast. A small city, it wasn't the kind of place where she envisioned Jackson settling down. But time changed people, and he must be far different than the younger guy who wanted to travel the world.

He still had the same smile, though. The same way of looking at her. The same draw. The same amazing body. She saw that firsthand this morning.

Argh. Stop already. Focus on the video.

"Let's look at this one more time." He stretched out his long index finger and tapped the play button, his arm brushing her side

She jerked away, earning a surprised look from him. She ignored it and squarely focused on the short clip. It was odd to watch herself pull open the door, the strap to her brief-case slung over her shoulder. She bumped into a man, his head down, hood up, even though the video was filmed in June. She couldn't make out his features, but she paused to stare after him and say something. His only response was to keep on moving.

"Do you remember what you were saying there?" Jackson asked.

She shook her head. "I was probably telling him his manners were appalling."

Jackson grinned. "I could totally see you doing that."

"You could?"

"Yeah, I mean you had the best manners. Probably still

do. Just like your dad. He was so polite. Proper. I felt like a big bozo around him."

"You never said anything."

"It was my problem, not his or yours. You are who you are. I am who I am. I just wished at times I was more like your dad. If so I wouldn't have..." He shook his head. "Sorry, you don't want to talk about our past."

Honestly, in less than a day she was leaning toward wanting to discuss it with him. "Even if I don't, your team should be here any minute, and you don't want to get into that now."

"True that." He stopped the video. "Okay, so we know this guy is the correct build for the man you talked to at Summit last night."

"Yes, though honestly, everything is so average about that guy, a lot of other guys will fit his build, too."

"We're not concerned about other guys, just the person in this video."

"It still seems like the odds of finding him are pretty low."

"If you can get a good sketch made this morning that will go a long way in helping."

She didn't like the incredible pressure that put on her, but she would do her best.

The doorbell rang, and she jumped.

He patted her hand. "Relax. Like you said, it's the team."

He closed the computer and headed for the entry. She got up and prepared herself to meet this group. Jackson told her enough about them this morning that she felt as if she already knew them. Still, she wasn't prepared for their entrance. They swept into the kitchen like hurricane force winds, and Jackson quickly introduced the trio.

Riley, Eryn, and Alex were physically strong. Intense.

Intimidating. Even Eryn, who was two inches shorter than Maggie, could obviously take her down in a flash. A good thing for her job, Maggie supposed, but when Jackson had told her one of the team members was a woman, Maggie hoped she'd have something in common with her, and it would make the whole bodyguard thing more palatable. But she was already intimidated by the woman's obvious physical strength.

"Anyone want breakfast?" she asked, needing to get out from under their intense scrutiny. "I'd be glad to scramble some eggs."

"Oh, yeah." Alex gave her a big grin.

"I'm in," Riley said.

Eryn smiled, her chocolate brown eyes creasing. "I could eat."

Jackson eyed Maggie. He knew she was running from them, but she didn't care if he figured it out. She felt compelled to do something, so she busied herself at the stove and sink. First she squeezed fresh orange juice and placed the pitcher along with glasses on the island where the team settled onto stools.

Jackson picked up the pitcher and started pouring. "Maggie's like this amazing cook. We better put this investigation to bed soon, or we're all going to gain weight."

Maggie wanted to comment on the way he talked about her in such a personal way, but she wasn't about to bring that up in front of the team. Instead, as they discussed her protection, she made toast and alternated with sloshing the eggs around in the pan and putting out silverware, napkins, butter, and homemade raspberry jelly.

When the eggs were fluffy and perfect, she plated them, then added toast. She turned to distribute the plates and found Jackson behind her holding out his hands. She let him take the plates, and he passed them to Eryn and Alex. Maggie handed another one to Riley and jabbed one in Jackson's hand, pushing at him and encouraging him to go sit on the far side of the island. He didn't take the hint but set the plate down nearby. He, along with the three amigos —as she was choosing to think of Jackson's teammates— prayed and dug right in.

"I appreciate the food." Eryn held a fork filled with egg near her mouth. "But don't think you need to feed us while we're here."

"Speak for yourself." Alex smiled as he spread jelly on his toast.

Maggie returned his smile. She only had to listen in on the team's conversation while she cooked to figure out that he loved to joke around. Eryn seemed to be the one who listened carefully and made sure everyone's point of view was heard. Maggie hadn't gotten a good read on Riley yet.

And Jackson? He was still blunt and told the truth even when it was hard to hear. Case in point, last night when much of what they discussed was difficult to bring up. That seemed to be the baton he carried with the group, too.

She gestured again for Jackson to join his teammates, but he remained by her side. She had to admit she was still succumbing to that attraction. It might even be stronger because of the years away from him, but she wouldn't give into her feelings, and that meant putting distance between them at all times.

She took her plate and coffee cup and sat next to Riley. He smiled at her, his slate blue eyes lighting up. Why couldn't she feel some sort of attraction to him? Or to Alex? Maybe then she could forget about Jackson's gaze that remained pointedly locked on her.

He glanced at his watch. "Sketch artist should be here soon."

Maggie nodded, her mind going to the task. She would have to recall in detail the man who likely attacked her, and now her breakfast felt like a hockey puck in her stomach.

"While you work with him, we'll have a look around the exterior of your house to formulate a security plan," Jackson continued, not seeming to notice her rising anxiety.

This was her home he was talking about. Her sanctuary. The place she was born and raised in. Her roots. She really didn't want to think that she wasn't safe in her own home.

Riley took a long sip of his coffee. "After that, you'll be heading to the morgue, right?"

She nodded.

Alex looked at Jackson. "You want help on that trip?"

Jackson shook his head. "I'd rather have the three of you assess the Summit neighborhood before Maggie goes back there."

Eryn set down her slice of toast and met Maggie's gaze. "How late in the day do you plan to work at Summit?"

"As long as there's daylight."

Jackson dropped his fork to his plate with a clank. "Any way I can convince you to leave before the sun sets?"

She stared at him pointedly. "I'm already losing precious time on the sketch and the morgue trip. I hate to waste even more of the day and drag out this recovery. Not with families waiting for news."

"It would be far easier for us to protect you if you would cut out a bit early," Eryn added.

Maggie wanted to stick to her guns, but she couldn't very well do so now. Not when she could make things easier for these people who were voluntarily making sure she didn't come to any harm. "What say we leave a half hour before sunset. Will that work?"

"Yes. Thank you." Eryn smiled. Her face came alive with it, lifting high cheekbones that most women would love to have. She possessed this amazing strength, and yet her long, silky black hair and riveting dark eyes, gave her a feminine look at the same time

The doorbell rang, and Maggie got up to answer.

Jackson held up his hand. "Let me get the door."

"It's probably just the sketch artist."

"I know, but we have to be cautious."

Jackson headed for the door. On the way, he nodded at Riley who got up and went to the entrance. He wore a gun in a holster at his side. All the team members did, but Riley snapped off a safety strap and planted his feet wide as if he were a human shield.

Alex and Eryn remained seated but swiveled to face the door. Their intensity ratcheted up—if that was even possible —and left Maggie feeling breathless. Her anxiety rising, she couldn't just sit there. She started to get up to put a beef roast in the crock-pot so there'd be barbequed beef for sandwiches when they got home for dinner.

Eryn shook her head. "Stay put, please."

These guys were serious, very serious, and Maggie's heart started hammering as she dropped back onto the stool and kept her focus on the entryway. She heard the door open, Jackson talking, and a man responding. Footsteps came their way. She knew in her heart that Jackson wouldn't lead her attacker in her direction, and this must indeed be the sketch artist, but now her heart was beating so hard she couldn't relax at all.

Jackson rounded the corner. A thin guy with a bald head

wearing jeans and a navy T-shirt followed behind. He carried a leather satchel and small wooden easel.

"This is Bobby Evers," Jackson said and introduced everyone.

Bobby's focus zoned in on Maggie. "Where would you like to set up?"

"The family room, I guess." She pushed off the stool and wasn't surprised her leg muscles were wobbly. "Would you like some coffee or juice?"

He patted his bag. "Brought my morning shake with me."

"Then follow me." She led the way to the family room and dropped onto the sofa before anyone noticed how unsteady the scare had left her. If she was going to survive this ordeal with a minimum of stress, she had to figure out a way to control her emotions.

Once upon a time, trusting God had helped. But since losing Alison, her talks with God were more about questions that she received no answers for, than about trusting Him to protect and help her.

Too many things had gone wrong in the past few years, and she lost the faith like a child that she once possessed. She didn't want to admit to this failure of faith, but there it was, and she couldn't deny it any longer.

Bobby unfolded his easel consisting of two boards hinged together with metal clips. It looked more like a wooden portfolio than an easel. He clipped a sheet of filmy paper on the right side, but nothing on the left. He selected a few pencils from his bag, grabbed a dark green sludge-looking drink, and sat across from her, resting the board on his lap.

He took a sip of the green glop. "Go ahead and describe this man."

As memories came flooding back, she fidgeted with her fingers. "He was...I don't...I mean..."

"Relax." Bobby's smile widened, and he set down the drink. "Try to forget what this man did to you. Just isolate his face in your mind and give me the details. It might help to close your eyes."

Right. Easy for him to say. Still, she let her lids close and concentrated on last night's conversation.

"What nationality was he?"

"Um...Caucasian, I think."

"What shape is his face? Bobby asked.

"Round. And he had a beard. It was thick."

"Color?"

"Dark brown. Almost black. Neatly trimmed. Maybe an inch long." She heard his pencil scratching over the paper and paused to let him catch up.

"What about his eyes?" he asked.

"He wore glasses. Wire rimmed. Oval. He had a professor kind of vibe or maybe a serious student."

"Good. Good." His pencil scratched frantically. "What color were his eyes?"

"I don't know. It was too dark. The same for his hair. The hood of his sweatshirt was up." She sighed and opened her eyes. "I trusted him. Not at first, but when he explained who he was." She shook her head. "How dumb was that? I was like out in nowhere. A strange man approached me, and I trusted him. If I hadn't, maybe I could have protected myself. Called 911. Done something so he wasn't still out there wanting to hurt me."

The thought of him coming to her house, maybe to the morgue or the neighborhood again, sent a tremor snaking through her body.

"I'm sorry this happened to you." Bobby's pencil stilled, and he looked up. "Try to clear that from your mind, though. Just focus on the physical features. Like you're simply standing back and observing someone. Maybe you can describe his nose."

She nodded and closed her eyes again. Clear everything out. Check. Focus on that face so he can be caught. Check. She let her mind go and recounted every detail she could remember.

Mentally exhausted, she lay back against the sofa and stared at the wood ceiling. She wished her dad was here. She missed him so badly. Her mom had been gone since Maggie's high school years, but the ache in her heart never went away, the pain so reminiscent of losing Alison.

Tears pricked Maggie's eyes. She willed them away and curled her fingers into a tight ball.

"Done," Bobby announced. "Take a look at this and let me know if it's accurate."

She sat forward, and he held out the paper.

She took a quick look. "No. No. That's not him."

"No worries." He smiled. "It's rare to get it right the first time. What seems to be wrong?"

"The shape of his eyes, I think."

Bobby took a booklet from his backpack, flipped it open, and handed it to her. "This is the FBI's Facial Identification Catalog. Try to find similar eyes in one of these pictures."

She studied the many faces on each page and finally saw a pair of eyes very like her attacker's. She pointed at the picture. "But his were a bit narrower. And so is his nose. Narrower than the picture you drew, that is."

Bobby erased and started sketching again. Maggie waited patiently and felt a yawn coming on. Despite the overwhelming fatigue from the adrenaline crash as Jackson predicted last night, she didn't sleep much. And recalling the man who'd attacked her was emotionally taxing, adding to her tiredness. She had important work to do today and couldn't let the weariness get to her. On top of that, she needed to be alert for danger, too.

Man, that was just crazy. Someone wanted to kill her. Really kill her.

"Okay, look at this." Bobby turned the board around.

She took one look at the paper, and her breath whooshed from her body. "Yes. That's him. That's the man from last night. My attacker."

Jackson stretched to work out the kinks in his muscles from sleeping on a too-small sofa and took a long look around Maggie's front yard. As he suspected last night, the pines were grouped as thick as a forest, providing far too many spots for an attacker to take cover. The trees also lined the drive winding up the mountain. Normally, Jackson would expect that the aerial view of the property that Riley was recording with their drone would help them formulate a strong plan. But in this case, Jackson thought aerial footage would simply display a forest encircling the small clearing holding Maggie's house.

That meant his visual inspection was more important than ever. He looked up at Maggie's front porch.

"I don't much like the overgrown shrubs around the foundation," he said to Alex.

He turned to face Jackson. "You still in love with her?"

Jackson shot him a look. "Who said I ever was?"

"C'mon, man. It's as plain as that ugly nose on your face."

Jackson rolled his eyes. "Not something I'm going to talk about."

"When did the two of you date?"

"Said I wasn't going to talk about it."

"Yeah, well, I didn't say I'd quit asking." Alex grinned and ran a hand through his hair. Of all the team members, he was the one who cared most about his looks. He had naturally curly hair, but used gel to tame it into submission and wore it spiked in the middle.

Jackson continued walking the perimeter and hoped that Alex would give up, but he was like a pit bull, and barring something else gaining his interest, he would keep trying to get details. They rounded the far corner of the house to discover a view overlooking the smoky valley covered in tall pines.

He headed for the back edge of the property, ambling down the incline that led to a large level back yard. A contemporary metal-and-wire cable fence sat at the rear of the property where the ground dropped off sharply. A large seating area with plush chairs was located near the fence. He stepped across the pavers and checked out the steep cliff.

"No one's coming up that rock face," Alex said from behind.

"Unless he's a climber." A long shot, but Jackson couldn't rule out the possibility even though it was remote.

He heard the sound of their drone taking flight and looked up to see it whiz overhead. Riley was an avid video gamer so operating a drone was really in his wheelhouse.

"Let's walk the rest of the perimeter." Jackson took a winding path across the yard to a large brick patio with a sliding door on the house's lower level. "Don't much like this door. It's way too easy to breach."

Alex didn't respond but took a few steps closer to the

foundation and squatted near a flower bed. "You should see this."

Everyone on the team possessed strong scouting skills, but Alex took it to a much higher level. Jackson joined him near a large footprint in the soil. Not hardly Maggie's shoe size and definitely not the petite Daria's, either. Alex got up to look around the area, and Jackson tried to see it from his teammate's Recon Marine viewpoint.

"Sprinklers ran recently," he said. "The footprint was made after that or the water would've obscured the edges."

"I heard the sprinklers come on at five this morning. Whoever made this print was out here after that." Jackson's gut knotted as he came to his feet and checked the slider to be sure it was still locked. "I don't see any other sign of an intruder, do you?"

Alex shook his head. "He must've come from the front yard. Maybe we'll see something on the west side."

"What do you think he was doing here?"

"If it was me, I'd be doing recon. But then I'm always doing recon." Alex chuckled.

Jackson found nothing humorous in their discovery. "We need to find a way to secure this patio door."

"Best way to do that is for one of us to take the couch down here tonight."

"You volunteering?"

"It's a cinch that you won't be leaving Maggie's side, so yeah, I can do it." He eyed Jackson. "About that. How long did you and Maggie date?"

"Nice try." Jackson shook his head. "Let's finish the perimeter and get Riley over here to cast this print."

As a former police officer, Riley was in charge of forensic collections at non-crime scene locations, but Gage was currently in the market to hire a forensic team member. Not an easy task when most forensic techs didn't get injured on the job, and Gage was sticking with that criteria for all team members. Something Jackson and the others appreciated.

Jackson continued along the foundation, looking for evidence.

"I will get it out of you, you know?" Alex said.

"I know," Jackson replied. "But I'm gonna make you work for it."

He climbed the incline but struck out in locating any additional signs of a visitor. "You mind tasking Riley with casting that print? I want to talk to Maggie about it."

"She's gonna freak."

Would she? "She's a strong woman. She'll be able to handle it."

"I don't envy you, man."

"Why's that?"

"With the personal connection, there's got to be a lot of additional stress for you."

Jackson stared him down. "More like pressure to find this guy before he hurts her."

Alex nodded. "After I talk to Riley, I'll hike out to the road to see if I can find any fresh tracks."

"Sounds like a good plan." Jackson left Alex behind and took the front steps two at a time. Eryn met him at the door. She was being overly cautious, but he appreciated her care and concern.

Bobby was just packing up his supplies from the coffee table. Maggie got up from the sofa, a drawing in her hand, and joined him near the entrance. Without a word, she handed over the paper.

The face looking at Jackson seemed innocuous enough, and he couldn't believe this guy could've bested him at the truck. Round face, glasses, and jaw covered with a thick beard, he looked like he could teach at Maggie's college or even be a student, not someone who would murder a woman. The only thing that would've made the sketch more valuable was if his hair wasn't hidden under a hoodie, and they could add hair color to his description.

"This's him, huh?" he said.

She nodded. "Not very scary looking, right?"

"No, but you can't let that make you relax." He met her gaze and held it. "You—more than anyone—know what he's capable of doing."

She shuddered, touching her bruised neck, and he instantly regretted his statement. He'd never been one to pull any punches, but maybe he should try to be less blunt with Maggie. She seemed to understand what she was up against now, and he could try backing off a little. If he saw signs of her letting up, he could start being more direct again.

Bobby tentatively crossed the room. "Let me know if you want to make any changes, and I'll be glad to come back out."

"Thank you," Maggie said.

Eryn walked him to the door and secured the lock behind him.

Jackson laid the sketch on the hall table, his focus on Maggie. "You don't have a gardener or anyone who would've come out here this morning, do you?"

"No. Why?"

"We found a footprint in the flower bed by the patio. It was made after the sprinklers ran this morning."

"He was here? Today?" She twisted her hands together.

"Him or someone else," Jackson said to try to ease her concern, but the lingering fear in her expression told him he didn't succeed. "Don't worry about that access point, though. Alex will bunk down by the lower-level door tonight."

She laid her hand on his arm, and her touch sent a jolt of emotions racing through his body. His attraction to her hadn't cooled one bit in six years. Not a drop. Not a pinpoint. It remained on high octane, and he had to admit he loved feeling this alive again. He didn't realize how emotionally dead he was since they broke up.

She smiled up at him, and he forgot everything. Forgot his defenses. Forgot the promise to himself to protect her without getting involved. Let it all go in favor of enjoying the soft, warm smile that replaced his concern with an awareness of her as a woman. Her curves. Her silky skin. Her full lips, soft, and ready for kissing. He knew the feel of them. The touch. Years ago. He wanted more than the memory now. Couldn't have it.

What are you doing, man, other than torturing yourself?

He forced himself to look away.

She squeezed his arm and removed her hand. "I'm so thankful you're here. I don't know what I'd do without you."

"Cook less," he said to lighten the mood and forget how his heart continued to betray his common sense.

"It's the least I can do for you." She exhaled loudly as if the touch affected her too. "So what happens next?"

Perfect. Move back to what they should be talking about. "Riley's finishing the drone flyover. We'll review that footage while he casts the footprint."

"What good will a cast do?"

"Every shoeprint is sort of like a fingerprint," Eryn said, giving Jackson a pointed look.

He totally forgot she was in the room with them. If her look meant anything, it said she saw his personal reaction to Maggie. Eryn was too polite to mention it now, but she would say something later. That, coupled with Alex's earlier comments, told Jackson that he had to do a better job of focusing on the investigation and Maggie's protection. If word got back to Gage that Jackson lost focus of his job when he was with Maggie, Gage might pull him from her detail, and he couldn't live with that.

Case in point—the shoeprint. That's what he needed to focus on. "Two people can wear the same brand and style of a shoe, but the wear pattern on the bottom will be unique for each person. This could also be an unusual style carried only by select vendors, and that could allow us to figure out where he bought it."

"And all of that could lead to your attacker's identity," Eryn added.

"Once Riley is finished with those tasks," Jackson continued. "He'll head over to the Summit neighborhood and take an aerial look there, too. That way we can plan our best defense for the day."

Maggie frowned. "In other words, I won't be heading out to Summit until you have a plan."

He nodded. "I wish we could move faster, but caution is the name of the game."

5

Jackson had never been in a morgue, but he wasn't surprised to find a sterile and clinical-looking room. Big stainless-steel sinks lined one wall and another wall was filled with lockers. Two stainless tables took up the middle of the room, and the bones recovered last night were laid out in the shape of a body. But even Jackson, with his limited anatomy experience, could see many of them were missing.

Dr. Owing stood by the table, her hair spikier today and her eyes bloodshot. She wore a clear plastic face shield, latex gloves, and a lab coat.

Maggie crossed to the table and set her tote bag on the floor. Jackson followed but hung back to observe. The last thing he wanted to do was interfere with their important work.

"The bullet." Dr. Owing held up an evidence bag.

"It did survive the fire, then." Jackson stepped closer. So much for restraining himself and hanging back.

Dr. Owing nodded. "I've been told by a gun enthusiast who works here that it was jacketed with a copper alloy."

"May I look at it?" Jackson asked.

She handed over the bag.

He held it up to the large light above the table and turned the bag to get a good view of all sides. "Appears to be in pretty good shape."

"If a gun is recovered," Maggie said. "Then Nate's team should be able to match this bullet's rifling to it."

He stared at her in surprise. He didn't expect her to understand that all bullets fired from a gun would have the same rifling marks, and no two guns created the same bullet lands and grooves.

"Don't look so surprised." Her eyes crinkled. "As a forensic anthropologist, I often have to identify the cause of damage to bones. Bullets are a big part of that. So big, that I took several classes at our local firing range to become more familiar with handling and firing guns."

Jackson would do well to remember that the woman he was looking at wasn't the Maggie he once knew. Shooting guns? He never expected that from her. She'd changed, and so had he.

He gave the evidence bag to the doctor and stepped back again. The door opened, and Nate entered the room. He nodded his greeting as he joined them at the table.

"Bullet." Dr. Owing held out the bullet to Nate.

Jackson was glad to see he gave it careful study. "This looks like it's in good enough shape to do some comparisons. If we recover a weapon, that is. If not, at least we can positively confirm this man died from a gunshot wound to the head."

"I wouldn't go so far as to say that's the cause of death," Dr. Owing said. "He could have died of smoke inhalation or other fire-related causes. Without organs to evaluate, I can't declare the bullet as his actual cause of death. I can rule the death suspicious, though."

Maggie took a ruler from her bag and cleaned it with the disinfectant wipes at the table. Moving to the skull, she rested it against a circular hole. "I measured this last night, but I wanted to double-check that the hole was made from a small caliber like the recovered bullet."

"Too bad you can't dial it down to the actual caliber," Nate said.

Maggie looked up. "Sadly, we can't now, but a current study discovered that the density of skull bones affects the size of bullet holes made in the skull. So with further research on bone density and diameter of the entry wound, we may be able to pinpoint the caliber in the future."

"That would be an amazing advance," Nate said.

Maggie nodded and shifted her attention to Dr. Owing. "Our first priority is to ID the victim. Have the dental x-rays been done?"

Dr. Owing nodded. "I've emailed the images to our forensic odonatologist who's been working the fire. He'll compare them to the films for the two missing men. We should hear back soon and may have an ID for John Doe in only a few hours."

"And if that doesn't pan out, can you collect DNA from the bones?" Nate asked.

"May be possible," Maggie said, tapping her finger on the table. "But I wouldn't hold my breath. Usually we can get good DNA from bones, but when it's extracted from burnt bone fragments, it can be highly degraded. That would make an amplification of genetic markers difficult or even impossible. And heavily burnt bones are prone to cont-amination with external DNA."

"That's a no then?" Jackson asked.

"No, it's a maybe with long odds." She set down the ruler. "I have a friend who's having success with MPS—Massively Parallel Sequencing—in her DNA work with burnt bones, and we could send her a sample to process. No guarantees, but it might work."

Jackson looked at Nate. "Is that something your DNA lab is doing?"

"Shoot, I don't know."

"I would highly doubt any criminal forensic lab is using MPS," Maggie said. "They've been slow to adopt the process."

"If it works, why not do it?" Nate asked.

Maggie rested her hands on the table. "First, it's slow. The currently accepted procedure takes six to eight hours to obtain twenty CODIS markers from a DNA sample. MPS technology produces ten times the data but takes at least twenty-four hours to do so. And then, practice standardization would be an issue if MPS was introduced in a court of law. However, in this case we're only looking to ID John Doe, not discover the killer's identity, so the courts are irrelevant."

Jackson thought he caught most of what she was explaining, but the whole court thing was still a gray area. Still, this wasn't related to Scott's investigation so he wouldn't waste their time by asking for clarification.

"Can you contact your friend?" Nate asked.

"I'll overnight a sample to her." Maggie bent to grab her bag. "In the meantime, I can give you an approximate height, age, and ethnicity so we can begin building a physical profile."

"But you're sure it's a man?" Nate asked.

She nodded. "A male's pelvis is heart-shaped and narrow like this one."

From her tote, Maggie took out a tool that looked like a

T-square with a sliding scale. She cleaned it, measured the femur, and entered data in a calculator. "He was five eight, give or take a couple of inches." She bent closer to the skull. "The narrow nasal root and bridge as well as the narrow face tell me he's Caucasian."

She moved on to the bones of the wrist and then studied the ribs. Jackson was very interested in this information, especially interested in seeing Maggie's expertise, but he couldn't lose sight of the fact that he wasn't here to help find the person who murdered this man. He was here to find Scott's killer and protect Maggie.

"I'd put him in his late twenties," she announced.

"So we have a Caucasian male in his late twenties about five foot eight who was shot with a smaller than .32 caliber bullet," Nate summarized.

Maggie nodded.

Nate tapped the screen on his phone and stared at it. "He fits the description of one of the two missing homeowners."

Maggie frowned. "I just can't see him being one of these men."

"Why's that?" Nate asked.

"If it is him, how would we explain the dogs lighting on remains in two other locations, and why was he in this shed, not on his own property? And why murdered?"

"No point in speculating until we hear from the odonatologist," Dr. Owing said.

"True." Maggie's eyes tightened as if she didn't want to let it go.

Jackson remembered her tenacious approach to life. Give her a goal, she achieved it, and usually did so in record time. She was extremely intelligent and motivated, which was how she attained her PhD in a shorter-than-normal timeframe.

"I need to get my forensic staff out there to process the scene ASAP," Nate said. "So where do you stand in releasing the scene to us?"

"We're missing bones, and I'd like to do one more pass of the area in daylight," Maggie replied.

"I have a deputy stationed out there to protect the integrity of the scene so just let him know when you're finished."

"Thank you, Nate. I will." Maggie turned her attention to the ME. "Would it be possible for me to come back here tonight so I can drop off anything I find at the site? Plus give all the bones a close examination."

Dr. Owing smiled, her long face widening. "I'm glad to meet you here. Just text me when you're ready."

Maggie looked at the doctor then Nate. "And one of you will let me know what you hear from the odonatologist?"

Nate nodded. "If there's nothing else you need me for, I'll head out."

"Go. Go." The doctor shooed him away with her hands, and he left the room.

"Before I go," Maggie said. "I'll need packaging materials to send the sample to my friend."

Dr. Owing nodded. "I'll get it."

"And I'll call Stacey to be sure she can process the sample before I send it on." Maggie stepped away from the table and made the call. Jackson was content to lean back against the wall and watch her as she talked. She twisted her hair in her finger as she often did on phone calls, one of the many things he'd found cute about her.

Dr. Owing returned and placed the packaging supplies on the table. "You ever been through anything like this?"

Jackson shook his head. "But I did see a lot of trauma in the army."

"Ah, a former solider. I know it's kind of trite to thank you for serving our country, but I have a lot of respect for soldiers." She sighed. "And I, too, have seen firsthand the damage war can do."

"Not trite at all, but none of us do it for thanks."

She gave a crisp nod. "My son would agree. He's career navy."

"Then you're the one needing thanks," Jackson said. "A soldier's family carries the heavy weight of service and the worry, too."

Jackson thought he saw tears form in her eyes, but she quickly cut her gaze to Maggie who was finishing her call.

She stowed her phone as she crossed over to them. "We're good to go. If it's okay, I'll select the bone in the best condition for DNA recovery."

"Go ahead. We've already photographed and inventoried every bone and fragment so no need to worry about that. I'll need your signature on our chain of custody log, but then you're good to go."

It took Maggie thirty minutes of picking up and peering at bones to decide which one to send, but once she did, she carefully packaged it, said goodbye to Dr. Owing, and met Jackson at the door. "I'd like to drop this off at a shipping place on the way."

"Sure." He smiled at her. "I'm really impressed by you. You sure know your stuff, don't you?"

She blinked rapidly. "What do you mean?"

"You're an expert in your field, and I can't get over all that you accomplished since I last saw you."

A blush crept over her face, and the urge to kiss her and intensify her blush was almost too strong to resist.

She held up the package. "We should get going."

"Right." Jackson lifted his hand to stop her from stepping out the door. He took a long cleansing breath as he moved into the hallway. Once he was sure it was clear, he motioned for her to join him.

She tucked the package under her arm. "You don't think my attacker could be here, do you?"

"No, but—"

"But we need to be cautious."

"Right. You get it."

"How could I not. You've reminded me of the danger plenty of times." She pinched her lips together. "I'm sorry. I don't mean to be cranky. I just have a ton to do to help the victim's family, and I hate to waste time thinking about myself."

"Think of it this way, then. If something happened to you, who would help these families?"

She looked at him. "They would just call in another forensic anthropologist."

"But would he or she be as good as you?"

"No." A grin found its way to her face.

He smiled along with her, but at the main exit, he held up his hand again and let go of his good mood so he didn't miss even the smallest detail and put her life in danger.

On the way to Summit, they dropped the DNA sample at a package delivery store with a guaranteed morning delivery, and Maggie hoped they would finally be on track to learn the deceased's identity. Of course, his DNA sample would need to be in CODIS for that to work. The FBI database held DNA for many criminals, but if their victim wasn't arrested or a prior victim of a crime that required taking a sample, then getting the DNA profile from this bone wouldn't help.

She decided to think positively and sat back as they sped down the highway heading for Summit. She felt weird with Jackson driving her SUV. Had felt odd last night, too, but she was too tired to think much of it. But today, she noticed every movement the guy made and driving was no exception.

What was it going to feel like with him standing at her side while she sifted through ruins?

Grr. She was placing far too much importance on his presence. Thinking about every little thing he said for way too long. Case in point, his compliment about her accomplishments at the morgue. She still felt a warm glow inside and wanted more of that sensation. Was she feeling this way because it was Jackson, or was she so desperate for a man's companionship that she lingered in the compliment?

Not that she hadn't been in a man's company since they'd broken up. She dated. Several great guys, in fact. Men who would make fine life partners, but she didn't connect on a deep level with any of them.

She sighed.

Jackson shot her a look, and she wished she'd controlled that sigh. He obviously was tuned into everything she did the same way she was noticing his every move.

"Everything okay?" he asked.

She nodded.

He eyed her. "Is it really, or are you just putting on a good front?"

She never could or wanted to lie to him. She shifted in her seat to face him. "The front, I guess. You being here has really thrown me for a loop."

"I feel the same way."

The comment sent a flash of satisfaction through her. Just the thing she was trying to avoid.

"I'm glad to see you, though," he added. "Real glad."

"Me too," she admitted and hoped by saying it aloud, her crazy emotions would no longer have any power over her. "Maybe when we split up we were too quick to say we'd never see or talk to each other again. If we'd taken time to talk things out, we might've had a better chance at moving on."

"Have you moved on?"

"Not really."

"Yeah. I get that." He fell silent. Perhaps thinking about the past or simply considering what to say next.

She should think about that, too. Should she continue this discussion? Hash out their past? They were only minutes away from Summit and getting into a discussion only to have it interrupted might not bode well for their afternoon together. But tonight? After the second morgue visit? Maybe they could talk then.

She turned to suggest it when the Bee Gees started belting out "Stayin' Alive" over the SUV's speakers.

Jackson shot her a questioning look.

"Don't look at me," she shouted above the song. "I didn't turn it on." She twisted the knob to completely lower the volume. The sound kept blaring from the speakers.

"I can't turn it down," she said.

His brow furrowed, and he reached for the knob. "Odd. Volume is all the way off."

The fan suddenly came on, blasting hot air in her face.

She looked at Jackson. "What's happening?"

"Looks like the car's computer is malfunctioning."

She frowned. "Of all the times for that to happen. If it breaks down—"

The small monitor on the dashboard flashed with a message. It read, "I TOLD YOU. I'M NOT GOING AWAY FOR MURDER."

Her heart dropped to her stomach. "What in the world?"

"It's not a malfunction. Your attacker must've hacked the car's computer."

Before she could even process Jackson's comment, the windshield washer fluid sprayed nonstop, flooding the windshield.

Jackson reached for the wipers. "Wipers won't turn on."

She grabbed the dashboard, trying to get a good view of the road, but the liquid blocked her view. "Can you see?"

"Barely." His tense tone sent her heart racing. "I'll slow down and pull over ahead."

The engine suddenly accelerated, and the vehicle sped up.

"You didn't do that, right?" she shrieked over the still-blaring song.

"Right," he replied, the one word deadly intense. He slammed on the brakes. The SUV continued to speed up. She glanced at his leg. He pumped the brakes again. And again.

She clutched his arm. "Jackson?"

"We don't have any brakes, and I have no control over our speed."

The speedometer continued to climb. He fumbled with the switches, and it stopped accelerating.

"What did you do?" she cried out in relief and slumped back.

"I turned off cruise control. Maybe we'll be able to coast to a stop now."

"Yes, good."

He jabbed a finger at his phone mounted in a holder on the dash. Eryn's name displayed on the screen, and she soon answered.

"Our car's computer has been hacked," he yelled over the music. "Use GPS to track us. We need help."

The steering wheel suddenly cranked right, jerking the vehicle toward the side of the road.

Maggie screamed and shot up in her seat.

"Jackson." Eryn shouted. "Turn down the music—I can't hear you!"

Jackson grabbed the wheel, and Maggie saw him try to jerk them back onto the road.

"I have no control over the steering," he yelled so Eryn could hear.

"No!" Maggie clutched the door handle. "Oh no."

"Jackson!" Eryn's voice was faint.

He shot out an arm in front of Maggie. "Brace yourself, honey. We're going to crash."

6

Jackson kept his arm lodged in front of Maggie. He used his other hand to wrestle with the steering wheel. Fat lot of good it did him. The SUV hit the edge of the pavement and jerked harder, sliding on the gravel and dragging them toward the ditch.

He cranked the wheel more to the left, but his efforts didn't change their course by even an inch. The ditch was a few feet ahead. A large lake another ten feet after that. He pounded the brakes frantically.

No response.

The vehicle dropped into the ditch and kept going. The lake loomed ahead.

God, no. Keep us safe.

Five feet. Three. A foot.

The vehicle plunged into the lake, hitting hard. Jackson's body flew forward and jerked back. His bum knee smashed into the gear shift. He bit down on his tongue not to yell and worry Maggie.

She screamed again.

"Jackson?" Eryn cried out. "What's happening?"

Maggie jolted against his hand. He tried to hold her back, but he couldn't. His airbag slammed into his face. Hers into his hand, pushing it tight against her body.

"Hold on, honey," he called out. "Just hold on. We'll get out soon."

The SUV rocked. Groaned. Floated. The front dropped fast. Water washed over the hood and seeped into the vehicle at an alarming rate. His airbag started deflating. Eager to check on Maggie, he punched it down the rest of the way. Thankfully, the music stilled and the fan quit pumping hot air into the car.

"We're in the lake, Eryn," he shouted, and hoped she was still connected. "We need help now!"

"On it," Eryn replied, and he was so thankful he'd thought to call her.

"You okay, honey?" he called to Maggie.

No answer.

Fear settled in his heart, twisting and turning in anguish. "Maggie!"

He reached for his seat belt and snapped it off. He leaned across the console. His knee felt like it was on fire, but he ignored the pain and pressed the bag from her face.

She lifted her eyes to his. Hers were wide with shock, her face bright red from the airbag slap.

"Are you hurt?" He searched her face, her body, looking for any injury.

"I don't think so." She grabbed his hand. "Are you okay?"

He ignored the throbbing pain in his knee and nodded. Over her shoulder, he saw water lapping at her window and seeping into the vehicle.

They had to get out of the vehicle—now!

"Can you get your seat belt off?" he asked.

She reached for it. "Water. Oh no. Water. It's filling up. We'll drown!"

"Listen to me, honey. Get that seat belt off—now—while I get us out of here."

She fumbled to find her belt. "Can't we just open the door?"

"No—don't even try! Water pressure's too strong, and we'd just sink faster."

"Then what?" Her voice was high with anxiety.

"Don't worry. I've got your back." He turned around and jerked out the headrest. "You have that seat belt off yet?"

"Yes."

"Okay. Listen carefully." He faced her. "On your side of the car, I'm going to jam the metal part of the headrest into the window where it meets the door. That should break the window. When it does, I need you to take a big breath and swim out through the rushing water."

"And what about you?"

"I'll be right behind you."

"Okay. I can do that."

"That's my girl." He smiled at the trust replacing fear in her expression.

She didn't return his smile, but impulsively, he kissed her. She didn't balk or pull away so he deepened the kiss, pouring out every ounce of his past feelings for her. She returned his kiss with passion.

Stunned by his reaction, he pulled back. He'd kissed her. How crazy was that. Likely a reaction to the shock. Fear of death. Death—he had to get them out of there!

"Ready?" he asked. "Lean toward me and cover your face."

She obeyed.

He rose up as high as he could and slammed the headrest into the window. Cracks climbed up the glass and it crumbled. The shattering sound was music to his ears. Water poured through the window.

He dropped the headrest. "Deep breath and go!"

Maggie gulped air and planted her hands on the frame to pull her body out of the vehicle. She floated upward, and he pushed off after her. Once out, he took her hand and hooked it onto his belt. A stronger swimmer than she was, he propelled them toward the light.

He broke the surface and breathed deep. She popped up next to him. Gasped for air. He pulled her into his arms and treaded water with his feet.

"We made it! Thank you, Jackson. You're amazing." She flung her arms around his neck and nearly took him down with her exuberance.

"Let's get to shore." Adrenaline buzzing through his body, he towed her toward shore. He kept swimming until he figured it was shallow enough and stood. His feet sunk into deep muck, but he kept holding her and slogged to the shore where he settled her down on the grass. She fell back against a tree and panted heavily.

A gunshot cracked loud in the silence, and a bullet whizzed past—right where she'd just been standing.

Jackson grabbed her and dropped to the ground behind a felled tree, covering her body with his. He reached for his phone to call in backup and then remembered it was in the car. They were on their own now, and he had to figure a way out while keeping Maggie safe.

"Was that a gunshot?" she asked, her teeth chattering.

"Yes."

"Fired at us?" Her voice pitched higher.

No. You. But he wasn't going to tell her that now. He lifted his body, making sure to keep his head below the log, and waited for her to meet his gaze. "Shhh. I need you to stay down while I check this out."

She clutched his arm. "But you could be shot."

He looked her square in the eye. This was life-or-death. The slightest mistake would kill them both. His voice was firm. "I'll be fine, but I need you to stay right here. Head down. Body prone. Behind this log. Can you promise to do that? No matter what you hear or see. Stay down."

She nodded.

"That's my girl." He kissed her forehead and didn't think twice about the second kiss in such a short time.

She squeezed his arm and released him. He rolled to his side, crawled along the log to a thick tree, and quickly took cover behind it. He poked his head out to take a quick look and jerked back. No response from the shooter. He tried it again. No gunshot.

He dropped to his belly, drew his weapon, and slithered in the direction from where the shot was fired. He saw movement across the road. A man. Muscular. Wearing jeans and a sweatshirt, hood up. He didn't wear glasses, but his face was round, and he had a beard. He could easily be Maggie's attacker.

Jackson waited for the guy to turn away before bolting across the road. He tried to move in silence, but he stepped on a twig, the snapping sound reverberating through the trees and sending birds in flight. The suspect looked back. Caught sight of Jackson. Took off running.

Jackson kicked it into high gear but darted from tree to tree to protect himself from a bullet to the chest. His covert movements soon had him falling way behind. If he hoped to catch the shooter, he had to be more aggressive.

He charged out from behind the tree and ran no-holds-barred after the man. Jackson's knee protested but he kept going and gained on the suspect.

Twenty feet. Then fifteen. Ten. Five. Almost there.

He lifted his arms, ready to reach out and tackle the man.

Pain sliced through Jackson's knee, and it suddenly gave out.

No! Not now. He pitched headfirst into the scrub. Somersaulted. Once. Twice. Landed flat on his back, the breath knocked out of him. He dragged in some air and pushed to his feet. Pain ripped through his knee, stealing what little air he managed to take. He stood for a moment. Took a few tentative steps. Felt like his leg would collapse beneath him. He couldn't keep running. Not with this stupid knee.

He started limping back toward the lake as sirens sounded in the distance, winding through the air. He alternated hopping and limping. He didn't realize how far he'd traveled, but it seemed like miles on his gimpy knee with his soggy clothes weighing him down. When he reached the road, he spotted Maggie sitting in the front of Eryn's rental car. She jumped out when she saw him but stayed near the vehicle. He swallowed hard and tried to walk as normally as possible. He didn't want Maggie to think he wasn't up to protecting her.

Eryn rushed up and fell into step with him.

"Have the responding deputy put out an alert on the shooter," he said. "Shooter's around six feet. Two hundred pounds. Wearing jeans and a black hoodie. Fits the sketch from this morning."

"Roger that." She pulled out her phone and turned away.

Maggie rushed to him. Her hair hung limply over her shoulders, and her clothing melded to her body, revealing

84

her curves. He wanted to linger on that view, but he forced his gaze back to her face.

She brushed her hair back, and gave him a quick once-over, her focus lingering on his knee for a long moment. "Are you okay?"

He nodded and was thankful that Nate pulled up just then, drawing her attention. Jackson put all his weight on his good leg, and waited for the sheriff to exit his car and join them.

Stopping next to Jackson, Nate ran his gaze over Jackson's wet and dirty clothes, then stared down the embankment where Jackson's teammates were squatting by the tire tracks from Maggie's SUV.

Nate faced Jackson. "Give me a rundown."

Jackson did. Straight and to the point. If Maggie wasn't standing there, he would elaborate, but he didn't want to raise the worry he knew she was already feeling.

He hated that he didn't catch the gunman, but he wasn't going to dwell on it. They had to move forward which meant gathering evidence to locate the suspect. "Slug's in the water."

Nate nodded. "I'll get my team on thermal imaging, and we may get lucky and find it."

"What are the odds of that?" Jackson asked.

"Since it's soon after the shot, we have a better chance."

"And if you don't recover it?"

"Then we'll move on to more expensive options like divers or dredging if my budget can take the hit."

"Our team leader is a former SEAL, and I'm sure he'd be glad to do the dive if it comes to that," Jackson offered.

"Appreciate it. I'll also arrange to get the vehicle out of the lake. Then I'll have my tech guys look into the hack."

Eryn possessed skills far superior to the average county

computer tech and Jackson wanted her in on it. "Can our tech person work with your team? She's a former FBI agent and served as a cyber security professional for them."

Nate nodded. A good sign when many local sheriffs might resent the offer. "I'd appreciate the help."

"Eryn," Jackson called out. "Mind joining us?"

She got up, brushed off her pants, and started toward them. Jackson was always thankful for his teammates, but now that he was working an investigation with personal ties, he was even more thankful. And speaking of personal, Maggie smiled at him, and he suddenly remembered that he'd kissed her. Not once, but twice. Could she be thinking about it, too?

Talk about losing his focus. They'd had one, maybe two minutes to get out of that car, and he paused to kiss her like some middle school boy with a crush.

Eryn stopped in front of the group, her gaze darting from one to the other. "What do you need?"

Jackson introduced her to Nate and explained. "Nate will hook you up with his team."

Nate nodded, seemingly tongue-tied as he stared at Eryn. She had that effect on men. She was a very striking woman yet tough, exuding strength that warned she could take on a guy in a boxing ring. A combination that took Jackson some time to get used to.

"So—your people," she said pointedly.

Nate pulled out of his trance. "Right. If you want to hang out here until we bring up the vehicle, you can follow me back to the station, and I'll get you started."

She looked at Jackson. "Can you spare me at Summit?"

He nodded. "We're not going back there until I have some answers."

Maggie frowned. "But I—"

86

"Need to help the families," Jackson interrupted and tried his best not to snap. "I know you're committed to them. Trust me, I wouldn't get in your way if I didn't think it was too dangerous to go out there right now."

"Speaking of Summit," Nate said. "John Doe's dental x-rays aren't a match for either of the missing men."

"So it's official." Maggie's voice was strained. "We have a third victim. Though we have to suspect John Doe wasn't a victim of the fire but died before it."

Nate gave a quick nod. "I'll get on the phone with the homeowners of the property where he was discovered and tell them about John Doe. Maybe even try to get them to come back to town so I can interview them properly."

"Is it really necessary to cut their vacation short?" Maggie asked.

"Body language can tell us a lot more about their involvement than I'll get from a phone call."

"Will you show them the sketch for my attacker, too?" Maggie asked.

"Yes, and I have a deputy showing it to everyone who stops by Summit today. Plus, we're trying to contact every Summit homeowner to see if they recognize him."

"Glad to hear that," Jackson said.

"What about missing persons in the area?" Eryn asked. "Can you request dental records for any that might fit John Doe's build?"

"Already done. We're looking at two potential men, and I'll let you know if they pan out. If you'll excuse me, I'll make arrangements for the imaging and the SUV." Nate spun and strode over to his deputy who stood next to his car, blocking the road.

Eryn moved closer to them. "Maggie brought me up to speed on your adventure."

Jackson nodded. "If only I could have stopped it."

"Actually," Eryn said. "If the ECU's been compromised, there's nothing anyone could have done."

"ECU?" Jackson asked.

"Electronic Control Unit." Eryn widened her stance as she often did when she got going on her favorite subject. "We're dealing with a very capable hacker here."

"How can you tell that?" Maggie asked.

"Basic car hacking like turning on the radio and fan isn't difficult, but compromising a vehicle's so-called Electronic Control Unit—or ECU—that's tougher. The hacker had to use the CAN network to spoof messages to the SUV's steering and brakes, and that takes greater skills. The ECU sends legitimate commands to those components, so the hacker would have somehow paralyzed that innocent ECU and sent malicious commands to the target component without interference."

"In English, please?" Jackson smiled.

Eryn wrinkled her nose. "With this hack, the vehicle's computer is telling it to do one thing, and the hacker is telling it to do something else. This basically knocks the other computer offline, and the hacker takes control. I haven't seen this complicated of a hack done remotely, but it's not far-fetched to believe it happened."

"Even if it was remotely hacked, the guy had to be tailing us if he knew when to take that shot at Maggie." Anger at Maggie being in such danger had Jackson seeing red, and he ground his teeth.

"We'll need to get a look at any traffic or CCTV cams in the area," Eryn said. "I can take care of that."

Maggie glanced from one to the other, her focus settling on Jackson. "If all of this is true, we're looking at a fairly talented computer person, right? Scott could've been friends with computer students at the college."

"Good point," Jackson said. "When we get back to your place, I'll review our earlier interviews to see if there's a lead there. If so, we can head to campus and run it down."

Maggie waved a finger between them. "We—as in you and me? Like you'll actually allow me to leave the house?"

Jackson resisted sighing. "You know that I'm not trying to be difficult, just trying to keep you alive, right?"

She ran a hand through her tangled hair. "I know, and that came out snippy. I didn't mean it that way. I just want to go with you to campus."

Given a choice, he'd put her in a bulletproof bubble, but he had no right to let his unreasonable fears dictate his actions as her bodyguard. "Depends on the lead, and if you're needed. I may not go myself. Might send Alex or Riley."

But would he send someone else?

Not likely. Not with a chance to make some headway on this investigation and get this killer off the street before he struck again.

7

In her kitchen, Maggie stood before the crock-pot, inhaling the savory scent of beef that had roasted all day and filled the house with a tantalizing aroma. She shredded the meat and mixed in barbeque sauce for their dinner. As much as she complained about going home instead of returning to Summit, her body ached from the seat belt cutting into her chest and abdomen, and she couldn't imagine kneeling over the ruins and sifting through debris. She was far better off taking time to recuperate, swallowing some aspirin to bring down the swelling, and returning to work in the morning.

And of course, getting out of the wet clothes so she could quit thinking about the accident. About the gunshot. About the kiss. Correction—kisses.

She was shocked at first, but then she readily welcomed Jackson's kiss. She forgot all about the sinking SUV and their lives being in jeopardy. She returned his kiss for all she was worth. She would always care about him, but until they reconnected, she'd thought all romantic feelings had ended.

Footsteps approached the kitchen, and she turned to see Jackson entering the room. "Thought I'd find you in here."

All those thoughts of kissing him had her gaze traveling to his mouth, and she jerked her focus away. "The kitchen is still my go-to place to relax and unwind."

"I never liked to see you stressed, but my stomach always benefited from it." He patted his perfectly flat abdomen and grinned.

She didn't want to smile. Didn't want to enjoy being with him or she might find herself wanting to kiss him again. But he had the best smile, and it was hard to resist. It was one of the things she'd fallen for on the spot. His whole face came alive. Bright white teeth. Full lips. And eyes that gleamed, the skin crinkling at the edges.

He took a step toward her. Lifted his hand as if he planned to touch her. She jerked back. His smile fell, a stony look replacing it for a moment, but he quickly cleared it away and took a seat on a stool.

He watched her for a long time, his index finger tapping on the granite countertop. "You asked earlier if I thought we did the wrong thing by splitting up and not working through our loss together. Is that what you think?"

Wow, she didn't expect him to bring that up right away. "I don't know. Maybe. What about you?"

"I've been giving it some thought. I doubt staying together would've helped. Not with the way you blamed me."

"Blamed you?" She rested her hands on the island. "I never blamed you. The accident was my fault. If I hadn't gotten mad and grabbed your arm, the car would never have gone off the road. It's all my doing. We would have a beautiful daughter if I hadn't lost my cool."

He shook his head. "Don't be so quick to take the blame. If I'd stepped up to my responsibility as a father right off the bat, we wouldn't have even been in the car that day, much less arguing. I blew it when I said I wasn't ready to be a dad. Made it worse when I took off and left you alone to figure things out on your own. That's the real issue here."

She sighed, letting out years of anguish in one breath. "We're both to blame."

"I guess," he said, but he sounded skeptical.

She sat on a stool and swiveled to face him. "You don't think so?"

"Maybe...I don't know. If I'd just done the right thing—"

She grabbed his hand. "Stop. Now. You did nothing wrong. It just took you time to react to the news. But you came back to do the right thing. That's what's important here. Forgive yourself and let it go."

He raised an eyebrow. "Like you've forgiven yourself?"

She jerked her hand away.

He spun to face her. "That was uncalled for, I'm sorry. I'm just lashing out at you when I'm mad at myself."

She slid closer and took his hands in hers. The touch of his skin reminded her of the day they'd split up, and she'd grabbed his hands to beg him to reconsider his decision. She was so young and foolish. She thought she could change his mind. But now she knew he'd had to walk away back then and figure things out in his own time. "Seems to me that even if we didn't break up that day, we would've had this same talk over and over and eventually split up."

He stared down at their hands. "You're probably right. Maybe we can never get past it."

"Couples do learn to accept a loss like this and stay together. All the time."

He flashed his gaze to hers and held. "And they don't, too."

Her heart hurt at the pain she saw in his eyes, and she

wished she could offer comfort somehow. But she never found it for herself, so it wasn't hers to offer.

"What are you thinking?" he asked.

She shrugged.

"Come on. You can tell me anything. You know that, right?"

"Once, maybe. Now?" She shrugged again.

"That hasn't changed. I still want to know your thoughts."

"I just wish...my faith. I should've been able to find comfort there. Let it help me through the loss, you know? But no matter how hard I prayed, I felt like I was falling and falling. I waited to hit ground and find firm footing, but even after all this time, I'm still falling. I still think God got it wrong. That I wasn't supposed to lose Alison. I mean, we only had a month to go. Just thirty days, and she would've been born."

Sudden pain like a knife to the chest stabbed Maggie's heart. Her voice dropped to a whisper. "I don't know. Maybe God wasn't watching over me that day. Or maybe He was punishing me."

Jackson didn't say a word, but stared at her for the longest time, emotions racing over his face. "I thought the same thing. Except it was my fault. We shouldn't have been intimate before marriage. But I know God wasn't punishing you. Me, maybe, but not you."

"I was there, too, right along with you."

"So maybe He wasn't punishing either of us. Maybe losing the baby was just a tragic fact of life. Many people lose loved ones in accidents. Maybe God didn't protect us, but I know He wanted us to turn to Him afterward for healing and comfort."

"Did you do that?"

He sat back, breaking contact with her and resting an elbow on the countertop. "I suppose it made me who I am today. But getting close to God? Turning to him? No...I went the other direction. Doubting Him at every turn."

"Yeah, me, too. I mean, honestly, I think of Alison every day, but I try not to analyze things anymore. I'm afraid if I do, I'll go back to that terrible time again when she died, and I can't go back there. I almost didn't make it. Emotionally, I mean."

"I'm so sorry, honey." He lifted his hand to cup the side of her face.

She welcomed his touch now and leaned into the warmth of his palm.

"If only I'd stayed around for you," he continued. "Sure, we might've broken up later, but I could've held you after Alison died. Tried to make things better for you."

"Jackson, I..." She didn't know what to say, but his touch felt so emotionally healing. Like a salve for the raw pain. The ache that she'd tried to bury, and yet it remained close to the surface. She couldn't pull away.

He looked deep into her eyes and slid forward on his stool. She should turn away, but couldn't even if she wanted to, and she didn't. Just like in the sinking SUV, but then she'd been terrified and wanted to cling to him. Now? Now she just wanted him to move closer. Slide his arms around her waist and draw her into his arms. To feel the way she once felt with him.

The timer dinged. The sandwich rolls she'd previously baked and froze were done toasting in the oven. The timing couldn't have been better.

"I need to get the rolls," she said and fled from him as if he was her attacker and not the man she clearly still had feelings for.

~

Okay, how was Jackson going to do this? To go on with Maggie as if nothing had passed between them in the kitchen while his heart ached over her anguish. With his own pain, too. It didn't really matter, he supposed. Not when they still shared so many issues over losing the baby. After all these years carrying the guilt and grief, he doubted he would ever let it go. It seemed as if Maggie felt the same way. So, a future for them? No, it wasn't possible.

He glanced around the dining table where his team-mates devoured the barbeque beef sandwiches, salad, and sweet potato fries as if they hadn't eaten in years. The closest most of them came to home cooking was dinner at Gage's house. After he married Hannah, she took pity on the team and started a weekly dinner. Jackson had to admit it not only fed their stomachs, but their souls in a way, too. Seeing Gage, Hannah, and the kids so happy gave them all hope for such a life. Likely Hannah's ulterior motive.

Hope, yeah, right. His hope was in vain. Hannah and Gage hadn't lost a child. As he and Maggie discussed, even strong couples struggled to survive such a loss, and he and Maggie were far from a strong couple.

"Any updates on my SUV?" Maggie set her sandwich on her plate. She'd only taken a few nibbles and pushed the rest of her food around her plate. Jackson was starting to worry about the small amount of food she consumed at each meal. She had to keep up her strength.

"It turns out there was a software recall for that model a few years ago," Eryn said, her fork mid-air.

"I didn't own it back then," Maggie said. "I bought it used just six months ago. Guess the people who sold it to me didn't pay attention to the recall."

Eryn nodded. "If they had, this hack wouldn't have been possible."

"Does this mean automotive companies have found a way to prevent computerized vehicles from being hacked?" Maggie asked.

Eryn reached for her iced tea. "No, that was just one little patch for this particular model. Computerized cars can still be hacked. And are. There's bound to be more in the future. That you can be sure of. So pay attention to recalls." She looked around the group. "That goes for all of you. You guys might think you're invincible and a little recall doesn't mean a lot, but Jackson can tell you that it does."

"We need to listen to Eryn." He paused to place emphasis on his next words. "For once."

He grinned, and the guys laughed.

She swatted a hand at him but looked at Maggie. "See what I face on this team? I get no respect."

So she said, but her tone didn't convey the same meaning. She knew they were teasing her like a kid sister, and she always rolled with the punches. She was a great teammate and totally one of the guys.

But he would take pity on her and move them on. "Maybe now would be a good time for you to update us on anything you learned about the hacked computer."

She took a sip of tea and set the glass down. "First, you should know that Nate's forensic team recovered the bullet from the lake, but without a weapon it doesn't do us much good right now. Second, they found a GPS tracker in a wheel well."

Jackson slammed a fist to the table, making everyone jump. "Sorry. I don't like the thought that this creep knew where we were today."

"Explains how he found you to take a shot at Maggie," Riley said in disgust.

Eryn nodded. "And on the computer, as I suspected, the hacker put the second ECU into 'bootrom' mode, allowing him to paralyze the factory ECU and send malicious commands to the target component without any interference."

"Really?" Alex said, a big grin forming. "You don't know better than to speak computerese with us after Jackson's crack?"

"It's precisely the reason I did." Eryn wrinkled her nose at him.

"Touché." Alex held out his hand for a fist bump. "Now can you explain or—better yet—just tell us what the impact is?"

Her smile disappeared. "It means that I'm now certain an attack like this isn't possible via a wireless connection. At least not yet. Sure, the wipers, radio, and image can be done wirelessly, but the hacker had to physically tinker with Maggie's car to accomplish the attacks on her steering and brakes."

Jackson shot a look at Alex. "The footprint. Maybe that's why the guy showed up here, and the print by the back door was meant to lead us astray if we heard anything."

"He messed with my SUV when we were home?" Maggie asked before Alex could respond. "How did we miss hearing him doing it?"

"You don't have an alarm on your vehicle," Eryn said. "So all he had to do was use the hack to gain access to the vehicle and modify the computer under the dashboard. That wouldn't have made much noise. That's likely when he installed the GPS, too."

"Why didn't the hack kick in on the way to the morgue?" Riley asked.

"Good question," Jackson said. "The hacker couldn't have known where we would be headed this morning so he couldn't have planned the location where he could shoot at us."

Eryn swallowed her bite. "He coded it to occur the second time the engine was started."

Jackson was baffled. "But why?"

"Only he can tell you that."

Alex frowned. "Maybe he wanted to be sure you were far enough away from home before the computer failed. That way he could tail you to fire off that shot, and the rest of us wouldn't spot him."

"Maybe." Jackson added the mystery to the other facts they just couldn't explain until they found this guy and made him talk. Jackson faced Riley. "Where are we on that footprint?"

He wiped his mouth with a plaid napkin. "I gave the cast to Nate for his staff to evaluate, but it has to cure for seventy-two hours before they can clean and evaluate it."

"That long?"

"Sorry, man. You can't rush things without destroying the cast."

"Anything else on the SUV that might move us forward?" Jackson asked Eryn, almost hating to hear her response.

"Nate has his forensic staff processing the computer console and car for fingerprints, but honestly, I think this guy is smart enough to wear gloves, don't you?"

"He didn't when he attacked me," Maggie said.

"Yeah, that's odd, isn't it?" Jackson said. "He comes out to Summit planning to kill you, why not wear gloves? Or a mask to cover his face just in case you get away and can ID him."

Riley rested his elbows on the table. "Maybe he's not as smart as we think."

"He might not be street smart, but his computer programming skills are top-notch," Eryn said.

With all this talk about their suspect, Jackson lost his appetite, and he pushed his plate away, earning a concerned look from Maggie. She knew it took a lot for him to lose his appetite, and he was probably adding to her worry. He should've just choked down the rest of the sandwich, but the damage was done now.

He polished off his glass of iced tea. "Before dinner, I reviewed our interviews with Scott's friends. A few have computer backgrounds, but they didn't mention anything about programming or computers in conjunction with Scott. I still want to talk to them again tomorrow."

"What are their names?" Maggie lifted a fry to her mouth.

"Right, you might know them." Jackson tapped his phone and opened his note screen. "Hugh Reinhardt and Garrett North."

Maggie swallowed her bite. "I know Hugh. He took my Intro to Anthropology course last year. Bright guy, but all I know about his computer skills is that he used a laptop to take notes. A common thing these days."

"Since you know him, he might open up to you, and I'd like you to accompany me on the interview. If you didn't flunk him, that is." Jackson smiled, trying to turn back time before their talk in the kitchen left them even more uneasy with each other.

"He was an A student." She quirked a half smile. "I'm also friends with the assistant professor in the computer science department. We could ask if he knows any students who are into hacking."

"Good idea," Eryn said. "If you need me to evaluate anyone's computer skills, let me know."

"I've been thinking," Maggie said. "It might help me figure this out if I knew more about Scott."

Jackson was glad to change the subject from the danger and their suspect's abilities. "Scott comes from a wealthy family. His dad's an advertising executive in one of the big five companies in New York. Scott wanted to follow in dad's footsteps and majored in marketing."

"And he came to college in Medford?" Maggie asked. "That seems odd."

"Did to us at first, too," Jackson said. "But then we learned his high school girlfriend moved to Oregon in her senior year of high school. That's when Scott decided to attend college here."

"Ah, love." Alex gave Jackson a pointed look. "The things we do for it."

Jackson ignored his teammates and turned back to his notes. "Scott was a good student despite the fact that he liked to party and smoked his share of weed. With pot being legal in Oregon, that wasn't a red flag."

Maggie tilted her head. "Any other drug use?"

Jackson shrugged. "His buddies didn't say anything. Could mean he wasn't into it, or if they admitted to the use, it might incriminate them, too."

"What about the girlfriend?" Maggie asked.

"They broke up after six months. We considered her current boyfriend to see if he might be involved in the murder, but from what everyone says, her breakup with Scott was amicable, and there's no indication that the boyfriend is involved."

Maggie stared ahead for some time before meeting Jackson's gaze again. "I never asked. How did Scott die?"

"He was strangled."

She gave a resigned nod as if she was recognizing that the killer used the same method to try to kill her. "Scott seemed like a nice guy. Who would want to do that to him?"

Jackson wished he could answer that question. "Hopefully our interviews tomorrow will help us figure that out."

8

As Jackson pulled into the faculty parking lot, Maggie looked up at the old campus building in Medford where she'd taught for two years. The college had graciously given her time off to work the forest fire and being back on campus after a few days' absence felt like coming home. Odd. She only took this teaching job to support herself while she was in town caring for her father.

So why was she still in Ashland?

There was nothing to keep her here now. Not with her father passing away a year ago. She wouldn't have to sell the house, but she could move on and find a full-time job in forensic anthropology again. Maybe she felt compelled to stay because she felt closer to her parents here. Could be she simply wasn't capable of getting over losing people close to her. First as a teen, losing her mother. Then Alison. And now her father. Who knows, maybe she still wasn't over any of them enough to be emotionally whole.

A sigh begged to escape, but she let it out slowly so she didn't catch Jackson's attention, causing him to fire off questions she had no desire to answer.

He shifted into park. "I don't have to tell you that we need to be careful, right?"

"Right." She forgot about her past and focused on the campus—deserted except for a few students racing toward early morning classes.

Just the way Jackson wanted it. He said it would be easier to spot any problems with fewer students moving around. Looked like he was right.

He got out, and she met him at the front of the old truck he'd borrowed. Together they walked past the building where her usual classroom was located and down a tree-lined common area before stepping across the street to a popular dorm.

Jackson pressed the doorbell. When a female voice came over the intercom, he explained their purpose. She buzzed them in, and Maggie followed him to a young woman who sat waiting for them at the reception desk. She wore thick glasses and an economics book lay open in front of her. Dark circles under her eyes said she worked the night shift at the front desk.

Jackson grinned at her, and a wide smile crossed her face in acknowledgement of his potent charm.

He held out his ID. "I know Garrett's room is 301. Mind if we go up?"

The girl's smile wavered. "Is he expecting you?"

"He knew I might be coming back to talk to him again." Jackson leaned over the desk. "Just between you and me, this is about Scott Dawson's murder. Our team was hired to find the killer."

She gaped at him. "You don't think Garrett is involved in that, do you? I mean he was friends with Scott. And he's a great guy. Garrett, I mean. Scott was, too."

"Both great guys as far as I can tell." Jackson smiled

again, and Maggie didn't know how the poor girl was putting two thoughts together under his megawatt charm. "You don't know if Garrett was into computer hacking, do you?"

"I don't think so. At least I never heard anything about it. But I'm kind of a nerd. You know, study or work most of the time to pay my tuition. Garrett and Scott had money so they could afford to mess around."

Jackson leaned closer. "So...it's okay for us to head up, then?"

She nodded. "But don't tell anyone I let you in or I could get in trouble. I can't afford to lose my work-study job."

"Promise." Jackson turned to Maggie and gestured at the elevator on the far side of the lobby.

She hurried across the space before the girl realized she'd fallen under his spell and changed her mind. The moment the elevator doors closed, Maggie shook her head. "You worked that poor girl shamelessly."

"I feel bad about it, but surprising Garrett is far more effective than being announced."

She nodded, but as a woman who once succumbed to his charms, she didn't like to see him turn it on someone else. Sure, his attention to the girl wasn't romantic in the least, but it still left Maggie wondering if she'd just been a conquest to him, and she'd fallen for it hook, line, and sinker. One thing was for sure. She wasn't about to ask him and take them back into the personal realm.

The doors opened, and Jackson gestured for her to go first again. She suspected he was protecting her back. As he'd told her so many times in the past, he "had her six."

She located room 301 with a door plastered with party pictures. From the look of things, they were pretty rowdy parties.

Jackson reached over her shoulder and knocked loudly. The warmth of his body urged her to turn toward him, but she held her position. When Garrett didn't answer, Jackson pounded loud enough to wake the entire floor.

"Alright, already." A deep voice grumbled from behind the door. "I'm coming."

Jackson stepped back, and a shirtless guy wearing jogging shorts jerked it open. He was tall, chubby, and his brown hair was matted to the side of his head. He locked gazes with Jackson.

"You." The word sounded like an accusation.

"Told you I might be back. We have some questions for you."

He looked at Maggie. "We?"

"Assistant professor, Dr. Maggie Turner."

"Right. Right." He appraised her. "Thought you looked familiar."

"Can we come in?" Jackson asked.

"Place is kind of a mess and my roommate is still sleeping. How about we go to the lounge?"

Jackson nodded his agreement.

"Lemme grab a shirt." He turned back and started to close the door, but Jackson's foot stopped it. Garrett eyed Jackson. He didn't even blink and kept his foot wedged in the doorway. Garrett cast a frustrated look at Jackson then shrugged and went to find a shirt.

"What's up?" Maggie asked quietly.

Jackson bent closer. "Best to keep an eye on him. Our visit might encourage him to hide or even destroy something important."

She would never have thought of that, but then her training in the criminal discipline was in evaluating the bones of deceased individuals, not interviewing the living.

Garrett shrugged into a wrinkled gray T-shirt with stains on the front and brushed past them. They followed him down the hallway to the lounge at the end. Sun streamed into the windows, highlighting the debris left from a party the night before. He pushed empty pizza boxes aside and slid onto a table.

"So what did you want to know?" He yawned as if their visit meant nothing to him.

Jackson pulled out a chair for Maggie, but he remained standing and alert. "You're a computer major, right?"

He nodded, looking a bit wary now.

"Did you and Scott ever work on computers together?"

Garrett didn't answer right away but picked at fuzz on his shorts. He finally looked up. "Yeah, we worked together. Scott was into using ad tracking to figure out people's movements."

"Explain," Jackson demanded.

"You know businesses track people's movements online, right? Like when you click on an ad, the company serving up the ad records your data and gives information about you to the company."

"Right."

"Well, it's even a bigger deal than most people think and has become more highly targeted and location-based. Scott was really into it, and he wanted me to try to use these ads to track people's physical locations."

If Jackson thought this was important, his expression didn't show it. "And did you? Track them, I mean."

"Yeah, man. It was sweet." Garrett grinned. "We targeted a few users, and I served up a grid of hyperlocal ads to figure out which ads got served to these users for a few weeks." He chuckled. "We tracked their clicks and apps and learned all kinds of things about them from religious beliefs to medical conditions."

It made Maggie sick that so much information could be collected about hers and other peoples' online movements. Problem was, she didn't want to stop using the Internet. It was an important part of her life, but she knew from Facebook that it wasn't a coincidence that ads for items she recently searched for suddenly showed up in her Facebook feed.

Garrett's smile disappeared. "But here's the thing. I mean doing the project with Scott was fun, but anyone with half a brain could do this to track people, and it could be used the wrong way. It's gonna be a big problem going forward. I hope to write a protocol to prevent the tracking and cash in on it."

Maggie could see that. Garrett seemed like he'd be motivated to live the highlife where he could spend a lot of time partying after he graduated.

"Could Scott have done this without you?" Jackson asked.

"He wasn't all that computer savvy, but I showed him how to do it, and he caught on. All he had to do was understand demand-side providers—DSPs—for advertising."

Jackson eyed the kid. "Why didn't you mention this the first time we talked?"

"I...um...well...you see. Scott might've taken it to extremes and tracked people so he knew when they'd be out of their house."

"And then?"

"Then he mighta...well...made himself at home in their places."

"At home, meaning what?"

Garrett held up his hands. "I think that's all I should say."

"Sure, if that's what you want." Jackson sounded far too accepting. "I can go ahead and bring in the local police to question you, or you can answer me now."

Ah, he was being sarcastic with his first comment.

Garrett crossed his arms. "And if you do, I'll have my lawyer waiting."

"You can at least share the addresses Scott visited."

"Um...no."

"What about hacking? You into that?"

Maggie thought it was a good idea that Jackson changed the subject, as clearly Garrett wasn't going to tell them anything else about Scott's visits.

"You mean illegal hacking? Nah."

"There's legal hacking?" Maggie asked.

"Sure. There are ethical hackers. They are called white hat hackers. They're often paid employees or contractors working as security specialists, and they use hacking to find security holes."

"You one of those ethical hackers?" Jackson asked.

Garrett cocked his head. "I've worked on a few projects."

Jackson took a step closer to the kid. "Any of them involve cars?"

Garrett blinked, then grinned. "Nah, man, but that would be so cool to take over someone's car. I can just see the driver's face when he figured out he couldn't control things anymore." Garrett laughed and slapped his knee.

Maggie knew how cool it wasn't. "Listen here, I just—"

"You willing to let our computer expert take a look at your machine?" Jackson interrupted.

Maggie had to figure he didn't let her finish because he didn't want her to tell Garrett about the accident.

"Which computer?" A snide smile slid across Garrett's mouth.

Maggie wanted to tell this guy off, but she resisted in favor of letting Jackson gain the information he needed from the little creep.

"All of them," Jackson said.

"I've got nothing to hide, but no thanks." Garret settled his feet on the floor and stood. "I like need to get to class now, so time to take off."

He didn't wait for them to respond but started for the hallway again. She saw Jackson fist his hands and knew Garrett frustrated him, but hopefully the kid had provided enough information to give them a strong lead.

In the elevator, she glanced at Jackson. He'd been silent on the walk down the hallway and now his face held a pensive expression. She had to wonder if his thoughts mirrored hers.

"Do you think that Scott may have learned something in the visits to these houses that he shouldn't have known and that's what got him killed?" she asked.

"Sounds like a good possibility, and one I intend to explore."

The interview with Hugh Reinhardt had been the polar opposite from their questioning of Garrett North. Maybe it was because he knew Maggie, but Jackson suspected Hugh was just a down-to-earth college student working hard to get good grades. He worked with Scott on a couple of homework assignments, and they played basketball together, but that's all.

"I hope Wallace can help us." Maggie pulled open the

door for Ridley Hall where they would meet with the computer professor Maggie mentioned.

Jackson stepped into the air conditioning behind her and took a moment to enjoy the cool air giving them relief from the humid temperatures outside. Temps that weren't helping in the fight to control forest fires.

His phone rang, and he glanced at the screen. "Hold up. It's Alex, and I need to take this."

"What's up?" Jackson answered.

"Thought you'd like to know Summit's been quiet all morning, and it looks like the risk to Maggie is low so you can head over here."

After the accident and potshot yesterday, Jackson still couldn't fathom taking her to Summit and leaving her exposed to another shot. "I'll think about it."

"You'll think about it as in a member of our team, or you'll think about it as a man who's still got a thing for Maggie?"

"Goodbye, Alex," Jackson said pointedly and hung up.

Maggie ran a jerky hand through her hair. "That was quick."

"He just wanted to tell me it's been quiet at Summit."

Excitement raced across her face but was instantly replaced with a skeptical look. "And your comment to him about thinking about it means you haven't decided that I can go back to work this afternoon."

Jackson didn't want to start a discussion on the subject, so he answered with a quick nod and gestured for her to step over to Wallace's office.

She didn't move and kept her focus pinned to him. "Are you leaning in any direction?"

He resisted blowing out a long breath in frustration. After all, he didn't want to encourage more questions. He also wouldn't tell her that given his choice, he'd put her in a protective bubble, leaving him with avoiding a direct answer. "Let's wait to make a decision until we find out what your professor has to say."

She planted her hands on her trim waist. "He's not my professor."

"Okay," he said and pointed at Wallace Waverly's door again. Just the name alone made Jackson think of an old guy with gray hair, but the guy was an assistant professor, so he was more likely a younger man.

His door was open.

"Knock, knock," Maggie said before entering.

"Maggie! Good to see you. We've missed you around here." The guy sounded far too enthusiastic to see her if she was just a fellow colleague.

Jackson entered the small office. The man standing behind the desk had his gaze locked on Maggie and didn't seem to notice Jackson at all. He looked to be in his early forties, tall, thin, with sleeked-down black hair, thick glasses, and an oversized smile. His skinny mustache stretched thin as he beamed at Maggie.

What kind of guy grew something like that? If you were going to have facial hair, grow a full beard, or a goatee, but not a weaselly little thing that looked like one of his students swiped a marker across his face.

Wallace was clearly infatuated with her, rubbing Jackson the wrong way. He didn't like the guy's lecherous look. Didn't like it one bit.

Wallace suddenly turned his gaze on Jackson and gave him a quick once-over, his expression saying he found Jackson wanting.

Well, bully for him. Jackson didn't much like the look of Wallace either. Not his pleated khakis and white short-sleeved dress shirt pressed so stiff it would stand up on its own. He'd paired it with a striped tie pulled so tight at the neck Jackson doubted the guy could take a deep breath.

Maggie introduced them.

Jackson hid his dislike and shoved out his hand. When Wallace looked down his nose at Jackson, he gripped Wallace's hand more firmly than needed. Wallace winced, but it was barely noticeable. Jackson had to give the professor credit for not crying out.

He freed his hand and gestured at the chairs in front of his desk. "You said you were looking for information on hackers."

"We are." Maggie sat and crossed her legs, the delicate sandal on her foot swinging. "And not the ethical kind."

Wallace looked horrified and pushed up his glasses. "If we had any black hat hackers in our community, I would have reported them, and they would no longer be students here."

"We want to know about anyone who's shown even a hint of interest in car hacking." Jackson planted his hands on the back of Maggie's chair and leaned forward. He waited for her to shoot him a look, but she didn't move.

Wallace got the hint though, his body angling away. Jackson was staking his claim. Not that he had a claim to stake, but there was something about this guy that Jackson didn't like, and he couldn't stomach the thought of Maggie dating Wallace. Okay, fine, Jackson couldn't stomach the thought of her dating anyone, but the professor even more so.

"We've discussed hacking in class, of course, but no one has shown an unusual interest in it." He met Maggie's gaze. "What's this all about, Maggie?"

"Scott Dawson's murder."

"Scott Dawson. Oh...oh...goodness." He grabbed the knot on his necktie and fidgeted with it.

"The company I work for has been hired to find the killer." Jackson pushed off Maggie's chair and took out a business card. He handed it to Wallace and briefly considered leaning over Maggie again, but Wallace had gotten the point, and Jackson didn't want to irritate her.

Then maybe you shouldn't have done it in the first place.

Wallace glanced at the card and let it flutter to his desk. "Scott was good friends with Garrett North. Did you talk to him?"

"We did," Jackson replied before Maggie revealed any information shared by Garrett. "Did you ever see them together?"

"Sure. All the time in the lab. They were working on some marketing project for Scott's independent study."

"At least that's what they told you," Jackson said.

"Am I wrong?"

"Let's just say the independent study was far more independent than you might think."

Wallace's face blanched. "It wasn't for a class?"

"No."

"Goodness. I hope I don't take the fall for it. I probably should have supervised them more closely, but you know how it is, Maggie? Right?" He paused and looked for agreement. "We've got far too much to do and not enough time to do it, and yet, we're expected to publish brilliant papers." He released his tie to press it against his chest.

"Could we take a look at your lab computers to see if there's anything in the history to help us find the killer?" Jackson asked.

Wallace shook his head. "Student privacy rules. I'm sure you understand."

Jackson opened his mouth to protest, but Maggie sat forward and pressed her hand on Wallace's hand splayed on the desktop. "Please, Wallace. I don't want to put you in an awkward position, but it would mean so much to me."

Jackson was impressed. She was playing Wallace much the same way Jackson charmed the girl at the desk. Difference was, the girl at the desk didn't really imagine she'd be dating him, where Wallace's face was lit as bright as any IED Jackson had the displeasure of seeing ignite.

"Of course. If it's that important to you." Wallace smiled and covered her hand with his.

"I'd like to have our computer expert join us if you don't mind," Jackson said, not only to get permission, but to wipe that dreamy look from the professor's face.

Wallace looked like he did mind. Very much.

Until Maggie smiled at him. "Will you sit with me and help me understand what we're looking at?"

"I'm always glad to help you."

Yeah, including breaking privacy laws.

Jackson waited for Wallace to leap over the desk and take Maggie's hand, but he stepped around and waited for her to rise.

"Lead the way," Jackson said. "And I'll text Eryn to meet us at the lab."

Wallace stepped into the hallway. Maggie followed, pausing only long enough to give Jackson the evil eye. Okay, fine, he deserved it, but come on. The guy was super creepy, and so in love with her it almost made Jackson nauseous. How could she stand it?

He trailed the pair into the basement of the building. Wallace paused by a door and dug out his keys. While waiting for him to open the door, Jackson fired off a quick text with the room number and told Eryn to join them

ASAP. Before Wallace got the door open and lights turned on, she responded that she was on her way.

The room temperature was even cooler down there, and the hum of computers filled the space. Rows of desktop computers sat at workstations and larger computers were housed in metal racks along one wall. Servers, he guessed, but he really had no idea.

"Nice setup," Jackson said to Wallace hoping to repair any damage he might have caused with his he-man tactics upstairs.

"We do have a wonderful department for a small school, and I'm proud to be part of it. I just hope I can secure tenure, here." Wallace glanced at Maggie. "You want that, too, right?"

"I'd be most happy for you if that happened."

"No silly." He swatted a hand at her. "I meant you want tenure, too."

"Oh that." She glanced at Jackson for some reason. "Yeah. Sure."

"Do students have assigned computers?" Jackson asked Wallace.

He shook his head. "All of our machines are networked so students save files to the server or a flash drive, not the desktop hard drives."

"And where would the Internet history be stored?"

"On the server. That way when you log in under your user name, your information is retrieved. We've set it up this way so if a student tries to cover up inappropriate actions by deleting files on the desktop, we'll have the files on the server where the students don't have permission to delete or overwrite them."

Jackson nodded his understanding. "Are there any particular machines Garrett and Scott used often?"

"Yes." Wallace jetted across the space to the last row of computers. He tapped two monitors. "They used these machines every time. I should have figured they were up to something when they sat in the back all the time."

"Can you log us into these computers?" Jackson asked.

He nodded. "But I'll have to remain by your side at all times."

"No worries."

"Okay, then," Wallace said. "We'll start with Garrett. Give me a second to query the user database to locate his login so you'll see only his files."

On the first computer, Wallace opened a database window and entered a query to find the login as promised. He then logged out and signed in again as Garrett.

"There," he said. "You can see the files that Garrett accessed and modified."

Jackson dropped down behind the monitor. Wallace gestured for Maggie to take a seat behind the second computer and watched her every move until she was seated.

"I'll bring up Scott's account on this machine." Wallace leaned over her and Jackson couldn't help but notice that Wallace's typing slowed, and it took a lot longer to get this computer going than the first one.

But he finally had Scott's account up on the screen. He slid another chair close to her and sat. Jackson considered changing computers with Maggie, but he suspected Wallace would just move his chair.

"Let's start with their Internet history." Jackson opened the browser. He didn't know if they'd find anything of interest as both guys were likely smart enough not to leave behind a trail if they were up to anything illegal, but then, college students weren't always the smartest. Not even computer geeks who should know better.

Jackson sorted the history by date and started reviewing it. Garrett hadn't opened the Internet since Scott died. Not necessarily a red flag. There were gaps in dates when the Internet hadn't been accessed even before Scott died.

Jackson looked at Wallace. "How often does Garrett come into the lab?"

Wallace tilted his head. "Twice a week. Maybe three times. More when Scott was alive."

Just as Jackson thought. He continued to scroll through the list of sites that were mostly about computer programming and advertising, but still Jackson visited each one to see if it might hold a lead.

Before long, the door opened, and Eryn stepped in.

"Good. We can use your help." Jackson introduced Eryn to Wallace who'd come around the workstation and stood watching Eryn cross the room. If Jackson were Eryn, Wallace's unyielding attention would creep him out, but she held out her hand to him. "Eryn Calloway."

Wallace muttered his name and clasped her hand. Eryn gave it a firm shake as she always did, and the poor guy winced more for her than when Jackson had gripped it like a vise.

She let go of his hand. "So what do we have?"

"This," Maggie called out. "I don't know what it means, but it's interesting."

Eryn stepped behind Maggie, and Jackson leaned over to see the screen. She opened a website for a do-it-yourself workshop called You Can Do It. A place where you could work on site and rent everything from metalworking tools to 3-D printers to industrial sewing machines.

"What would Scott want with this place?" Maggie asked. "Was he into woodworking or hobbies like that?"

"Not that I know of," Wallace answered.

"This is a membership place," Eryn said. "If you'll let me take over the computer, I'll see what I can find out."

Maggie got up to stand behind the chair, and Eryn took her place. Surprisingly, Wallace remained seated, his gaze on the screen. Eryn entered a monthly membership into the shopping cart and opened the cart.

"Mind explaining what you're doing and why?" Jackson asked.

"If he was a member and bought something, I'm hoping the shopping cart remembers his information and we can use that to access his files." She pointed the cursor at the name field and nothing happened. She typed "SC" in the box. Scott's name popped up. "Perfect."

She added his last name and tabbed to the address field. "I'll need his dorm address."

"I can get you that." Wallace took out his phone. He tapped a few buttons and rattled off the dorm's physical address.

Eryn typed in the first letter. "That's odd. Nothing pops up."

"Maybe he's not a member," Maggie said.

"He entered his name, but he could've abandoned the cart, or maybe he used a different address."

"What about a PO Box?" Maggie asked.

"Good thinking." Eryn typed "PO" in the address field, then "Box," but nothing further came up. "Okay, I'm going to enter one number at a time to see if an address pops up."

Jackson watched as she started the number sequence. In today's digital world, he was so thankful that Eryn was on their team. Gage had really thought things through before starting his business, looking for experts in the areas they would need to perform at a high level. Perhaps he could use a forensic anthropologist on the team, too.

Now where did that thought come from? Focus, man.

Eryn went through the numbers in order. When she inputted "8," an address displayed.

"Bingo. I'll plug this address into Google maps to see what we have." She opened a browser window, and Google displayed the address as belonging to a mailbox place. "He does have a box. Just not one at the post office. There might be something in his box that can help us. I need to get logged in to see if we can somehow pick up his mail."

"Can you do it?" Maggie asked.

"I can try, but we'll need a password, and that might be tough to get."

"Too bad the police never located a laptop for Scott," Jackson said. "If he had one, it could've given us something to go on."

Eryn glanced up at him. "They also didn't find a mailbox key, but it's clear he had a box, so maybe someone took the laptop."

Jackson nodded. "I'd put money on the killer taking it along with the mailbox key."

"If the killer has the key," Maggie said. "Wouldn't he have emptied the mailbox already?"

"Possibly," Jackson replied, but he continued to hold out hope.

Eryn opened the account page. "We have Scott's email address from our initial interviews with his friends, but the police never found anything questionable in his account. Or anything related to this place. He most likely had a second email account."

Maggie turned her rapt gaze on Eryn. "How do we figure that out?"

"Same way. We hope he logged in with it using this computer." She typed in the letters "SC" in the email field and an address popped up. "Not the address we knew about."

"That's not uncommon." Wallace piped up.

"Of course. Many people use different emails for different uses. Hopefully we'll get lucky, and this will be the one we need. Now a password. People are creatures of habits and that goes for passwords, too. They like to use the same one over and over again even though that's not at all safe."

"Why not?" Maggie asked, looking a bit guilty.

Eryn swiveled toward Maggie. "If one of your accounts is hacked, and you use the same password, the hacker can get into other accounts, too."

"I never thought of that."

"Most people don't, but if you've set up your accounts this way, you should change them. Especially financial accounts." Eryn started to swivel but turned back to Maggie. "And don't use 12345 or 'password' or your name or birthday for your password. Create something random."

Maggie frowned. "But then I'd have a ton of logins. How would I remember all those passwords?"

"Get a good password keeper app on your computer and lock them in there. Or write them down so that they are not on your computer at all. Looking up a password each time you log into an account takes one more step, but keeping your money and information safe is worth it."

"Thank you." Maggie smiled at Eryn. "I'll take care of that tonight."

"There are many other security safeguards I can teach you," Wallace offered. "Perhaps we can get together tonight."

"Umm...I...well..." Maggie's gaze wavered.

"Maggie will be busy with us tonight," Jackson said and didn't feel the least bit guilty when Wallace frowned.

"Okay, so moving on," Eryn said. "Let's try the password Scott's dad helped us figure out."

Eryn plugged in his dog's name plus the date he died, and the screen opened. "Bingo. He has a membership and placed a custom fabrication order." She clicked on the order to open it.

Jackson leaned forward. "What in the world? He fabricated four Glock 19 slides and receivers and had them shipped to his PO Box."

Eryn looked up at him with an incredulous stare. "Most interesting."

"So those are parts of a gun, right?" Maggie asked. "Why would he want them?"

Jackson looked at Eryn. "Ghost guns?"

"Could be."

"What in the world are ghost guns?" Wallace asked.

Jackson turned to the professor. "It's a slang term for guns that don't have a serial number. These guns aren't built in a factory, but are fabricated in a shop like this or a person's home."

Wallace's eyes narrowed behind his glasses. "But why?"

"These guns don't require a background check, and without a serial number they can't be traced."

"I worked an investigation involving ghost guns a few years ago," Maggie said. "But it would be far-fetched to believe it's related to Scott, right?"

Jackson nodded. "But we should still consider it."

"Look." Eryn tapped the screen. "The slides and receivers were just shipped. Maybe they're at the mailbox place waiting for pickup."

"We need to get into his mailbox account to figure out a way to gain access to the parts and any mail he might have."

"I'm on it." Eryn surfed to the mailbox place's address. "Odds are good he used the same email and password."

She plugged them in, and his account opened. "Just like you thought. He has two packages waiting."

"Can we pick them up?" Maggie asked.

"I would expect that he has some security in place to prevent that." Eryn stabbed a finger at the menu. "Looks like there's a field to add people authorized to pick up packages." She opened the screen. "I can add someone. Want me to add you, Jackson?"

He faced Maggie. "Mind if we put your name here?"

"I don't mind, but why?"

"Two reasons. The mailbox staff is less likely to question a woman. And, if the killer knows we're investigating Scott's murder, connecting my name to the mailbox might tip them off."

Maggie gave a resolved nod. "Okay, my name it is."

Eryn typed in Maggie's name. "I'll need your driver's license number."

Maggie fished her wallet from her purse, and Jackson sat back waiting for Eryn to finish.

"Done," she said. "Maggie can now retrieve these packages."

9

Maggie didn't know if she could do this. Her hands were shaking and her palms moist. She was so not cut out for espionage or doing anything even the least bit questionable. She had her parents to thank for that. Honesty at all costs. That's what they'd taught her, and it was rarely a problem. But now, at the mailbox place...man, she couldn't even make herself open the door.

But the team needed her to accomplish this task. They'd also tried to find any address for homes Scott may have broken into but struck out. Getting a win here could buoy everyone's spirits. Wallace promised to keep working on searching their computer histories, but Eryn said if she didn't find anything, there was nothing to be found. And Maggie believed her. Even Wallace seemed to be impressed with Eryn's computer skills.

Okay, Maggie. Go. You've put this off long enough.

She took a deep breath and pulled open the door. A wall of mailboxes sat to her right and a large counter with packing supplies behind it took up the back of the space. A young guy in his early twenties with blond hair and a neatly trimmed goatee stood behind it pouring packing peanuts into a box.

She stepped up to the desk.

He looked up. "Can I help you?"

"I'm here to pick up two packages and the mail for one of my students." She quickly laid the package pickup form on the counter and slid it to him.

As he looked at the form, she lowered her hands to her sides so he didn't see they were shaking.

"Scott Dawson, huh," he said.

Please don't let him know Scott or watch the news to know that he was murdered.

The guy caught her gaze. "Haven't seen him in a while. He doing okay?"

She couldn't lie. She'd never pull it off and had to change the subject. "This is the form I need to pick up his packages, right?"

The young man nodded. "Let me get 'em."

"Hey, could you give me his mail, too? I don't have his key, but I'd like to help if I could."

He eyed her, and she concentrated on not looking guilty, but she felt exactly the way she'd felt when she was six and tried to steal a candy bar. Her parents stopped her dead in her tracks and grounded her for a week. This, however, held much bigger consequences.

Guilt gnawed at her stomach, but she forced a smile to her mouth.

"Why not," he said. "But I'm not s'posed to do it, so you can't tell anyone."

She mimicked zipping her lips.

He chuckled and stepped through a doorway in the back.

The moment he was gone, she let out a gush of air and

sagged against the counter. Jackson thought it was a good idea to send her in here, but he was wrong. Way wrong.

She heard the guy's footsteps plodding toward her. She drew in a deep breath. Blew it out and flexed her fingers. Her hands were still shaking. What should she do? He was sure to notice them trembling when she took the packages. She quickly rested them on the counter, clamped them together, and feigned a relaxed pose.

He set two boxes in front of her. "I'll just grab the mail."

He moved to the right where the boxes were located and returned with three envelopes. "Not much here, but then Scott never gets much mail."

"It's interesting how you know the mailbox customers so well," she said to distract him.

"You work in a place like this long enough and you get to know them." He laid the envelopes on top of the boxes.

"Thank you so much." She didn't have to fake her appreciation for his cooperation.

He nodded. "Say hi to Scott for me."

She grabbed the packages and mail and fled the building. It felt as if his gaze was lasering into her back, and any moment he would realize she shouldn't have the mail and come after her. She hurried down the street and slipped into the old pickup truck where Jackson sat behind the wheel. Letting out a long breath of relief, she nearly tossed the items at him. She half expected him to have the truck running like a getaway vehicle, but he sat there calmly, the engine silent.

"I'm not cut out for this undercover thing." She held out her shaking hands. "My parents raised me to be far too honest to do things like this well."

"Hmm, so what does that make me?" Jackson laughed.

"Someone who's good at investigating, I guess." She tried

to laugh it off but wondered if the emotions he displayed since they'd reconnected were all fake, too. He sure had motives to want to gain her cooperation, and what better way to do that than sweep her off her feet a second time.

He didn't seem to notice her ongoing unease, or at least he didn't say anything about it, but glanced at the envelopes. "Junk mail."

She nearly started laughing hysterically. She risked getting caught for junk mail? Priceless.

Jackson pulled a knife from his pocket and sliced into the larger of the two boxes. He lifted out four grips for a handgun.

"Receivers for a Glock 19." He put the pieces back into the box and opened the other one and took out a long narrow metal piece. "Same thing except for a Sig Sauer." He shook his head. "So we have parts for eight guns here. Why does Scott need eight unregistered guns?"

"He doesn't, right?"

"Right. Unless he's a big-time criminal with flunkies working for him. Or I suppose he could be selling them."

"Is it legal to do that?"

Jackson shook his head. "He'd be breaking the law for sure."

"It's crazy to me that you can even have parts like these made." She shook her head. "I've thought that since ghost gun investigation I worked on. In that case, a guy killed his mother with a ghost gun. If companies like the do-it-your-self place didn't make the parts, that wouldn't have happened."

Jackson's forehead furrowed. "I don't know about that. Most likely he would've found another gun or killed her another way."

"I suppose."

"Do you have records on this investigation that we can review?"

"At my place."

"Then let's review them tonight." Jackson closed the box and ran his finger over the return address label. "Did you see the company's located in Rugged Point?"

She shook her head as she hadn't noticed anything while in the store other than her heart pounding in her head.

"It's just up the coast from Cold Harbor. Might be a good idea to talk to the owners about Scott."

"Sounds good. A company who makes gun parts is your thing, and you can schmooze them, right? Especially if we run into any females." She hated that she felt a need to add that last comment, but she did.

"Hey," he said. "You were doing your own schmoozing with Wallace back there."

"True."

"You know he's half in love with you."

Boy, did she. "It's not really a secret. But honestly, it's really not me. I think he'd be infatuated with any female who paid attention to him."

"He does seem a little socially awkward."

"And that's putting it nicely." She thought about her many stilted conversations with Wallace in the past, and his clumsy attempts to ask her out. "Still, he came through for us today so I owe him."

A hint of frustration shadowed Jackson's eyes. "Well don't make the repayment a date."

"Why not?"

He watched her for a very long time, his gaze heating up, and she felt like squirming under his intense focus. He suddenly looked away.

"I just don't want you dating him, okay?" he muttered barely loud enough to hear.

She didn't know what to make of his comment. Could he be jealous? It certainly would explain his behavior in Wallace's office. She thought of him dating another woman, and Maggie didn't like the thought. Not at all.

"We could get Riley to fly us there right now."

She shook her head. "As much as I want to help find Scott's killer, I need to work at Summit this afternoon. Nate's people are waiting for us to turn it over. Plus I need to catch up on the other work there."

Jackson returned his attention to her. "Let me make sure the team is in place at Summit before we head over there. Then tonight after you do your morgue thing, we can take the chopper to Cold Harbor. We can spend the night at the compound and be at You Can Do It's door when they open in the morning. Does that work for you?"

Locked in a helicopter with him so she couldn't walk away if things got personal? She didn't know if she was up for that, but she did want to visit this company and move the investigation forward.

"Maggie?" he asked.

"I've never been in a helicopter," she blurted out the first thing that came to mind.

He watched her. "Does that worry you?"

"No way. It sounds fun."

He patted her knee. "That's my girl."

She wasn't his girl. His woman. His anything except maybe his expert anthropologist and the woman under his protection. She was about to argue when he took his hand away to start texting. But his behavior—this closeness and touching—was exactly what she was worried about in the helicopter. Sure, Riley would be with them, but he would be busy flying the chopper.

"Will the whole team come with us?" she asked.

"Yeah, I'm sure they'd like to spend a night at home," he said not looking up from his phone. "Especially, Eryn. I'm sure she misses her daughter."

"She has a daughter?" Maggie was surprised Eryn hadn't mentioned the child.

"A four-year-old." He tapped the screen a few more times then looked up. "I'll get us on the road. If you take my phone, you can read the team's responses to me."

She took his phone, and he started the old truck. It huffed and sputtered but then finally caught with a big plume of smoke shooting out the tailpipe. He got them on the road and it was only moments before the first response came from his team.

"Eryn says she's back at Summit and everything is fine."

The phone dinged two more times in succession. "Alex, too, and Riley's still on overwatch—whatever that means."

"He's a former police sniper, and it's his job to keep an eye on things through his rifle scope and report anything suspicious. He's taken a stand up in the hills and has been watching the property all morning. Also, in the event of an overt assault, he'll take out the attacker."

Craziness. Pure craziness. "Just the thought of needing a sniper to keep an eye out for me is totally weird. And especially if he needed to shoot."

Jackson held her gaze for a moment. "I'm sure all of this is odd to you, but trust me—it's necessary."

"I trust you." With keeping me alive, at least, but not messing with my emotions? Not so much.

"You don't sound convinced."

"Oh, I am. You're like this fierce warrior. If I didn't know you were extremely capable before, I do now. And so is the team. I'm in good hands."

He pulled his shoulders back but didn't respond.

If she didn't know better, she'd think her opinion of his skills was still important to him, and he was preening under her compliment. But she doubted he really cared about what she thought of his skills.

You do, though.

Right, she liked it when he complimented her at the morgue, so maybe it wasn't so far-fetched to think he respected her opinion as well. Maybe these sparks flying between them weren't all physical. Maybe it ran deeper.

Not something she was even willing to contemplate and surely wouldn't discuss.

"You really like working with this team, don't you?" she asked to change the subject back to business.

"Yeah, I mean it's the closest thing to the Berets that I could hope to find. It's amazing and challenging at the same time. People are depending on you, so you show up and get tested every day. No other day or other mission matters. It's what you do today. Everyone on the team gets that, and it makes for a good working situation."

His body suddenly stiffened, and his breath seemed to catch.

Something was wrong. Really wrong, and a heavy feeling settled in the pit of her stomach. "What is it? What's wrong?"

He took a shaky breath and blew it out. "Here I am feeling guilty over letting you down, but it just hit me that behavior goes against who I am as a team member. It's about what you do today, not the past. I need to let all of that go. The blame. The regret. Focus on today."

Wow. What a realization. One she wished she could

have, too. But he left out one really important thing. "You didn't mention Alison. It applies to losing her, too, right?"

"That's a different thing all together." He sent a glowering look her way, and the open expression closed down.

She knew that look. He didn't want to talk about it. Would refuse to talk about it. Just when she thought they could be making headway, he clammed up. She was such a fool. When would she learn to avoid personal issues and stick with talking about his job and his protection services?

Now. She'd start now and move them back to a safe topic. "Everyone on the team seems to like each other."

His shoulders relaxed. "We have our moments, but yeah, we get along. You learn pretty soon in special forces if you aren't liked in the teams, your career will most likely be cut short. I saw guys dropped for that. You can't just be tough and give it your all, you have to perform and gain the trust of your teammates, too."

She could imagine teamwork, but when your very life depended on it? That was a whole other story. "When you were deployed, your career seemed so foreign to me. I couldn't even fathom what you did. But this...um...this situation...has helped me see more of your work and get to know more about you."

He nodded but didn't respond. He likely didn't want her to know more about him—just as she shouldn't want to know more about him.

She started to sigh, but when he glanced at her, she turned to watch out the window for the rest of the drive. The closer they came to Summit, the destruction increased. She didn't like seeing it, but at least working would occupy her mind.

When Jackson parked and switched off the ignition, she removed her seat belt.

From the console, he grabbed a microphone, hung it around his neck, and put an earbud in his ear. "For communicating with the team. As you know they've already cleared the property and there aren't any visible threats, but we still need to be on alert."

He tipped his head at the window. "Eryn's got the entrance covered. I'll be at your side, and Alex will stick close to us. And like I said, Riley's up in the hills. You won't see him, but he'll be there."

They both got out and entered the subdivision. Eryn nodded as they passed her. She was stopping people and asking for identification and the purpose of their visit. Surprisingly, the volunteers didn't question her, but simply provided the information. Eryn's amazing confidence was likely the reason people believed she should be there and had a right to demand their ID.

The search and rescue coordinator marched up to her. Roy McCall, a sixty-something male, shoved a hand into his thinning gray hair and looked like he might pull out what was left of it. "Thank goodness you're here. We've finished two houses since you were here last, and we have a ton of fragments needing your review."

"Lead the way." She gestured ahead.

He stepped down the road to the fourth house on the right. Well—to the house's ruins—before he veered off into the debris where Alex stood at the road, his feet planted wide. He wore mirrored sunglasses which hid his eyes, but his lips were in a tight line and his head was constantly on the move. His intensity scared Maggie as much as it comforted her. He remained at the street while she and Jackson followed Roy onto the property.

About fifteen feet in, Roy's team had erected a tent with a card table and chair, and next to it, they'd stacked bins holding bone fragments. Each bin was numbered, and a corresponding flag was placed in the ground where they'd located the bone fragments. A clipboard sat on the table with a list of the same information.

"Thanks, Roy, I'll take it from here," she said dismissing him, as he tended to stand and watch her, making her uncomfortable.

He departed, and she put down her things before sitting and picking up the first bin. Jackson settled sunglasses on his nose, the same mirrored kind Alex wore, and he came to stand behind her, far too close for her comfort. She thought he wanted to see what she was working on, but even more so, she suspected he wanted to watch the road.

"What exactly is your job here?" he asked, his deep voice rumbling over her shoulder.

She set down her bin and swiveled to look up at him. "The first thing we do is have the dogs search the rubble for human remains. When they light on something, the area is cordoned off, and I excavate the ruins. The search and rescue workers follow behind us and sift through other debris areas. They then put what they believe to be bones in a bin. But rocks and burnt clay can often look like a bone fragment, so if an item's in question, they put it in a bin. I'm trained to distinguish bone fragments from other objects, and I either confirm or deny their findings."

"So each of these bins have potential bone fragments?"

"Yes." She took latex gloves from her bag and snapped them on.

"Mind sharing with me what you find as you go?"

She shot him a questioning look.

"I like to learn everything I can. Never know when it might come in handy in my line of work."

"Sure, I'm glad to share." She set to work, filling Jackson

in on her findings as she went along. Time flew past, and he didn't move from his location. He had to be getting tired of standing there. Alex, too, still out at the road in the blazing sun for hours. Maybe she should suggest a break.

Her phone rang. She snapped off a glove and grabbed it from the table.

"It's Nate," she said to Jackson before answering.

"We received the dental records for one of the males that was reported missing in the area," Nate said. "But they're not a match to the victim you found."

Her heart dropped at the news. She'd been counting on a match. "And the other man?"

"His records are coming from out of state. They're actual films, not electronic files, so we won't get them until tomorrow."

She'd just have to wait. There was no other choice. "I sent the DNA sample off to my friend, and it could be ready as early as ten tomorrow morning. If I haven't heard anything from you on these dental records by then, I'll follow up on the DNA."

"That would be great." He paused for a long moment. "You finding anything else at the scene?"

"I haven't had a chance to work the area where we recovered John Doe yet. The search and rescue team needs me to process some fragments first so they can move forward. But I hope to finish the crime scene before leaving today."

"I really need to get my forensic staff on this." He sounded irritated.

"I know, and I'm sorry. I'll do my best to finish the work. I promise." The pressure of all the demands on her time was starting to get to her. Couple it with some lunatic trying to kill her, and she really could use a short break to hydrate and be able to focus again.

She disconnected the call and relayed the information to Jackson. Standing, stretched. "I could really use some water. Maybe you and Alex would like some, too. Is it okay if we head back to the truck to grab a bottle?"

He nodded. "Let me tell the team."

He pressed a button on his microphone. "Bravo one heading for recovery truck."

He suddenly shot a look around the area. "Let me know when we're clear."

"What's going on?"

"Riley spotted a guy with binoculars in the hills watching us. We need to take cover."

Cover. Right. Like there was any in these ruins. Jackson hated their location. A little table wasn't going to protect either of them, but he carefully cleared off the bins and tipped over the table. Alex backed toward them, his head on a swivel looking for any danger. Maggie stood watching, and Jackson grabbed her hand to pull her down behind the table with him.

He didn't know what it was with civilians in situations like this, but they often stood gaping as if the threat wasn't real. On his bodyguard assignments, he'd experienced it far too many times to count. But today, his feelings brought it home like never before. He should've thought to make Maggie wear a vest. The rest of the team, too. If they got out of this alive, he would insist on it.

He drew his weapon and waited for an update from either Riley or Eryn. She was the closest to the target and had gone to investigate. Thankfully, Gage approved extra staff for this protection detail. If he hadn't, Jackson would've had to figure out a way to keep Maggie home. As it was, he should try to limit her exposure even more. Maybe she could arrange to have the bone fragments brought to her house.

"Half a klick from the subject," Eryn's voice came over Jackson's earbud.

"Any sign of a weapon?" he asked.

"Negative."

"What's happening?" Maggie whispered, worry shading her usually bright eyes.

"Eryn's about a half klick away from binocular guy."

"A klick?"

"Around a third of a mile."

"Does he have a gun?"

"Neither of them has seen one. They'll let me know if they do." He worked hard to play things down, but the worry for her life made his gut hurt.

"I'm sorry you're in this position." She met his gaze and held it. "Eryn, too. Going to check out a man who might be armed."

"Riley's got her six. Ours, too," Jackson said, but in reality, they were sitting ducks and he could do nothing about it with the danger coming from a long distance. "After Eryn neutralizes the threat, I want you to wear a Kevlar vest."

She nodded so obediently, it broke his heart. She was a spirited woman, and these recurring scares were erasing her confidence bit by bit. He was glad they were heading to Cold Harbor today. A night in one of the compound cabins where she was completely safe should help her relax and get a good night's sleep.

And when they returned tomorrow? Then what? Then he had to tighten things down. "When we get back here tomorrow, can you arrange to have the bone fragments brought to your house? Or any building for that matter. Somewhere where we can better protect you. The morgue maybe."

"Yes...yes...of course. I don't know why I didn't think of that. I would still like to work the area where we found John Doe before we leave today, but only if you think it's safe to do so. Otherwise, I'll call Dr. Owing to do it."

"Why don't we hold off on deciding that until we know what's going on with this guy?"

"Sure, but I don't want to stay if it means others are in danger." She gently touched his arm, her gaze zeroing in on his and holding. "Thank you for all you're doing for me. With our past, I wouldn't blame you if you'd chosen to sit out this detail, and it means a lot to me that you didn't."

"Oh, honey, don't you know." Volatile emotions tumbled through his words. "I could no more sit this out than I could stop breathing. You mean too much to me for that."

Her eyes teared up, and they sat that way, connected by an invisible thread, until Jackson's earbud squawked.

"Guy claims to be watching the progress with the ruins," Riley said, drawing Jackson's focus to where it should be. "Eryn's detained him just in case. She'll wait with him until a deputy can sort this out."

"Roger that." Jackson shook off his concern and relaxed his shoulders. "We're good. Just a neighbor watching the progress over here."

She exhaled a long breath and offered him a tremulous smile.

He stood before he let that look suck him into a place he had no business going. He held out his hand to her. She slipped her slender fingers in his, and he tugged her to her feet. He should let go of her hand, but they locked gazes again.

"Seriously, thank you, Jackson." She pulled him closer and gave him a hug.

It started out platonic, affectionate, but their connection morphed into so much more, and he clung to her like life itself. He remembered the feel of her from the days when he had a right to hold her so closely. The way she fit so well in his arms. The way he always liked knowing she was his. But she wasn't anymore. Would never be again.

The thought made him pull away. He caught sight of Alex in his peripheral vision. Alex lifted his sunglasses to stare at them with an I told you so look on his face.

Regretting the hug even more, Jackson took another step back from Maggie.

"So can I stay?" she asked.

He picked up the chair for her. "Let me talk to Alex, and we'll see where we go from there."

He lifted the table into position then stepped out from under the tent, the sun hitting him hard. Felt like the temps had shot up ten degrees since they arrived. Alex had to be suffering under the heat while the tent shaded Jackson. If Maggie stayed, he would offer for Alex and Eryn to switch places with him to get some relief. Maybe so he could get some relief from the heat sizzling between him and Maggie, too.

"What's the plan, boss?" Alex asked.

"Maggie wants to stay to excavate the area where she found John Doe. It's just as exposed as this spot, and I'm not sure I like the thought of it."

"We've been here for hours now with no real threat," Alex said. "I say she's good to do the work."

"We'll set up at the other site, then. You stay with Maggie in the tent. Alternate with Eryn. I'll spell you."

Alex watched him, but he didn't say anything.

"Thought you two might want a break from the sun," Jackson explained.

"Sure, man, if you can pry yourself from Maggie's side." Alex socked Jackson in the arm.

He ignored it and turned back to Maggie. The moment he saw her, the warmth of her hug came rushing back. The feel of her body in his arms. The worry when Riley reported the watcher. Jackson's heart constricted, and his mind clouded again.

He wasn't fooling himself, was he? He could step away for the afternoon and let Alex take over her immediate care, right?

10

Maggie lifted a trowel of debris onto her square sifting screen and watched as fine dust and particles fell through. She'd been following the same procedure for hours now under the watchful eye of either Alex or Eryn, while Jackson replaced them at the road and entrance.

She had no idea why he changed from standing beside her, but she suspected it was related to his recent admission that she meant so much to him that he had to be by her side. Maybe he was proving to himself that he could leave her to someone else's care. Or trying to show her that he could do so. Perhaps he was afraid she would fall for him all over again, and he didn't want that to happen.

The thought hurt, which was odd since she didn't want it to happen again either. She feared she was too late on that, though. Or maybe she never stopped caring about him. Sure, she wanted him to be happy. To have a good life, and to that end, she cared. But her reaction to his moving away from her this afternoon revealed so much more.

She sighed and turned back to her work.

"Sounds like you're frustrated," Eryn said.

Maggie nodded, but kept her attention on the screen.

Eryn moved closer. "This devastation is something else. I've seen a lot of tough things in my career, but never anything like this."

"I haven't either." Maggie looked up at her.

"You seem to enjoy your job, though."

"I'm not sure enjoy is a word I would use. It's hard to say I enjoy this." She gestured at the devastation. "Committed to helping people is more like it, and I enjoy the commitment."

"I've noticed that you like to help others outside your job, too." Eryn smiled. "Like feeding all of us."

"I guess it's just who I am. My parents were missionaries when I was younger, and they set a good example for me."

"So you're probably like this super Christian, then."

"Hah! Not even close." Maggie shook her head over her faith failures of late. "But I want to do better. Just not sure I can."

"You sound like me." Eryn frowned. "I lost my husband before my daughter Bekah was born. Now I've got this crazy worry that I'm going to lose her, too. It's completely side-tracked my faith."

Maggie set down her trowel. "I totally get the worrying thing."

"Seems like Jackson feels the same way, but I don't know why. The guys are pretty closemouthed about their pasts." Eryn shook her head. "Shoot, they're just kind of close-mouthed about most everything except the job."

"Is it hard working with all of them?"

"Hard? Nah. They're great. And since Hannah married Gage, there's another woman at the compound, so that's good."

"From everything I've heard, she sounds like a special person."

Eryn nodded. "She's like the mother hen of the team. I fill that role on the job. Guys don't much like it, but sometimes they need to be reined in."

Maggie imagined the team on a covert mission, and Eryn lecturing them about something like doing their dishes. "Do they listen?"

"Of course, they do. I might be smaller than they are, but I'm fierce." She chuckled.

Maggie laughed along with Eryn, the lighthearted time with this amazing and unique woman renewing Maggie's spirits. She felt able to return to work with enthusiasm and forget all about that tired sigh that had started the conversation.

She dug in with her trowel and hit something hard. Felt like metal. She set aside the trowel and gently swept the debris to the side. She felt a small chain and lifted it from the soil to reveal a keychain with a single dangling key. The heat burnished the metal, but everything was intact.

"Look at this." She held the keychain up to Eryn, the key fob dangling and swinging in the breeze.

Eryn squinted. "Is that a greyhound dog on the ring?"

Maggie took a good look at the fob. "Looks like it."

"Do you think it belongs to John Doe?"

"Could be. Or the killer could have dropped it, I suppose." Maggie laid it down in the spot where she located it and got out her phone to snap pictures. She stood to take wide shots. "We need to get the deputy on duty over here so he can enter it into the evidence."

"I'll tell Jackson." Eryn repeated Maggie's request in her microphone. "Roger that."

She looked at Maggie. "Jackson's on his way, and he'll bring the deputy with him."

"Jackson doesn't need to come over here," Maggie said without thinking.

Eryn studied Maggie for an uncomfortable moment. "Is there a reason you don't want him to join us?"

"No...I mean...he..." She shrugged. "He's the one who didn't want to be here."

"Because he wanted to give Alex and me some relief from the sun," Eryn said, keeping her voice low. "But if you're thinking he doesn't want to be with you, you're wrong. It's eating him up not being over here."

"Oh, I..."

"Look, it's none of my business, but I just want to say I hope the two of you can work through your past and get together again."

"Get together? No. We—"

"Save it." Eryn held up her hand. "The only people you and Jackson are fooling are yourselves. You're clearly meant to be together."

Maggie was stunned into silence. Not only at Eryn bringing up this personal subject but at her statement.

Maggie shot a look at the road where Jackson took long strides toward her, moving far faster than he needed just to escort a deputy over to the scene. Was Eryn right? Did he want to be by her side? Were they meant to be together?

She always thought they were, but if they wanted to reunite, they'd have to work through their loss of Alison to move forward.

Problem was, from what Maggie could see, neither of them seemed any closer to doing that than the day they lost Alison.

∽

Jackson was relieved to be at the morgue. A thought he never imagined would pop into his head, but he was glad to get Maggie out of potential danger. They'd stopped by her place to pack a bag and get the files for the ghost gun investigation she'd once worked on. Now, while she studied each bone under bright lights, he sat at a desk in the corner reviewing the files...stopping only to watch her when she didn't know he was looking.

He was stunned by how much he was enjoying having her back in his life. Not only did she make him feel alive inside again, but he had someone to share his thoughts with. He wasn't a big talker, but he could tell her things he didn't tell the guys, and he liked having that outlet.

She looked up from entering data in her laptop and caught his gaze. A shy smile slid across her face, and it seemed as if her lips were begging to be kissed. It took all the discipline learned in the army not to get up and cross the room to kiss her. He flashed her a quick smile and turned his focus back to the ghost gun files.

A male, Uriah Ingman, killed his mother using a gun and silencer that he built with parts purchased online. He probably figured since he never bought or registered a gun that he wouldn't get caught if he used a ghost gun. Problem was, as he was trying to get rid of their mother's body, his sister Yvette walked in on him, and he convinced her to help him bury the mom in the backyard. And most importantly, he also convinced her to keep his secret.

Years later, Uriah's new girlfriend moved in with him. Unbeknownst to him, she started digging a garden in the backyard, unearthed the bones, and called the police. When interrogated, Yvette caved and told the truth. They both went to jail. She received a much shorter sentence and was recently released.

Jackson looked up from the file. "What kind of man kills his own mother?"

Maggie set down a fragment. "There's no excuse, but she did abuse them as children and continued to belittle them as adults. That's the only reason Yvette went along with covering it up."

"And now she's out of jail."

Maggie nodded. "I think she's been out for a few months."

The need to be closer to Maggie was nearly unbearable so Jackson got up and crossed over to the far side of the table. "And your role in this investigation was to identify the mother?"

She met his gaze. "That's right, though Uriah continued to claim I was wrong. That their mother had taken off. But then the police recovered the gun with his prints all over it, and the slug recovered from the grave matched the gun. Uriah claimed I planted the bullet, and that I was lying to put him in jail."

"But the sister confessed."

"Yeah, but she later recanted and supported him in his claims." Maggie sighed. "They were both so angry at me."

"Do you think she might still be mad and seeking revenge?"

Emotions paraded across Maggie's face, and she drummed her gloved finger on the metal table. "I suppose it's possible, but obviously Yvette wasn't the one who attacked me at Summit."

"She could have arranged for someone to do it for her. Like a husband?"

"She wasn't married and said she would never get married. Not with the way her mother and father argued. She didn't want to be like them."

He planted his hands on the table and leaned closer. "Then a boyfriend or a cousin. Some guy she hired. No matter what, we should talk to her."

"Agreed, which is why I already had Eryn search for her address online. She lives in Medford."

Jackson was impressed by her forward thinking. He glanced at the clock. "We have time to talk to her and still get to Cold Harbor at a reasonable hour."

"I'm finished here." She closed her laptop. "Let's go."

"I want another set of eyes so I'm going to ask Alex to accompany us."

She nodded and almost looked relieved. Maybe she didn't want to be alone with him or maybe she was more afraid than she was letting on. Either way, he felt better about having Alex watching their backs.

Later as they walked up to the rundown apartment in a not-so-nice part of town, Jackson was even more thankful Alex joined them and stood sentry at the end of the walkway.

Maggie knocked on the bright red door. The woman who opened it was short, thin, and was obviously unsteady on her feet. Jackson looked beyond her to the apartment and spotted several empty liquor bottles, dirty dishes, and piles of trash in the living room.

"Yesh," she said, slurring the word and teetering even more.

"Hello, Yvette. I'm Maggie Turner. Do you remember me?" Maggie's tone was warm and kind, something Jackson couldn't have managed if he were in her position.

Yvette shook her head and nearly toppled over before grabbing the doorframe.

"I'm the anthropologist who recovered your mother's remains," Maggie said.

She cast a skeptical look at Maggie. "Mother's dead. Uriah killed her."

"I know, I testified at your trial."

"Oh-h-h, right. The bone lady. Uriah hates you."

"What about you?" Jackson asked. "Do you hate Maggie, too?"

"Nah. You got Uriah out of my life. I love you." She made the shape of a heart with her hands and laughed.

Jackson needed to know if she was in touch with the brother and he was manipulating her into going after Maggie. "Do you visit your brother?"

"No. No way." She shook her head hard, her stringy hair slapping her face. "He killed mother. Don't want to see him ever again."

"But you supported him at the trial," Maggie said.

"'Cause he said he'd kill me if I didn't." She frowned and drool slid down her chin. She swiped it away. "He woulda if I didn't. But now he can't touch me."

This woman wasn't a threat. She obviously had a problem with alcohol and could hardly take care of herself, much less orchestrate a plan to kill Maggie. He glanced at Maggie to see if she was thinking the same thing. She subtly shook her head.

"Okay, thanks, Yvette," he said.

She looked up at him, her eyes trying to fix on his. "You never said your name so I'll call you handsome. Tall, dark, and haaaaannnndsome." She smiled and wobbled.

"Let's go," he said to Maggie.

"Aw, don't go," Yvette called after them. "I'm just getting to know you."

As they headed down the sidewalk toward Alex, Jackson couldn't help but feel sorry for the woman. She was obviously lonely and in bad shape. All because of a terrible mother. He was thankful his parents were good role models even though his dad hadn't been around much.

"Well?" Alex asked.

"She's not much of a threat," Maggie replied, sounding relieved.

"Not much of one at all," Jackson added, but didn't know if he was happy about that fact because it meant Scott's killer was the most likely person trying to end Maggie's life.

And when a man killed once, it was so much easier to do it a second time.

11

The helicopter whisked over the Oregon countryside, the rotors thumping steadily overhead. Maggie wished they'd flown in daylight so the scenery below was visible, but when they returned home tomorrow she should have a clear view.

"ETA five minutes," Riley announced over their headsets.

She glanced at Jackson who sat next to her in a row of three seats. Alex and Eryn sat facing them on the other side of the helicopter. Maggie felt out of place as the team members chatted easily among themselves using terminology she didn't recognize. She almost felt like she was heading to a foreign country, and she had no idea what to expect once they landed.

She glanced at Jackson. "Are you sure it's okay for me to stay at the compound?"

He smiled. "Of course. Why wouldn't it be?"

"I'm not paying for it."

Something flashed in his expression, but his smile remained. "Gage's fine with it. You'll see for yourself when you meet him."

She was starting to get nervous about stepping into Jackson's everyday life. She didn't know why, but the unease was there in the pit of her stomach. "Which will be when?"

"His wife Hannah invited us to breakfast with their family."

Interesting and unexpected. "Do they have breakfast with clients often?"

Jackson shook his head. "First, you're not a client. Second, you're more than a client."

Even more interesting. "Does he know about our past?"

"Some of it."

"If you look below, Maggie," Riley's voice interrupted before she could ask Jackson for clarification. "You'll see the lights on our helipad. We'll touch down in a minute or so."

The chopper started to descend, and Maggie leaned over to stare out the window. She spied the circle lit up in a clearing in the middle of dense woods. She was both excited to see the compound and terrified that Riley might miss the small opening. But he soon set the helicopter down in the middle of the circle with barely a bounce.

She glanced at Jackson for direction on what to do next. He took off his headset and hung it on a hook behind him. She followed suit.

Eryn removed hers and jumped up. "Home sweet home, and my little sweetie awaits. See you guys tomorrow." She saluted and whipped open the chopper door before Maggie could even say goodbye.

Jackson chuckled, the sound nearly swallowed up by rotors still whirling overhead. "She's eager to get home to Bekah."

"She really doesn't talk about her much, does she?" Maggie asked.

"Not on the job, no. Sometimes people think less of her

skills because she's a woman. Then if she mentions that she's a mother, things can get even more challenging for her. So she doesn't bring Bekah up."

"That's too bad, but she seems to be fine with all of it."

Alex grabbed his bag. "You two need to get a move on, or I'm gonna make you walk."

Jackson rolled his eyes. "Nice try, but we have to wait for Riley to tie down the rotors and go through his checklist."

"Actually," Maggie said, an idea coming to mind. "It's a nice night for a walk. If it's not too far to the cabins, I'd like the exercise."

"Couple of miles," Jackson said.

"I can do it if you can," she issued the challenge she knew Jackson wouldn't refuse.

"I'm up for showing you up." He grinned, a devilish glint in his eyes. "We'll dump our bags in the utility vehicle for Alex to drop off and be on our way."

The rotors above settled into a slower, but regular thump as he grabbed their bags and jumped down from the helicopter. He shifted the bags and offered his free hand to help her down. He clutched her fingers tightly, and when she hit the landing pad she waited for him to let go, but he continued to hold on.

"Just until your vision adjusts to the lower light," he said as if reading her mind.

She didn't need his help, but she wasn't going to make a big deal of it in front of Alex and Riley who'd gotten out and were unpacking little boots with straps attached. She assumed they were for securing the helicopter as Jackson mentioned.

He dropped their bags in the back of a small utility vehicle with a hard top.

"Catch you later," he called over his shoulder to his teammates.

Maggie looked ahead at the moonlit path lined by soaring pine trees. She glanced up to see the sky flooded with stars, and her mind betrayed her by going to thoughts of how romantic this walk could be. She willed away the thoughts and only hoped she could make the long trek without letting the ambience get to her and doing something she regretted later.

∼

Jackson was happy to be home. Even happier to have Maggie by his side. Even if she looked uneasy about something.

She spun to smile at Alex and Riley. "Thank you for the ride and for all your help today."

A pang of jealousy bit into Jackson. Why, he didn't know. There was no logical reason for it. He knew she or they didn't have any romantic interest in each other. Maybe he wanted that simple, sincere smile directed at him. Or even more, he wanted to be the one to make her smile again as she'd frequently done before losing Alison.

He was always more serious—serving as a Green Beret did that to him. But Maggie? Man. She'd once been so fun loving. Such a joy to be around. She pushed away his angst and all the ugliness he saw in the line of duty and helped him enjoy life again. That was one of the reasons he came back to her. He wanted to live a life of joy. To experience that with his daughter, too. He knew, just knew that would be even more joyful. Until it wasn't.

"What're you scowling about, Lockhart?" Alex asked. "I'm the one left behind to help Riley tie this thing down.

You get to take a romantic stroll in the moonlight with a beautiful woman."

"On that note, I'll say good night." Jackson gestured for Maggie to precede him down the road before Alex added any more romance comments. "And don't run us over when you're in such a hurry to get back to your new seventy-five-inch TV."

"Seventy-five inches, really?" Maggie glanced over her shoulder at Alex.

"It's not a TV if it doesn't fill up an entire wall." Alex chuckled.

Jackson had to smile, too. He loved his teammates. Not that he'd tell them that, but they knew. It was assumed among them. Well, maybe not all of them. Coop was once pretty standoffish, but since he and Kiera got engaged, he 'd opened up and was coming around.

"I like your team," Maggie said as they set off down the winding road.

"They're good people. By the way, I should warn you that beyond the hangar is our shooting range. We have classes in session so don't be surprised if you hear gunfire in the morning."

She shook her head. "Your world is so foreign to me. I can't even imagine what else goes on here."

"Up ahead you'll see our training building and a city street with plywood building fronts. We use it for urban training. It resembles a Hollywood movie set."

"Your operation sounds so professional."

"Yeah, thanks to Gage. We owe him a big debt of gratitude. I don't know what I'd be doing now if it wasn't for him."

She frowned, surprising him. "I don't like that you're still putting yourself in danger."

Right. That. She never liked the risks he faced as Beret, but she found a way to accept it when he knew many women couldn't do so. "Someone has to do this job or the bad guys win."

"I know, and I'd never suggest you change. Not when you obviously love what you do. It's just hard to think about you getting hurt."

He glanced at her and concern marked her expression. He wanted to say something. Maybe take her hand, but slipping back into the personal realm wasn't good for either of them.

They walked in silence. He felt so at home. Really at home. Inside and out. He never imagined he would walk this road with Maggie. He'd always been comfortable at the compound, but right now, his inner peace gave the place a new meaning for him.

He glanced at her. She was looking ahead and frowning. Obviously, she wasn't at peace. Was it the talk of him being in danger, or didn't she want to be here with him? Could be either, he supposed.

Headlights came from behind, and he urged Maggie to the side of the road. The utility vehicle slowed alongside them, Riley driving and Alex riding shotgun.

Alex leaned out the window. "Still want to walk?"

"Yes," Jackson said, not giving Maggie a chance to answer. He wasn't about to give up this peaceful stroll. The quiet calm would vanish soon enough when the cold light of day reminded him of the many reasons this romantic walk was just an illusion and he and Maggie couldn't be together.

Riley sped off, the small vehicle jetting forward. The simulated town was just ahead, and Jackson led Maggie to the sidewalk so she could get the full feel of the place.

"This is so realistic." She turned in a circle to take it in, her eyes alight with her discovery. Big. Wide. Luminous. Captivating. Drawing him closer.

He sucked in a breath and shoved his hands in his pockets before he took her hand again, making things awkward between them.

"Who built all of this?" she asked.

"Gage was in charge, and he hired some of it out, but the team did most of the work." Memories of the first few months on the job came flooding back, and Jackson smiled. "It was hard work, but we had a lot of fun doing it. Alex pulled daily practical jokes, and we all got to know him real well. And the rest of us bonded when we came up with payback. Gage had his hands full keeping us on task. I think we made him work a few extra hours."

"How did his wife deal with all that?" she asked.

"He wasn't married at the time. His first wife died a few years earlier."

"Oh, gosh, I'm sorry. When did he marry Hannah?"

"Less than a year ago. He has a daughter, Mia, and Hannah has a son, David."

She looked surprised at that. "How old?"

"Mia's seven. David, six."

She suddenly fell silent, and her body seemed to fold in on itself as if collapsing.

He moved ahead to look her in the face. "What's wrong?"

"Alison," she said barely above a whisper. "She would've been six this year."

And just like that, her joy, his joy, evaporated. Sadness hung over them once again, and he had to wonder if they could ever get past the pain and move on.

Maggie would not cry. She couldn't. Not in front of Jackson. She never imagined she could still be this emotional about losing Alison after so many years, but she was tired and stressed from the attacks, and with Jackson in her life again, her heart was vulnerable.

She peered down the road, searching for something, anything to change the subject and saw a barn-sized building. "Is that your training facility?"

Jackson gave her a knowing look. She hadn't fooled him with the change of subject. Of course, she hadn't. They were once so in tune with one another. Jackson may be this big warrior and tough protector, but he had a heart for people, especially underdogs, and that made him intuitive and observant.

Still, she wouldn't get sucked into a personal conversation. Not tonight. Not when she was exhausted and weepy.

"What kind of classes do you hold there?" She started walking again.

"Most of them are a combination of classroom and practical application. We do tactical, close combat, and concealed carry. Plus, long guns, urban sniper. Oh, and survival skills. Coop even holds air assault classes."

"I'm impressed." She looked across the street ahead and saw a grouping of small cabins. And she counted six men sitting in lawn chairs around a fire pit. "Do your trainees stay in the cabins?"

He nodded. "We have a small class of deputies right now."

"And where do you live?"

"There's another section of cabins ahead for staff." He looked at her. "You can either stay in one of the guest cabins or you can bunk with me. I mean...not with me. In my bedroom. I'll take the couch."

Right. His place. She wanted to see where he lived. Wanted him close by. Sure, she was safe in the compound, even more so with these deputies next door, but she didn't want to be alone tonight. "I'll stay with you, if you don't mind."

He didn't answer but his mouth quirked up, and she knew he didn't mind in the least.

He gestured at the buildings. "I don't see your bag sitting by a cabin so it looks like Alex already figured that's what we'd be doing."

"He knows about us, right?"

"Kind of. A little anyway."

"About Alison."

Jackson shook his head. "No one knows about her. Not even Gage, and I'd like to keep it that way."

She understood. Her guilt kept her from talking about Alison with other people, too, and she wasn't about to share that personal information with the team members, who—though she liked—were nearly strangers.

"No worries," she said. "I won't say anything."

He gave a clipped nod. "We've got another klick or so to go."

She nodded, and now eager to end this walk and get some sleep, she sped up. Jackson kept pace with her and didn't say a word until they approached a grouping of larger cabins, each of them constructed in a unique style.

"We designed and built our own cabins," he said as if reading her mind. "Mine's the third one on the left."

She turned to look, but her focus landed on the first one, an A-framed cabin with a massive picture window in the front, the moon casting a bright glow on the roof. Lights flickered through the window. She assumed it was a TV, and it was a good chance the place belonged to Alex. Plus, the utility vehicle was parked out front, too. Next door was a cabin made of logs with a front porch and a small bicycle out front—most likely Eryn lived there.

She moved on to the next place, Jackson's home, a contemporary square box with stairs leading up the side to what she had to assume was a rooftop deck. Thin slatted siding ran horizontally across the building and big sliding doors served as his front door.

"I like your place," she said. "It's practical looking, like you."

He quirked an eyebrow. "I'm practical looking?"

"No, you're gorgeous, but your personality has a practical bent to it. You're no-nonsense and sensible." She couldn't believe she told him he was gorgeous but resisted the urge to clamp a hand over her mouth.

"Practical, except when it comes to you." He locked gazes. "I wasn't very sensible at all and ruined things for us by taking off."

"We both had a part in that."

He shrugged and grabbed their bags from the utility vehicle. He slid open his front door and flipped on a light revealing contemporary furniture in muted colors. Comfy, practical furniture just as she'd described him. He set her bag down and reached behind her to close the door. She caught a hint of lingering minty soap and the scent made her even more aware of him as a man.

He set down the bags. "Would you like something to drink?"

"Water would be good, but I can get it if you tell me where the glasses are."

"Third cabinet on the right. I'll go ahead and change the sheets while you get it."

"I don't want to put you out. Why don't I sleep on the couch?"

"You know I'd never let you do that."

"I know, but I had to offer." She grinned at him.

His mouth lifted in a playful smile, and his eyes sparkled with humor. She felt his reaction right to her bones. Felt their old life, the time before their loss, rising up and replacing the sadness and pain.

She moved closer to him, and though she knew she would regret asking a personal question, she needed to know the answer. "Do you think it would be possible for us to be happy together again?"

He didn't respond at first but ran a hand over his face. "Honestly, I don't know. I've felt a hint of it these last few days. So maybe. But it doesn't matter, does it?"

"No, I suppose not."

He gave a resigned nod and turned. "I'll be right back."

She watched him take his usual long strides across the dark wood floors of his home. His home. She was in Jackson's home. Over the years, she often wondered what had become of him. Where he was living. If she would ever run into him again. But he was from Florida, and with an entire country sitting between them, she always doubted they would cross paths.

The odds were so long that they'd meet again, and yet, here they were. Not only crossing paths, but she was spending the night at his place. Had God brought them back together? She could ask God, she supposed. If her relationship with Him was on solid ground.

She changed her focus to Jackson's place, taking a better look at the large living space. He was a minimalist for sure.

His furniture was of good quality, most of the wood pieces made of warm teak. A sleek fireplace filled one wall, a modest-sized television mounted above. She turned to the kitchen with natural wood cabinets. The doors were flat panels without handles. She pressed on the third cabinet and it opened as she thought it might.

She grabbed a glass and filled it from the sink. She drank the entire glass and refilled it. Then she got one for Jackson, set them on coasters in the living area, and went to find him. He was bent over his sleek platform bed spreading out a blanket. The bed was lacquered a light gray color and had glossy metal feet. Two nightstands matched the bed.

"I like your furniture choices," she said.

He shot upright.

"Sorry. Didn't mean to scare you."

"I'm not used to having people here."

"No girlfriend."

"No." He went back to the blanket.

She should look away, but she liked seeing the arch of his trim body as he bent over the bed. He wore his clothes so well, as if they were custom tailored to fit him, and he exuded such a manly vibe that seeing him making a bed made her giggle.

"What?" He glanced over his shoulder.

"You. Engaged in domestic chores."

He tucked in the final corner and stood to look at her. "Why's that funny?"

"You're this big hunk of a guy, and you look like you're more at home on a battlefield than making a bed."

"You'd be surprised at how domesticated I've become."

She laughed again.

"Now what?"

"I'm imagining you with an apron and feather duster."

"Is that so." He smiled, wide and tantalizing as he crossed toward her.

She knew she should back up. Run the other way, but she was locked in his gaze and couldn't move.

He stopped inches away and tucked a strand of hair behind her ears. "Now what are you imagining?"

"You kissing me," she said on a breath.

"Do you want me to?"

Unable to say the word, she nodded.

He didn't take his eyes from her but slid his hand around her waist, his touch igniting delicious waves of emotions. He pulled her to him and held her gaze. Slowly, ever so slowly, he lowered his head, and when she thought he would never get to that kiss, his lips touched hers.

She was instantly catapulted back in time, and she forgot all their emotional baggage, all their pain, and she cupped the back of his head to draw him closer. He deepened the kiss, and it felt like she found her way home at long last and couldn't get enough of him. Enough of the feelings warming her heart and erasing any lingering pain.

He drew her even closer and ran his hands over her back. She was lost in the feel of him. Helplessly lost and she wouldn't end this kiss for anything. Didn't want it to end for anything.

His phone rang from his pocket, and he jerked back. His heavy-lidded gaze met hers, and he shook his head before he stepped away to answer his phone.

She gulped in a long breath and blew it out but didn't take her focus off him. He clamped a hand on the back of his neck. She knew that move as well as she knew him. He was frustrated.

"What time?" His long fingers kneaded his neck. "Yeah, thanks. We'll be there."

He turned and shoved his phone into his pocket. "That was Gage. Breakfast is at seven so we should turn in and get some sleep." He gazed at her longingly before turning around. "I'll grab your bag."

He headed for the door, not a word about the kiss. It seemed all they could share was a kiss and regrets.

12

The next morning, Hannah and Gage answered the door arm in arm, and Maggie couldn't help but think how adorable they were. If you could call a guy built like a mountain "adorable." But their obvious love for each other left Maggie feeling even more devastated than last night.

She had to admit whenever she pictured herself with a husband, it was always Jackson who came to mind. But this morning, he was cool and reserved. All business. She could chalk it up to having breakfast with his boss, but he acted the same way at his place, too. Bidding her good morning then quickly racing past her to shower and get ready for the day while she drank a cup of coffee. Not uttering even one word on the drive over. Whatever the reason, they weren't in a good place this morning and it hurt.

Or maybe she knew the reason and just didn't want to admit it. The past was just too large of an obstacle to allow them a future.

Small footsteps came running down the hallway taking her attention. A good-looking young boy slammed into Gage's side and threw his arms around him. A girl dressed in pink shorts and a bubble gum striped T-shirt tried to keep up with him, but her gait was awkward, and she fell behind. When she did reach them, she took one look at Maggie, clutched Hannah's hand, and quickly hid behind her.

Hannah picked the child up. "This is Mia."

The child laid her curly pigtailed head on Hannah's shoulder. "Mia, say hello to Maggie. She's Jackson's friend."

"Hi," she said but seemed to snuggle closer to Hannah.

"Hey, kiddo," Jackson said.

He got a cute little smile and a 'hi' in return.

"Let's all take a seat at the table, and I'll get the food," Hannah said.

"Can I help?" Maggie asked.

Gage rested a hand on his wife's shoulder "I've got it. You sit."

She beamed a smile up at him, and he kissed her forehead.

Yeah, they were a happy couple all right, and they proved it all through breakfast. When they'd consumed the last of the spinach quiche, fresh fruit, and ham, Gage pushed back his chair and looked at Jackson. He clearly wanted to talk to his boss, likely about Scott, but she doubted he would do so with the kids at the table.

"Can we go play?" David asked.

"After you clear your dishes," Gage replied.

Both children got up, picked up their dishes, and headed for the kitchen. Maggie watched them go. David left the room without incident, but Mia stumbled, and the silverware on her plate rattled. She was a clumsy little thing, but oh, so adorable. Maggie turned her focus back to the others and caught Gage carefully watching her, a very intimidating look on his face.

Hannah didn't seem to notice but pushed to her feet. "If you'll excuse me, I'll clear the table and get you all more coffee."

"Let me help clear," Maggie offered.

"That's not necessary. You're our guest."

"I have the feeling these guys want to talk anyway." Maggie grabbed Jackson's plate and stacked it and his silverware on hers.

"Thanks." He looked up at her, but his blank expression kept her from getting even a hint of his thoughts.

She carried the dishes into the kitchen, set them on a large island and returned for others. Together, she and Hannah cleared the table in minutes and were alone together in the kitchen.

"Would you like another cup of coffee?" Hannah asked.

Maggie nodded.

Hannah gestured at the stools near the island. "Have a seat, and I'll grab the pot."

Maggie sat and checked out the homey kitchen. White cabinets and quartz countertops plus stainless-steel appliances could make the room look cold, but Hannah warmed it up with rich red accents.

She returned with the pot. "So you and Jackson go way back."

Maggie nodded.

"Did you date long?" Hannah probed.

"Three years."

"And the breakup? Was it amicable?"

Maggie didn't want to answer. Not only because she didn't know Hannah, but because she didn't think Jackson would want her to.

"I'll take your silence to mean it wasn't that pleasant."

Maggie opened her mouth to reply, but Hannah held up

her hand. "It's really none of my business, but I thought we might have that in common. Gage and I had an earlier relationship, too. We split up because I wanted a deeper commitment, and he wasn't ready. I didn't handle it well. Gave him an ultimatum. Commit or we were through. He took off."

"He left you?"

"Yes, with no explanation." Hannah sighed. "I can tell you I was hurt big time. Took me ten years to forgive him."

Maggie cupped her warm mug. "But obviously you did."

"Yes, but it wasn't easy. I had to figure out that I was partly to blame by giving him that ultimatum. I should've taken what he had to offer at the time and allowed him time to figure out what he wanted."

"I can totally understand that." Maggie sipped the rich coffee.

Hannah filled her mug. "So something similar happened with Jackson?"

"Similar?" She thought about it. "No. It was worse. Much worse."

Hannah's eyebrow rose, but she didn't say anything. She was waiting for Maggie to explain, but she promised Jackson she wouldn't mention Alison to anyone.

Hannah kept looking at her. She took another sip of the coffee and then another.

"Are you a woman of faith?" she finally asked.

Glad to have the subject changed, Maggie nodded. "Though honestly I haven't really trusted God since Jackson and I broke up."

"Oh, I get that. I was married before Gage. My husband died. I was so upset at God for the longest time, even though I know God didn't cause his death. It just cut so deeply, you know?"

"Yes," Maggie replied, the subject so close to her feelings on Alison it was almost frightening.

"I spent years asking God why. Demanding an explanation." She poured cream into her cup and stirred, a faraway look on her face. "It took Gage to teach me that God doesn't promise to explain everything to us. Sometimes we get answers, most of the time we don't. We just have to keep moving forward and trust that God can see further ahead than we can. And that He has our best interest at heart, and it will all end up good for us."

Maggie's heart constricted. "I can't see that. Not at all."

"Maybe you're not there yet. I mean, I don't know what happened with you two, but even if there isn't a physical loss of a partner like Nick, the loss of a relationship involves grief. Grief has many stages to overcome. Takes some of us longer than others to work through it."

Maggie set down her cup. "But it sounds like you have, and you've gotten used to the loss."

"Gotten used to it?" Hannah shook her head hard. "No, you never get used to losing someone you love so deeply, but you learn how to cope. Memories still come flooding back at the oddest times, and you have to consciously remember that God will work it all for good. I don't know how people without faith survive such a thing."

Hannah placed her hand on Maggie's and locked gazes with her. "God always gets it right. When we worry or question Him, it's like we think He's gotten it wrong."

Maggie sat there stunned. It was as if Hannah had taken the words right out of her mouth. She felt so alone after losing Alison and Jackson, but now she could see that God had actually been there with her the whole time. If not, she couldn't have been questioning Him. Oh, man. He was there all along, and she did nothing but distrust him and let anxiety get the best of her.

"Thank you," Maggie said, vowing to give this conversation some additional thought. "Your words helped a lot."

"I'm glad." Hannah lifted her hand and smiled. "I'll tell you a secret. I'm so incredibly happy with Gage and our little family that I want everyone on the team to feel the same way. So I've become the team busybody. Butting into their lives. Trying to do some matchmaking. One of these days one of them is going to tell me to mind my own business." She chuckled.

Maggie laughed along with her, and knew if she ever ended up living here that Hannah would be a good friend.

Mia came running into the room in her different gait. "Can David and I watch Veggie Tales?"

"Of course," Hannah said.

"Yippee." Mia tottered off.

Maggie's thoughts turned to Alison and the same sadness crept to the surface. She thought about her talk with Hannah. This woman, this Godly woman across the island was filled with joy and such hope even after losing her husband. She found a way through the loss and made a good life for herself. Maggie wanted that. She'd been without hope in her life for far too long, a mere shell of a person, not really living.

Maybe it was time to pray again and believe God had something good in store for her. Depending on herself had accomplished nothing, so why not listen to Hannah and try talking to God again?

She closed her eyes, feeling so uncomfortable with the thought of praying after all these years that she had to search hard for words.

Father, please help me lean on you and see the good from this awful tragedy.

She tried to expound on her statement but nothing came. Okay, fine. Not much of a prayer, but a start. She was so out of the habit that she didn't even know if it would work. But just reaching out to God and the chance at hope that life might get better helped ease her distress. Nothing seemed earth-shatteringly different, but a smidgen less pain gripped her soul.

She opened her eyes to find Hannah watching her intently.

Maggie searched for anything to say to take the focus from herself. "Mia seems like a happy girl."

"She is. For the most part, anyway, but she has her challenges. She was in the car accident that killed her mother. Mia suffered a brain injury and has residual effects like her halting gait."

Ah, that explained it.

"And she's painfully shy. It took some time for her to warm up to me, but now I couldn't imagine life without her."

Maggie nodded. She couldn't imagine life without Alison either, but she lived it for the last six years. Maybe today was the day that she could turn a corner and could once again imagine her future, too. Maybe.

Jackson was surprised at the You Can Do It building. It was about the size of a large gymnasium with concrete floors and block walls, but the lobby was professional with a long reception desk and small sitting area with black leather furniture. The sound of machinery hummed in the distance, and Jackson could easily imagine men or women working on the industrial equipment.

He approached the older woman behind the desk. Her salt and pepper hair was curled like a cap on her head, and she wore reading glasses with a long chain hanging around her neck.

Jackson smiled at her but got a blank stare in return. She glanced at Maggie, seeming unimpressed with what she saw, and turned her focus back to him. "Help you?"

"Is your owner or manager in?" Jackson asked.

"Not if you're selling something, he's not."

Jackson widened his smile, but it had no impact on the woman. "I promise I only want to ask him a few questions about the business."

"You law enforcement?"

"No, why would you ask?"

"They come in here sometimes wanting to know what people are making. Harry tells them to show him a warrant or take a hike."

"Harry sounds like an interesting guy. Can't wait to meet him." Jackson held his breath and hoped she would decide to get on the phone to her boss.

She picked up a microphone. "Harry, you're needed at the front desk."

Her voice came over loudspeakers, and soon, a man with a large belly, short legs, and a shiny head entered the lobby from a door in the back.

He ran his gaze over Jackson, a scowl following. "You with the cops?"

Jackson shook his head and gave him one of his business cards. "Could we have a word in private?"

He eyed Jackson, and it looked like he was going to say no.

Maggie stepped closer and introduced herself. "It would mean so much if we could have just a minute of your time."

He let his wandering gaze rove over Maggie, and when a captivated look crossed his face, Jackson wanted to deck the guy. Maggie, on the other hand, stood there without so much as blanching.

"My office is this way." He spun, his black work shoes squeaking on the polished concrete.

Maggie shuddered.

"Sorry he's such a creep," Jackson whispered.

"That's okay. Hopefully I can use it to our advantage."

Jackson didn't want her to put herself in an uncomfortable position, but he did appreciate her willingness to help.

By the time they got to Harry's office, he was standing behind a desk way too large for the small space. Somehow, he also managed to cram a credenza and three chairs in the minuscule office. Every flat surface held mounds of paperwork.

"'Scuse the mess. Agnes doesn't like to file." He cleared two chairs, putting the folders in a precarious position on the credenza. He dropped behind the desk and sank so low he looked child-sized. "Now what's this about?"

"One of your customers, Scott Dawson," Jackson said as he took a seat. "He was murdered, and my company was hired to find the killer."

"Killed!" Harry snapped his chair forward. "Man, that's rough. He was just a kid."

"He was one of my students," Maggie said.

"You're a teacher, huh?"

"Assistant Professor of Anthropology."

"If they'd made 'em like you back when I was his age, I'da gone to college for sure." He winked at Maggie.

Jackson had to give her credit when she didn't wince at

the comment but offered a tight smile. "We were hoping you might help us figure out who killed Scott."

Harry leaned his chair back again and raised pudgy arms over his head. "Don't know how I can help with that. He came here to use our CNC machine to fabricate gun parts and had us ship them to him. That's all I know, and I suspect you know that, too, or you wouldn't be here."

"What's a CNC machine?" Maggie asked.

"Stands for Computer Numerical Control. In a nutshell, someone brings in their own computer software, plugs it into the machine, and it does all the work to manufacture their object. You don't have to have any skills to operate the equipment. Our only rule for gun makers is they can't assemble firearms in the building. Which Scott didn't do. Like I said, he had us ship the pieces."

"Isn't that odd that he wanted such small parts shipped when he could easily have taken them with him?" Jackson asked.

Harry turned his attention to Jackson, seeming disappointed that he remained in the room. "Kind of odd, yeah, but his partner paid us a generous fee for the shipping so I didn't ask questions."

"He had a partner?" Excitement coursed through Jackson's body at the new lead, but he resisted sitting forward and letting Harry know this was an important fact.

"Yeah, an older guy."

"Do you have contact information for him?"

Harry crossed his arms. "I do, but I'm not going to give it to you."

"Please, Harry." Maggie leaned closer to the desk and rested her hands on a stack of folders. "This could help us find his killer."

"Maybe but..." He shrugged.

"The killer is coming after me." She untied the scarf around her neck and pointed at the angry purple bruises from the attack. "He tried to strangle me. And he shot at me. Maybe with one of these guns."

"Now that just plain makes me mad. A pretty little thing like you doesn't deserve this kind of treatment. You should be cherished." He snapped forward. "At least I'd cherish you."

Jackson nearly hurled, but Maggie nodded. "I can tell a sweet guy like you knows how to treat women."

He suddenly jerked back, pulled open a file cabinet, and ran his fingers over folders. He slapped one on the desk and drew out a form to give to Maggie. "This's the partner's address. Lyle Vetter. He lives on a boat he rents at a local marina."

Jackson took out his phone and recorded the address before Harry changed his mind and snatched the folder away.

"Thank you," Maggie said. "Tell me. Did this Vetter guy seem like he might be capable of murder?"

Harry shrugged. "All I know is of the two guys, he seemed to be the one in charge."

"Did he ever mention his job?" Jackson asked.

"Works in the computer field. Not sure of the actual job, but he was the one who always programmed the CNC machine, and he told me he worked with computers."

So he was skilled with computers. Meant he could have hacked Maggie's car. "Ever hear him talking about computers in cars?"

"Nah. It's not like I hang out with these people, you know. I have a business to run."

"Did the pair ever expand beyond handguns to rifles?" Jackson asked.

Harry shook his head. "Nah, don't have many people running rifle receivers here."

Jackson didn't much like Harry's nonchalant attitude about manufacturing guns. "Here's the thing I don't get, Harry. How can you let these guys make these guns? You know they're up to no good."

Harry crossed his arms. "If they didn't make them here, they'd make them somewhere else."

"Not really a very good answer," Jackson grumbled, but it looked like he'd gotten everything he could from Harry, so he stood. "I appreciate the information."

"Didn't do it for you." Harry scowled at him as if he just realized by sharing the name and address with Maggie, it meant he also gave it to Jackson.

Maggie dug her business card from her purse and laid it on the desk. She stood. "If you think of anything else that might help, I'd appreciate if you'd give me a call."

"Will do." He grinned at her, a knowing look on his face. "And I'll look you up next time I'm in your neck of the woods, too."

Jackson expected Maggie to turn green, throw up, or run away at the thought of it, but she nodded and calmly exited the office. Jackson followed her through the lobby and outside.

She hurried toward his truck, the wind whipping her hair around her face. At the passenger door, she turned, and gave an exaggerated shudder. "I need a shower. Maybe a soak in some disinfectant."

Jackson faced her. "I don't like that you gave him your business card."

"It only has my office number, not my cell."

He unlocked the door for her. "I still don't like a lecherous guy like Harry even knowing your name, much less where you work."

She turned to look at him. "I appreciate your concern, but I'm sure you have nothing to worry about."

He leaned against the doorframe and held her gaze. "You haven't changed. You take things like this in stride and move on when I always want to do something about it."

"You know why you do that, don't you?"

"No," he said, wondering what she might say.

She swiveled to face him. "Because your biggest fear has always been that you'll let someone down. I don't pretend to know where that comes from, but it's there."

"You're way off base here."

"How's that?"

"If my not being there for people is my biggest fear, how could I walk out on you the day you told me you were pregnant with Alison? And leave you for good?"

The wince he expected to see with Harry materialized now. "I can't explain that, but you came back and you were there for me at the hospital. At least the first few days."

"Yeah," he said. "But I should've stayed with you, and I bailed. Makes me a first-class jerk in my book."

She took his hand and clutched it tightly. "We were young. We both made mistakes."

She stared over his shoulder, a faraway look in her eyes and sad resignation on her face. He waited for her to speak, but she didn't.

"Maggie," he said to gain her attention again. "What're you thinking about?"

"Alison. Being with you has brought her death back to the surface, and I feel like it was just yesterday. That day in the hospital keeps replaying in my mind." She looked down at their hands and sorrowfully shook her head. "I can still feel her in my arms. Her little body so fragile and lifeless. Her tiny hand in mine. It was…"

Her voiced tapered off on a sob, and she looked up at him, her eyes awash with tears. "I was so desperate for more time with her. I'd barely met her in person, and I didn't want to let her go."

"I know, honey," he said, unable to come up with anything else.

He'd held his precious little girl, too. Once. Only once. For an hour. Then they'd taken her, and Maggie crumpled to the floor. He picked her up and held her instead, but she pushed from his arms, crawled into the hospital bed in a fetal position, and told him to leave.

His heart died twice that day.

"Why did she have to die?" She let go of his hand and doubled over as if the pain was too intense to stand upright.

And it was for him, too. Or at least it had been back then. Now it wasn't at quite the same level, but still an aching reality for both of them. He helped Maggie to her feet and drew her into his arms. He held her. Tightly. Close to his heart. Feeling the same awful, terrible despair.

"I just can't understand any of it," Maggie said. "Her life was so short. It was the hardest thing I've ever faced."

He felt tears of his own begging for release. "Even though she's gone, I'm convinced we'll see her again someday. We can hold her then. See her smile. Giggle. Laugh. And our hearts will be filled with joy."

He could imagine his daughter's precious face, looking up at him. Filling his soul with the joy that had been missing since that day in the hospital. That day he'd gone home empty-handed, his heart empty as well.

Maggie pulled back, her watery gaze connecting with his. "Will we? Will I—after I've doubted God for so long?"

"Of course, you will. You may have doubted God's love, but you still believe in Jesus, right? That's all that matters in eternity."

She gave a resigned nod and laid her head against his chest. He stroked her back, felt his tears abate and soothing peace temper his anguish.

"It wasn't more than a few hours ago that I was convinced I understood this and knew how to deal with it. But look at me now." She lifted her head and shook it. "I'm a mess. and I don't know what I think anymore."

"Hey," he said. "You'll figure it out. Maybe I will, too, someday."

She blinked several times. "It was you, wasn't it? The person who puts the daisies on her grave every year on the anniversary of her death."

"Yes."

She looked up at him. "I'm surprised we never ran into each other."

"I came at sunup so you wouldn't have to see me."

"That was kind of you, Jackson. So sweet." She sighed. "But now that we've reconnected, I wish I'd seen you sooner. Maybe I could've shared my grief with someone who knew what it felt like."

"Did you ever try a grief support group?"

"Yeah, and it helped. I mean, the people understood, but you're different. You were there that day. You were Alison's father. Seems like we really should have stayed together. It would have been better."

He didn't know if that was true, but he did know he thanked God for this moment with her and would cherish it as much as he cherished the memory of Alison's sweet little face.

13

—————

Maggie waited for Jackson to hang up from his call with Eryn. He'd instructed her to run a background check on Lyle Vetter while they'd waited in the truck. If it turned out he wasn't dangerous, they could head over to his boat slip. But after their talk, tension filled the truck and Jackson climbed out to pace. He walked back and forth for nearly an hour. Maggie wanted to go to him, but she knew he needed space to think about what had just transpired between them.

He jerked open the door and slid behind the wheel. "Vetter's a computer engineer at a local company."

"Just like Harry said."

Jackson nodded. "And he doesn't have any red flags in his past. He's never been arrested. Doesn't have even a hint of anything illegal in his life and nothing to say he's into guns either."

"What do you make of that?"

"It's a bit odd, but then the guy doesn't have to like guns or even shoot them to sell them." He cranked the engine. "He's a low enough threat that we're good to talk to him."

Jackson got them on the road, and Maggie leaned her head back against the seat. She was emotionally wrung out, but she felt better after crying in the parking lot. Her mind was clearer than it'd been in a long time. Maybe she'd just needed to share the loss with Jackson.

She would never get over losing Alison just like Hannah had said. But Maggie was tired of rehashing the way the past played out and wondering how it could be different. It all ended the same way. It couldn't be different. Alison was gone, and nothing Maggie or Jackson could do would ever, ever bring the precious child back. Not wondering if she was at fault. If Jackson was at fault. If she and Jackson should have stayed together. None of it changed the cold hard fact that Alison died, and the sooner Maggie accepted that, the better her life would be.

She glanced at Jackson, sad to see his clenched jaw. Here she was thinking of finally moving forward, and she didn't get the same vibe from him. But then he didn't hear Hannah's take on things, which helped Maggie immensely. There was still time before reaching the boat slip for Maggie to tell him about Hannah's wisdom.

She shifted on the cracked vinyl seat to look at him. "I had an interesting conversation with Hannah in the kitchen this morning."

"Oh."

He didn't even ask for details. Maybe he knew the direction she was heading, and he was too wrung out to talk about it.

She couldn't let that deter her. "We were talking about our pasts."

He shot her a look. "You told her about Alison?"

She held up her hands. "No. You asked me not to, but

she's very intuitive, and she could tell there was something tragic in my past that I wasn't willing to talk about."

"Yeah, I should've told you about that. She's always after us guys to open up about our feelings." Jackson rolled his eyes. "She thinks we all have issues from our time in the service and says if we talk about it, it won't hold us hostage."

Not somewhere Maggie expected this conversation to go. "Do you have issues with that?"

He shook his head. "I saw things. Things I'll never forget and wish I could. But nah, I'm good. Not like some guys I served with."

"I'm glad about that." She placed her hand over his where it rested on the gearshift. He shot her a look, but she didn't remove her hand. "You already have the bum knee and you lost Alison. You don't deserve other issues to deal with."

"I wish Hannah would believe me as easily. As far as I know, Gage is the only person who shared anything personal with her, and that's because he had to."

"She's only trying to help. If you told her about Alison, Hannah would likely stop asking you to share."

"I don't want her to know," he ground out between his teeth.

"Why?"

He cast her an irritated look before snapping his gaze back to the road. "You mean other than it makes me look like a complete jerk?"

"We've been over that. The accident wasn't your fault."

"I'm not talking about the accident. I mean the way I bailed on you when you needed me."

She leaned closer, hoping he would look at her. When he didn't, she said, "You came back, Jackson. That's all that matters."

"Not to me." He freed his hand and planted it on the steering wheel. The fingers on both hands turned white from his tense grip. "It's like I don't even know that guy who left, you know? Like—what was I thinking?"

She couldn't explain the past, and she was tired of trying. "Maybe it was supposed to happen that way."

"What do you mean?"

"I mean, when I was talking to Hannah she said something I can't forget. She said God always gets things right, and when we worry or question Him, it's like we think He's gotten it wrong."

He clenched his jaw. "Well, didn't He?"

"I've thought for years that He did, but now I think what Hannah says is more likely. If we believe God got that wrong, then what else might He have gotten wrong? Us dating? Me getting pregnant? Our very lives? We thank Him for the good things and blame Him for the bad. God is consistent, so we're just tormenting ourselves by fluctuating as circumstances change."

"Maybe," he sounded unconvinced.

"One thing I do know," she said before he completely shut down. "I questioned God and was upset with Him over what happened, but through it all He was there. Waiting for me to see His plan for my life and come back to Him."

"And you can do that now?" he sounded so skeptical.

"I'm not sure, but I know I'm going to try."

"Just like that? Hannah says something to you, and you can forget about losing Alison?"

"Forget? No way! You just saw that I can't. I don't want to forget her. Ever. But hoping for a future that isn't quite as sad and lonely as my life is now? Yeah. I want to consider that."

He didn't respond and kept his focus on the road.

She wouldn't keep probing. It did no good. "I'm sorry. I shouldn't have brought it up."

"No, wait." He looked at her then, his eyes wounded. "I'm glad you did. It's...it's not just God that I'm mad at. It's me. I might be able to get to a place where I can let go of my anger at God. But I honestly don't know if I can ever forgive myself for hurting you like that."

Jackson pulled into the marina parking lot and couldn't quit thinking about Maggie's words. He wanted hope in his life again. He always had, but he also knew he didn't deserve to have it. He was glad Maggie was trying for it, though. She deserved everything wonderful, and if she was looking to the future, maybe she could get married and have a child someday. Just not with him.

He saw her then in his mind. With another man. In a cute nursery, holding that man's baby, Maggie's eyes filled with joy. Pain stabbed through his body, and he shoved the gearshift into park. He had to get out of this truck and move before he drove himself crazy.

He snapped his gun holster onto his belt and shrugged into a button-down shirt that would cover the telltale bulge of his weapon. No way he was going to freak people out with the sight of it. Especially not Vetter.

He faced Maggie. "Wait here, and I'll take a look around first."

She raised fear-filled eyes to his. "Sounds like you're worried this Vetter guy is going to try something."

"It's always a possibility."

"So you think he killed Scott?"

"Not necessarily, but if he's involved in selling illegal guns, I could see him panicking when we approach."

"Good point. I hadn't thought of that."

"Sit tight." Jackson wished he could offer her more comfort, but he was plain out of comfort for the day and knew it would come across as insincere.

He pushed out of the truck and scanned the area. In the distance, he spied a long dock with boats moored along both sides. The boats on the far end under aluminum awnings were huge and looked to be very expensive. Even if Jackson didn't know that Vetter's slip number was seven, he would've doubted that the guy lived on one of the bigger boats at the far end.

Jackson scanned the entire property. Several workers were painting the marina office exterior, and two men were heading down the dock with poles and nets over their shoulders. A perfectly normal day at the marina. At least Jackson hoped it turned out to be a normal day other than asking Vetter a few questions.

He strode around the truck and opened the door. "I didn't see anything unusual, but stay close to me, okay? And if I give you a direction, follow it without question."

He stood back so she could exit the vehicle. He rested his hand on his gun as he started for the marina. Maggie walked next to him. He glanced at her, enjoying the soft way her hair blew in the breeze. Despite the reason for being with her, he had to admit he'd been happier the last few days with her than he'd been in the six years without her.

Birds soared over the glistening water looking so care-free it made Jackson's gut hurt. He would like to feel that way. To revel in life again. To have that hope that Maggie talked about. But facts were facts. If he hadn't managed to find it in six years, he wasn't likely going to, and it was about time he accepted that.

They stepped onto the dock, and the wooden slats bounced underfoot. He searched ahead for slip number seven and found it on the left side. He pegged the speedboat at about a fifty-footer. An upper deck held the pilot's seat and controls and a lower deck had windows running the front half of the vessel. The boat was bigger than Jackson thought it might be, but it looked like an older model so maybe that's how Vetter could afford to rent it.

They approached, and a guy at the next-door slip looked up from washing his boat deck with a sudsy mop. Keeping his focus on them, he set aside the mop and stepped down from his boat with the pail in hand. He paused for a second on the dock. Jackson removed his hand from his gun so he didn't draw attention to it and nodded a greeting. The man seemed like he wanted to say something. Ask a question or two, but he passed them by and moved on down the dock.

"Do you think he knows Vetter?" Maggie asked.

"Maybe. We can talk to him after we question Vetter." Jackson steered Maggie toward a set of metal stairs leading up to Vetter's rental boat.

She grabbed the handrail and started up. Jackson trailed her, and at the cockpit door, she stepped to the side. He saw no sign of life so he knocked on the door.

No one answered.

"Hello," Jackson called out and knocked again. He stood there. Counting. Hit two minutes. "Looks like he's not here."

He tried the door knob. It turned in his hand. "Maybe he's here, and he's not answering."

He pounded hard on the metal door. He glanced down the dock. Saw the neighbor reach the marina office and look back. Maybe he was going to report them. Maybe he was just getting something or returning that pail, though Jackson thought it odd that the guy wouldn't have his own pail onboard. Jackson checked the other direction. There was no movement save the wind gently whispering over them and blowing little flags on a boat down the way.

A very picturesque scene, and Jackson waited for someone to come yell at them for making so much noise on this perfectly quiet day.

Getting antsy, he stepped to the side and peered into the window. The upper deck was basically an indoor living area with a big plush captain's chair sitting in front of a large console and a wide windshield above. He couldn't see anyone moving nor anyone sitting on the small sofa or plush chairs.

He turned the knob and pushed the door open.

Maggie grabbed his arm. "You're not going in there, are you?"

"Not yet." He poked his head in and looked around. As he'd seen through the window, no one was up top. Didn't mean Vetter wasn't down below.

"Vetter," he yelled. "I need to talk to you. It's important."

No answer.

"Maybe we should go," Maggie said.

"Not until I'm sure he's not avoiding us and really isn't here." Jackson cupped his hands around his mouth. "Vetter come up here. I need to talk to you."

No sound except the water lapping against the boat.

Jackson took Maggie's hand. "C'mon. Let's see if he's below deck."

"We shouldn't."

He took a step and froze. He looked down. His ankle rested against a wire. He'd tripped it, but nothing happened.

He glanced to the side. Saw the device. A timer. Bright red letters counting down from one minute.

He spun. "Run."

"What?" Maggie asked.

"Run now. As fast as you can to the end of the dock."

"But I—"

"Now!" He grabbed her hand and fled down the stairs. "This boat is going to blow in less than sixty seconds! Move!"

14

"Blow up?" Maggie asked, her mind trying to grasp Jackson's statement.

"Hurry!" Jackson took off running on the dock, her hand still in his. He led them. Pulling. Urging her faster. They had a long way to go, and she was falling behind.

Jackson tugged her hand. "Faster!"

She tried to pick up speed, but she was moving as fast as she could. She didn't want to slow him down. She released his hand.

He came to a stop. Shot her a look. Lifted her into his arms. Took off.

"No! I'm slowing you down. Save yourself." Even as she said it, she knew he wouldn't listen.

He raced forward, and she clutched tightly to his neck.

Thirty feet. Twenty. Ten.

"We're almost out of time," he declared, though she had no idea how he knew that.

He kicked up his speed, surprising her.

The boat exploded. A boom blared through the quiet. A

concussion of air slammed into them. Jackson dove for the grass. Landed on his shoulder. Rolled and covered her. Debris rained down on them.

Her heart raced, and she dragged in as much air as she could. She waited to feel pain, but none came. She was safe. She'd survived. Covered by this resilient man who was taking the brunt of the damage. He was such an amazing man. Her protector. Her hero. He always had been. Always would be if she needed him.

The thought hit her hard. They had a connection. A deep one.

Jackson lifted his head and frantically searched her face. "Are you okay? Did I hurt you when we landed?"

"No. I'm fine. Thanks to you again."

He frowned. "No thanks to me. I triggered the tripwire."

She couldn't let him take the blame for this. "You had no reason to think Vetter would have a bomb. And after you triggered it, you recognized what happened and got us out of there."

"If I'd lost you. I..." His voice broke, and he tucked a strand of hair behind her ear, his gaze locked on hers like a death grip.

She reached up and touched his cheek. Smiled her reassurance when her heart was still pounding with fear, but she wasn't going to let him see that.

"I need to call the sheriff and the team." He pushed to his feet and offered his hand to help her up.

She shook her head. "I think I'd better sit here for a while. My legs are kind of wobbly."

"Of course," he said, his frown deepening. "I should have thought of that."

She stared up at him. "Stop setting such impossible standards for yourself, Jackson. You're a man, not Superman. You can only do as much as you can do."

"But I..." He shoved a hand in his hair and shook his head. "Let me get the team out here."

Digging out his phone, he stepped away and lifted it to his ear. He stood there strong. Tall. Broad shouldered. A man's man. Tough, and yet he was so vulnerable inside. She never knew what drove him to fiercely protect others with no leeway for mistakes. She would say it was due to the loss of Alison, but he was that way before they'd lost her.

Maybe not this intensely fierce, but he was driven to protect others. It was his reason for not wanting to leave the Berets. He wasn't being selfish when he returned to his team, he was thinking of others.

Not her. Not their baby. He had no reason to fear for them, but the larger population of the world needed protection from terrorism and despotic leaders.

He came back and squatted beside her. He searched her face, his expression tender and concerned. "Are you sure you're okay?"

"Yes. And you? Are you hurt?"

"No."

"Did you get ahold of Gage?"

"He asked me to tell you he was sorry you got caught up in this mess today."

At first Maggie was intimidated by Gage, but she was beginning to think he possessed the same wonderful heart for service as the rest of the team. "What happens next?"

"Medics are on the way, and I want them to check you out."

"But I'm fine."

"Shock can cover up injuries."

"Really, I might be shocked, but I know I'm fine."

"Would you humor me and let them check you out?"

She met his gaze. "If you do the same thing."

"Me? No. I can tell if I'm injured, and I'm not."

"Right. Superman." She grinned to try to lighten the mood, but he was so disappointed in himself that his lips didn't even lift a fraction.

She didn't want to add to his worries. "I'll see the medics."

"Thank you." He squeezed her hand. "I need to talk to the guy with the slip next to Vetter's."

"You think he might know where Vetter went?"

"Hopefully. Do you want to wait here or sit in my truck?"

She wanted to be near him, not sitting in a vehicle in the distance. "Here."

He nodded as sirens sounded. "Likely Sheriff Jenkins— Blake. He'll have questions for you. We've worked with him a lot, and I know you'll like him."

"I'm sure I will."

"Okay, sit tight. I'll go meet Blake and bring him over." He walked away.

She watched his every step. She didn't want him to go. Not at all. She'd come to depend on him again. Depend on his nearness. His attention. And now she felt alone. So alone.

What would happen when they found Vetter—or whoever killed Scott—and Jackson no longer had a reason to stay with her? Could she recover from losing him again? Because one thing she knew for sure. He would go, and even if she might want to be with him again, he was just as far away from her as the day he'd left six years ago.

From the marina office, Jackson glanced at Maggie sitting on the ambulance bumper as the medic stripped off her blood pressure cuff. They'd pronounced her fine. No thanks to him. How had he missed that tripwire? A rookie mistake, and he was far from a rookie. Sure, their intel didn't give him any reason to expect Vetter would plant a bomb, but Jackson shouldn't have underestimated him. He was a killer after all. Or at least it looked like he was a killer.

Maggie's words came back to him. She said he was a man. Simply a man. He got that. Man, how he got it. There were too many reminders in his past for him not to know his limitations. But the worst thing he could do right now was focus on it and make another mistake. He had to let it go and move on. Problem was, he kept proving how bad he was at letting things go.

Perhaps this moment, right now, was a chance for him to do that. To start over. Vowing to try, he stepped over to the man who'd been scrubbing his boat deck. He stood staring at the dock, likely trying to determine if his boat was salvageable.

"I'm sorry about your boat," Jackson said.

The guy swung his gaze to Jackson and ran it over him, a hint of anger in his eyes.

Jackson handed him a business card. "I'm Jackson Lockhart. I work with Blackwell Tactical."

"Freddy Paulson." He bent to study the card. "What did you want with Vetter?"

"We're investigating his connection to a murder."

"Murder." Freddy's head popped up. "He killed someone?"

"We don't know for sure."

Freddy shook his head. "No wonder he set his boat to

blow like that. Was he covering up evidence? Or trying to kill you, too?"

"We don't know that either, which is why we need to find him."

Freddy shoved the business card in his pocket and clamped his hand on his neck. "I talked to him this morning before he took off."

"You did?"

"Was weird. He pulls up in this new speedboat. A real fancy one. Cost big bucks. He packed up his things and loaded them in the new boat." Freddy shook his head. "How he goes from renting an old boat to owning a pricey one like that one, I don't know."

"Did he say where he was headed?"

"Yeah. Up the coast to Washington."

"Any specific city?"

"Nah."

"When was this?"

"Just before you got here." He thought for a moment. "Maybe two hours ago now."

"You have any idea how fast this boat could travel in two hours?"

He smirked. "Yeah, I looked up the boat's specs the minute Vetter took off. Clocks in wide open around fifty miles an hour."

"Means he could be a hundred miles up the coast already." Jackson didn't like that Vetter had such a head start. He could've stopped anywhere along the coast, and they'd never know where. "Did he ever mention knowing anyone in Washington?"

Freddy tapped his chin. "No. I don't think so. He was kinda quiet."

Jackson took out his phone and displayed Scott's picture. "Did you ever see this guy with Vetter?"

"Yeah, sure. On weekends. He was the only friend Vetter ever brought around."

"Anything else you might know that could help us locate him?"

Freddy thought for a minute then gave a description of the boat. The size, color, features and more, right down to the make and model. "I hope this helps, and he's not too far up the coast by now."

Jackson agreed and thought about how they were going to bring this guy in. The helo was the only answer. The chopper averaged two hundred miles per hour. By the time they got airborne, they'd catch Vetter in an hour about a hundred fifty miles north of their location, which was right around Newport.

"Thanks for your help." Jackson quickly shook the man's hand and jogged over to Blake who stood talking to Maggie.

Blake was an inch or so over six feet tall, muscular, and fit, and Jackson respected him for keeping in shape when, as the sheriff, he rode a desk a lot of the time.

"Are you finished with us?" Jackson asked.

Blake eyed him from under his hat. "You got somewhere more important to be?"

"Yeah, going after Vetter."

Blake arched an eyebrow. "The neighbor tell you something?"

"Vetter bought a speedboat and is heading up the coast to Washington. We'll take the chopper and stop him."

Blake narrowed his eyes. "Trailing Vetter is better left to law enforcement or the Coast Guard."

"Really?" Jackson scoffed. "Can any of you have a

chopper in the air and launch a Zodiac and five trained operators within an hour?"

"Zodiac?" Maggie asked coming to her feet.

"An inflatable boat used by special forces," Blake said. "These guys will push it out of the chopper and follow it into the water. They'll have the boat up and operational in a matter of minutes."

Jackson had to admit he liked hearing the admiration in Blake's tone. "Something no other team in our immediate area can do."

"True," Blake said, crossing his arms.

Jackson got that Blake wanted to follow official protocol, and if he called in the Coast Guard in Newport, they could launch a chopper to find Vetter, then dispatch a boat to bring him in. But after making a huge mistake and triggering the bomb, Jackson needed to arrest Vetter as much as he needed to breathe.

Jackson stared at Blake. "I know you have to report this and call in the Guard. Just give us a head start."

"I don't know."

"C'mon, man. Let me make up for tripping that wire."

Blake's expression turned sympathetic, and he nodded.

"Thanks, man."

"Keep me informed of your progress."

"Roger that." Jackson grabbed Maggie's hand. "We have to move."

He started for his truck, walking so fast she had to jog to keep up, but he couldn't slow down. He had a killer to catch.

In the vehicle, he put his phone in the dash holder and dialed Gage on speakerphone to report the news as he got the truck going. "I need the Zodiac and scuba gear in the chopper by the time I get there. And have Riley and Coop get started on the preflight checklist so you're ready to take off."

"Understood," Gage said.

"Thanks, man," Jackson said, thankful that his boss didn't mind taking direction from one of his subordinates. But the guy didn't stand on ceremony when there was a job to be done, and one of his team members was in charge. Unless of course, they were headed in the wrong direction. Then Gage was more than glad to step in.

"I'll be there in fifteen," Jackson said.

"Roger that," Gage replied.

Jackson ended the call and got on the road.

Maggie swiveled toward him. "Tell me exactly what will happen on this mission."

"We'll fly up the coast until we see Vetter's boat. We'll travel a little further until we're out of his eyesight. On the way, we'll suit up in dive gear. Then, like Blake said, we'll drop the Zodiac and jump in after it."

"Just like that. You'll jump out of the chopper." She shook her head. "Will you have parachutes?"

"Nah. Coop or Riley will hover the chopper right above the water. Maybe ten feet or so. Our drop won't be far."

Worry flooded her eyes. "Can I trust this Coop guy with your life? I mean, I haven't even met him."

"He's the senior pilot of the two, so yeah, you can trust him." He met her gaze. "You can trust all of us. I know that sounds like a bunch of baloney after I nearly let Vetter blow you up, but each of us puts everything into our job."

"I know you're doing your best. I can't ask for more than that."

He believed she meant what she said, but he knew he could always do better. Be better. Faster. More capable. But with the entire team on this mission, there was no better force in the world. "We'll get this guy today. You can count on that."

"I know you will. But promise me you'll be careful and not take any unnecessary risks."

"I promise to be careful." And there was no such thing as an unnecessary risk to him. Either he needed to take a risk or not. Simple as that.

"I'm glad. Now that we've reconnected I'd hate to lose you again."

He glanced at her to see if her comment held a deeper meaning, but she turned to look out the window. Did that mean she wanted a future with him?

The feel of the explosion's hot wave came rushing back, reminding him of what he almost lost. He could lose his life if need be. For her. For others. But losing her? He couldn't abide that. Couldn't even fathom the pain he would feel. Something he might never recover from.

Stunned at the depth of his feelings, he glanced at her. Admired the curve of her neck. Her soft hair falling over her shoulders. He wanted to reach out to her. Just touch her and connect in a physical way, the urge nearly overpowering his good sense.

That shocked him even more.

Had he already come to need her in his life? He cared about her, that was never in question. Loved her and always would. But really love her in an ask-her-to-marry-him kind of way? Had his heart seriously gone there?

"Do you think Hannah would let me wait with her?" Maggie asked, not looking at him.

"That's a great idea. I'm sure she would. Use my phone to call her. Gage's home phone is in my contacts."

She reached for his cell, and he felt an almost overpowering urge to take her hand back. To hold it close to his heart. To tell her that when he came back, they could talk about a future.

But he couldn't.

As much as he wanted to do so, he hadn't worked through the loss of Alison, and he just wasn't ready to commit his whole future to Maggie.

15

Jackson wished there'd been time to stop at Gage's house on the way in to drop Maggie off, but every minute counted so he headed straight for the helipad. He heard the helo rotors before he saw them spinning, and Coop sat in the pilot seat, Riley next to him. Gage, Eryn, and Alex were still loading gear.

Maggie peered ahead. "That's Coop, huh?"

"It is."

"He looks a lot like the rest of you. Fierce with a go-getter attitude."

"Gage wouldn't hire anyone that wasn't." Jackson shifted into park and faced Maggie. "I'll come to the house the minute we get back, okay?"

"Can you call me first? You know, the second your mission is over, and you're out of danger?"

"Sure." He hated that he was putting her through this, but this was the life of a man or woman who loved a soldier, law enforcement officer, firefighter, or his team. The ones left behind had the difficult jobs. Far more difficult than Jackson's. He trained. Knew he was well prepared, and that he could do the job. And then he was actively doing it while the woman he loved would sit and wait.

Hold on. The woman he loved. He couldn't deny it—he loved her. But did she love him?

He looked into her eyes. Those big eyes that saw him more than anyone else ever had. He took her hand and squeezed it to reassure her. "Don't worry. We'll all be fine."

She reached up and cupped the side of his face. He leaned into the softness of her hand and ignored that his team waited for him. He drew her close for a hug and held her tight. Inhaled her unique citrus scent. Felt the warmth of her body next to his. Wanted to linger, but he had a job to do.

He released her, and without thinking, he kissed her. Nothing deep, just a peck on the cheek before spinning and exiting the truck, leaving the keys so she could take the vehicle to Gage's house.

He strode toward the helo, his feet dragging as he didn't want to leave. He resisted looking back, or he might change his mind and tell the team to go after Vetter without him. By the time he reached the helo, the others had boarded. Eryn and Gage dropped onto seats on the far side of the aircraft. He ducked under the whirring rotors to climb aboard and take a seat next to Alex.

"Saw you and the missus," he said for Jackson's ears only. "Kissing, huh? Things have moved along."

"Stow it." Jackson fired his buddy a warning look.

"Dude, you're the one who needs to stow it. Better not let Gage see your puppy eyes for Maggie, or he's gonna plant your feet at the compound and assign Maggie's protection to one of us."

"Zip it, man. I've got everything under control." The last thing Jackson needed right now was for Gage to pick up on his developing relationship with Maggie. But she wasn't here now, so he didn't have to worry about that. He just needed Alex to keep his mouth shut.

Jackson located the gear bag labeled with his name and tugged it over to his seat. He put on his headset while squeezing his feet in the small gap in front of him. Due to the added boat and motor—packaged tightly to about three by four feet—leg room was limited. Would make for a challenging ride, too. They would slip into their wetsuits and other gear with the big package in the middle. He noticed that Riley was already suited up. Made sense as he wouldn't be able to change in the small cockpit seat and he'd be joining them on the dive.

"We good to go?" Coop asked.

"Roger that." Jackson swirled his finger telling Coop to lift off.

He took them smoothly up into the sky which was now turning overcast and gray in the distance. They didn't get a lot of rain in the summer, but it looked like a storm was moving in from the north. Would make the op more difficult, but it wouldn't stop them. And who knows, it might slow Vetter down.

Gage stared across the chopper at Jackson. "Now's a good time to fill us in on your plan."

"We'll drop the boat north of Vetter. Let him catch up and pass us. Riley will take out Vetter's motor with a copper sabot slug." The special bullet would penetrate Vetter's fiberglass hull and cowlings to reach the engine block, stopping him dead in the water. "Most of us will keep his attention while one of us takes a dive and comes up on Vetter's flank to take him by surprise. That person will detain him until we can board his boat."

"I've already loaded the sabot slugs in my diving jacket," Riley said.

"Without an intel or recon, we're facing a lot of unknowns," Jackson said. "It's gonna be one of those ops where we have to play it by ear."

Gage locked gazes with Jackson. "I don't like that, and you know it."

"Your concern is duly noted," Jackson replied. "But we have to act or miss the opportunity."

"I get that. Just don't like it."

None of them did. It was far better to have good intel and a detailed plan at the get-go, but no matter the op, they always needed to improvise.

Jackson kept his focus on Gage. "You have a better plan?"

"Wish I did."

"Your SEAL experience makes you the best to take the dive, but if you don't want to do it, I will."

Gage glanced down at his injured arm that severely hampered his swimming abilities. He lifted it and didn't say a word.

"Hey, man." Jackson hated to see the look of disgust on his boss's face, though Jackson thought the same thing about his knee. "Injured arm or not, you're still better than any of us."

"I'm not so sure about that."

"You have more underwater experience."

"True that. We'll see." He frowned.

Jackson knew how he felt. Not a person on the team didn't wish to have their limitations removed. Coop had a bad back. Riley lost a kidney from shrapnel. Sure, he could still shoot, but with only one kidney, the police department wouldn't risk him getting injured on the job and ended his employment. Alex had hearing loss and Eryn wasn't able to clench her left fist. All injuries they needed to overcome, but not one of them was a quitter.

Jackson looked out the window to the ocean below. Even flying, it would still take time to catch up to Vetter, but Jackson wanted to be ready when they got there.

"Time to suit up." He hung his headset on a hook behind his seat and dug out his thermo hooded wetsuit designed for assault swimmers. With fewer seams, an assault suit allowed more range of motion, and he was glad Gage sprung for the extra cost.

Jackson turned the top of the front zip suit inside out and rolled it down before stripping down to his skivvies and T-shirt. He slipped his foot into a large plastic bag and tied it near his knee before sliding his leg inside. The others once razzed him about the bag, but a surfer friend taught him that it made sliding on the suit's tight legs and arms far easier. Now everyone used a bag, even die-hard SEAL, Gage.

Once Jackson had his suit on, he slipped on his dive jacket with emergency buoyancy and breathing options built in and tools mounted on the front, then checked to be sure their rifles were bagged and ready to deploy. He put his headset back on for the remainder of the flight and focused his binoculars out the chopper window as they skimmed up the coast. He spotted a boat and zoomed in.

"Looks like Vetter, due north," Jackson announced into his mic. "Let's drop for recon, but not low enough to spook him."

"Roger that." Coop took the chopper down slowly.

Jackson watched through the binoculars as they flew over. Vetter looked up at them, but didn't watch for long. Their chopper likely held no interest to him as it held no markings, and he probably assumed they were sightseeing. "Didn't see a weapon. Anyone else?"

Responses of "negative" came over the headset.

"As a ghost gun maker, we have to assume he's armed."

"Agreed," Gage said.

"We'll have to be mindful of that in our plan. Drop the boat out of sight and wait for him to catch up and pass. Riley takes out his engine block. Gage you're in the water and will apprehend Vetter."

Gage nodded his agreement, and Jackson was glad to see his boss agreed.

"We good to go?" Jackson let his gaze rove over the team pausing at each face. They nodded. "Riley, Coop?"

"Affirmative," Coop said.

"Ditto," Riley replied.

"Then let's get this door open, and the boat ready to deploy." Adrenaline raced through Jackson's body. He didn't wait for anyone to move but put on his goggles and shot to his feet to slide open the door.

Salty ocean air rushed in, slapping him in the face. He loved the feel of it. The speed of the chopper. The op just ahead. The danger. Yeah, he loved that, too. Maggie didn't like it. He could understand that and felt bad putting her through the worry, but he could never give this up. And there he was. Back at the point at which he didn't want to be a husband and father.

But as a Beret, he'd been gone on long deployments. Now, he didn't travel far from home and rarely was away for more than a week. That would allow him to be the husband and father he wanted to be.

Could he really find a way to have a future with Maggie, maybe have children with her?

He looked out the door at the choppy ocean. He would have to figure it out soon as they were about to take Vetter into custody, and she would soon be free to return to life as normal. Life without him.

~

Maggie didn't like being left behind to wait. Not even if it was out on Hannah's patio in the bright sunshine, a tall glass of iced tea in her hand, and the children playing on a structure that was built by the team. When she dated Jackson, he'd left her behind plenty of times, but back then she had no idea of his dangerous maneuvers. Today? She could easily visualize the helicopter hovering over the water. The doors opening, and Jackson plunging into the ocean depths. All the while, a man who made ghost guns coming up the coast toward him. She didn't even want to think about more.

She'd sat in the truck for the longest time, watching the helicopter swirl up into the air, her fingers pressed against the cheek Jackson kissed. He'd kissed her. Actually kissed her in front of the team. Nothing romantic. Just a quick peck on the cheek. But that was even more special to her. It was a kiss that said, I'll be back. Wait for me. Not one that said, This is dangerous, I don't know if I'll be coming back, and I need to kiss you with every ounce of my being.

And then he was gone. Now she needed to trust that he would return to her uninjured. However, after this situation was resolved, someone else would hire the team. They'd need protection, and he'd do something like this again. That's the kind of man he was.

"You seem lost in thought." Hannah set down her tea.

"I was thinking about Jackson. He has this tremendous need to protect others, and if he fails at doing so, it really eats away at him." She looked at Hannah. "Is Gage like that?"

"Yeah. Everyone on the team is. I've also seen it in Blake, too. But Jackson seems to take it to an extreme that the others don't."

"I thought that, too."

"Has he always been this way?"

She nodded. "But it's gotten worse."

"Have you ever asked him about it?"

"We talked about it a little, but he didn't seem to know why he did it. I'm hoping to ask him about it tonight."

"Are you in love with him?"

Maggie gaped at Hannah.

"Sorry, I have no boundaries when talking about the team. They protected me, and I'm alive because of all of them. So I feel like a mom who can ask anything to be sure they aren't hurt."

"And you think I'm going to hurt Jackson."

"Not intentionally, but you're both obviously struggling with something. I'd hate to see it keep you from finding that 'happily ever after' I think you both deserve."

Maggie wasn't sure about deserving any such thing, but she couldn't go against Jackson's wishes and tell Hannah about Alison nor explain her issues with Jackson.

"Are you worried about him?" Hannah asked.

"Of course. Don't you worry?"

"Yeah, sure, but I've come to accept that Gage needs to do this."

"Jackson does, too."

"If you want him in your life, you find a way to live with the danger."

Maggie's phone rang and seeing her friend Stacey's name, Maggie eagerly grabbed it in hopes that she'd been successful in recovering DNA. "Did you get anything?"

"Hello to you, too." Stacey laughed.

"Sorry. You're doing me a favor, and I haven't even said thank you for that."

"Glad to help, and yes, I do have a DNA profile."

"Yes!" Maggie jumped to her feet. "Can you email it to me so I can have the sheriff search CODIS?"

"Absolutely. I'll do it the minute I hang up."

"Then thanks and goodbye." Maggie chuckled.

"Call me when this is all over and let me know how it worked out, okay?"

"You got it." Maggie disconnected and dialed Nate. "My friend was able to get a DNA profile from the sample. I'll have it in a few minutes and will forward it to you."

"Perfect."

"Will you call me if you get a hit?"

"Of course."

As he disconnected, her phone alerted her to a new email. She found the message and attached the DNA profile from Stacey. Maggie forwarded it to Nate, then sat back down to wait for Nate to call back. Maybe soon Lyle Vetter would not only be in custody, but they'd have the murder victim's name as well.

16

Jackson hit the water. Plunged deep into the cold. Thankfully, their thermo suits could handle the frigid temps. And their suits were front zip. Meant they weren't even exposed to the cold that ran along the back zipper of many wetsuits.

He swam to the surface and looked for the boat through his goggles. He flipped on his side and started for it as did his teammates. Gage taught them all the combat sidestroke. CSS was a mix of traditional sidestroke, front crawl, and breaststroke developed by the SEALs. This stroke used core muscles and reduced body drag, meaning they could move faster.

He reached the boat first. He was familiar with Zodiacs from his days in the service, and they were still used by the military, law enforcement, and rescue squads worldwide. He immediately began unfolding it, the other team members joining him. Once it was open and the floor was secured properly, he opened the automatic inflation valve to start filling the buoyancy tubes with CO_2. Less than four minutes later, the tubes were firm, and they climbed aboard.

Jackson opened the case for the motor, and he and Alex

got it mounted on the back while Riley readied his rifle, and Eryn and Gage took overwatch.

Alex started the motor, and the team took their positions. Riley at the bow, his rifle resting on the boat, Jackson and Eryn behind him, their rifles aimed to his sides. Gage took his place on the floor to keep Vetter from seeing him. They counted on Riley's shot to distract Vetter, allowing Gage to slip over the side and hang tight while they pulled closer to Vetter.

Their bodies were protected by the boat, but water sprayed their faces as the boat road up the choppy waves and plunged down the other side. Usually on a mission this intense, Jackson's focus was fixed on the op, but the waves took his thoughts in an odd direction today. Waves of trouble had rolled into his life for as long as he could remember, and he'd failed at trusting God to keep him from sinking into the depths.

Wasn't it time he started clinging to God like he was clinging to this boat as he rode out the chop?

Maggie mentioned God being there even when she didn't feel His presence. Jackson had always known God was there, too, even when Jackson let the waves of trouble take him under. Wasn't it about time he started to rely on God more?

"Ready for the shot." Riley's voice came over the earbuds of their portable comm unit.

Jackson shifted his focus back to the op and lifted his goggles to his forehead for a clearer view ahead. "Gage, you're on standby."

"Roger that," Gage replied.

Jackson saw Riley shift, and his finger drop to the trigger. He popped off a shot. It found its mark. Vetter's boat slowed immediately. He turned to look back at the engine.

"You're a go, Gage," Jackson said.

He heard Gage slide over the edge of the inflatable tube, but hardly a splash sounded as he slipped into the water. Jackson was always amazed at how fluid Gage was, barely making the water move on insertion. SEAL training taught him incredible covert skills.

Alex raced their Zodiac past Vetter, and once on the south side of his boat, Alex swung around and came up on Vetter's stern. The Zodiac lightened as Gage let go of the boat. Alex continued to circle Vetter to draw attention away from Gage.

Vetter ran from one side of the boat to the other, his face confused, but he didn't call out. He just watched them, eyes wide.

Jackson saw Gage pull up on the boat. Vetter started to turn in Gage's direction.

"Ahoy, Lyle Vetter," Alex's voice boomed from a megaphone. "Prepare to be boarded."

"No way." He shoved his hand in his jacket pocket.

He was likely going for a gun. Jackson lifted his rifle, ready to take Vetter out if he managed to get a gun pointed in their direction. His hand came out of his pocket holding a weapon. He started to raise it.

Gage moved up on him. Three feet. Two. One. His good arm went around Vetter's neck, and the gun in his other hand pressed against Vetter's forehead.

"Drop the weapon," Gage shouted.

Jackson waited, holding his breath as one good shot from Vetter in their boat's direction could take out the inflatable tubes. But he dropped the gun, and Alex piloted them slowly forward until they were parallel with Vetter's boat. Jackson hooked it and slipped onto Vetter's boat. He took zip ties from a pouch on his dive jacket and restrained Vetter's wrists behind him.

"Told ya you could do it," Jackson said to Gage.

His boss grinned, and Jackson knew succeeding at something that was once second-nature was even sweeter now as they overcame the obstacle in their lives.

"Am I under arrest or something?" Vetter asked.

"Or something," Jackson answered as he stared at the man who'd attacked Maggie. With the guy's round face and beard, Jackson had no problem believing he was the man at the Summit subdivision.

"What do you think we might be arresting you for?" Gage asked.

"Selling guns."

"Yeah and what else?" Jackson asked going along with the fact that this guy thought they were the police.

"I dunno."

Jackson jabbed the guy in the chest. "How about killing your partner?"

Vetter cringed, and Jackson instantly knew this guy had indeed killed Scott. Vetter didn't need to confess. His eyes were already doing so. He opened his mouth.

"Don't bother denying it," Jackson said. "Guilt is written all over your face."

"But I—"

"But you should just confess the murder. It will go easier for you."

"I'm not going down for this alone."

Jackson couldn't believe he actually admitted to it. "You had help."

Vetter nodded.

"Who?"

"Garrett North."

Jackson's mouth fell open. He thought the kid was guilty of something illegal but not murder. "Garrett helped you kill Scott?"

Vetter nodded. "He's the real leader in our operation. Scott and I've just been making and selling the guns. We've done it for years. A few here or there. But Garrett hooked up with Scott for some marketing project and Garrett took over. He set up the darknet storefront, and we've had a hard time keeping up with sales."

Jackson was all too familiar with this deep part of the Internet. It was only available through a special browser where criminals hid their identities to sell any number of illegal things. "Why did Scott have to die?"

"He wanted out. Said he was graduating soon and didn't want this to follow him. I was cool with it, but then Garrett said Scott knew too much. That if we didn't want to risk getting caught we needed to get rid of him."

"And so you just went along with it?"

"He had a good point."

"Right. Like there's ever a good reason to kill someone." Jackson shook his head and caught sight of a Coast Guard cutter headed their way. Blake must've sent them to arrest Vetter, and Jackson had but a moment to get answers before the crew descended on the boat and took over.

Jackson looked back at Vetter. "So it was you Dr. Turner bumped into in the lecture hall the night you killed Scott."

"You know about that?"

"Saw the video."

He grimaced. "Just our luck that the university was recording things. We thought we were in the clear and then the video shows up out of the blue. There I was for the world to see. Walking into the classroom." Vetter shook his head. "Then she had to go and bump into me. I knew it happened, but hoped she forgot all about it. But when I saw the video, I panicked. I thought the police would talk to her, and she would identify me."

"Prepare to be boarded," the male voice came over a speaker as the cutter pulled up alongside them.

Jackson wanted to take a swing at Vetter, knock him senseless for all he put Maggie through, but he stood back to watch as the guardsmen took Vetter into custody. Blake and Nate would have to figure out who had jurisdiction over Vetter, but Jackson thought the murder would trump the explosion, and Nate would take over. Jackson would call Nate on the way home and tell him about Garrett, too, so Nate could arrest the jerk.

And then...then Jackson could breathe again.

Or could he?

Maggie no longer needed his protection—at least from a killer—and she was free to walk out of his life for good.

Still on the patio despite the overcast skies, Maggie's phone rang from the small side table next to her lounge chair. She'd been waiting for this call from Jackson, but she still jumped.

"Hello," she answered, surprised at how breathless she was in anticipation of hearing his voice.

"Op went perfectly. We apprehended Vetter, and the Coast Guard took him into custody. We'll be home in about an hour."

"Look at him calling the little woman like a rookie," Alex teased in the background.

She didn't like that Jackson was getting razzed, but she did like the sound of being the "little woman." Thing was, if that ever happened, she would insist on calls like this for every op, and that meant her guy would get teased all the time. She would feel bad about it, but he was man enough to handle it.

"Did Vetter admit to killing Scott?" she asked.

"Yes, and he said Garrett was part of it all."

"Garrett, really? I mean, he was a real jerk—but a killer? That's crazy."

"I know, right? Anyway, you don't have to worry anymore. Vetter can't hurt you."

She sighed out her relief. The threat to her life was over. Really over. She was no longer in danger and was free to go back home. Back to work. To leave without Jackson. She didn't like the sound of that, but she did have to go home. Not before they talked tonight, though. "Since I have your truck, do you want me to pick you up when you land?"

"I can get a ride with the team."

"I don't mind picking you up. In fact, I'd like to do it."

"Then if you want to, go for it. You'll hear the chopper. Just head over when you do."

"See you then." Excited about seeing Jackson again, Maggie got up and went in search of Hannah. She found her in the kitchen, the kids at the island having a snack of cheese slices and crackers.

"I heard from Jackson," Maggie said.

Hannah looked up. "Everything okay?"

"Yes, everything went fine, and now they're on their way back."

Hannah exhaled as she smiled.

"I have a favor to ask."

"Anything."

"The team will be back in about an hour, and I want to

cook dinner for Jackson. Could I raid your pantry and garden to find something to make for him?"

"Have at it." Hannah grinned. "I think Jackson is about to hear how you feel before the night is over."

Heat rose up Maggie's neck. "I'm still not sure what I plan to say, but yeah, we're going to talk."

"You'll have to come over for breakfast and tell me all about it. Seven o'clock."

Maggie didn't even want to think about the morning, because it meant leaving. "We'll be heading back to Ashland tomorrow, so that will be up to Jackson."

Hannah narrowed her eyes. "You're going? But why?"

"Vetter's in custody. Means the danger is gone, and I need to go back to work."

"Right." Hannah chewed on her lip.

"What?"

"Big ears in here." She gestured at the kids staring at them and quickly dragged Maggie out of the room. "You could join the team."

"What?" Maggie laughed. "That's craziness."

"No. Think about it. They could use your forensic anthropology skills."

Maggie actually gave the idea a bit of thought until she hit an obstacle. "They wouldn't need me full time, and I have to support myself."

"Then do what I do." Hannah clutched Maggie's arm. "I'm a sketch artist, and I work freelance. I take jobs when it fits in our schedule."

Maggie considered Hannah's suggestion. "It could work, I suppose. I already freelance outside my teaching job. But there's no need to move here. I can stay in Ashland and offer them my services when needed."

Hannah's hand dropped. "But then you wouldn't be here."

"You're assuming an awful lot here, Hannah."

"Like what?"

"Like Gage would need to offer me a job."

Hannah waved her hand. "All I have to do is suggest it, and he'll do it."

"You sound so certain."

"I am. We're still in the honeymoon phase of our relationship." She winked.

"Jackson would also have to want me here. And even with freelancing, there's not enough work. I'd still need my teaching income."

"Not if you were married to Jackson. You could live here on the compound." Hannah smiled. "I'd love to have you here. Eryn would, too. And Coop's getting married in a few months to Kiera. She'd like it, too."

Maggie gaped at her new friend.

"What? A girl can dream, can't she?" Hannah chuckled.

"And that's all it is since Jackson's not ready for more. Shoot, I may not be either." Maggie didn't want to continue this discussion when there was no point in it. "Now about that food."

Hannah started back to the kitchen. "I have a nice piece of fresh salmon if you'd like that."

"Jackson loves salmon, so that would be great." And Maggie had just the perfect marinade that was easy and quick. "Mind if I make a marinade for it here? I need soy sauce, brown sugar, vegetable oil, lemon pepper, and garlic powder."

"I have all of that. Let me gather it while you raid the garden." She grabbed a small tote from open shelving and passed it to Maggie.

Maggie gave Hannah a quick hug.

"Can I help?" Mia asked.

Maggie turned in surprise. "Sure."

Hannah stroked a hand over Mia's blond curls. "This one loves to pick veggies. Especially peas. Though I have to warn you that more of them end up in her tummy than in the tote."

Mia giggled, her sweet little tone tugging at Maggie's heart.

Hannah retrieved a large plastic bowl and handed it to Mia. She jumped down and started for the door. They hadn't gone more than a few feet when the precious child slipped her hand into Maggie's. Maggie's heart instantly melted, then pain came rushing in and replaced the joy.

Maggie looked at their hands together. She could be holding Alison's hand. If she'd lived. Maggie could have shared this moment, so many moments with her daughter. Going out to gather fresh veggies. Cooking or canning and freezing them.

Maggie always wanted to have her own garden and chickens. The scene unfolded in her mind. Early morning on their property under a glorious sun and puffy white clouds. Her child gathering eggs and coming inside to the family sitting down to a big breakfast of scrambled eggs. A family that included Jackson and two additional children.

She wanted a child. Really wanted one. The thought hit her upside the head, and she stopped at the patio door. She was shocked, and at the same time, overjoyed that she could think such a thing. Of course, Jackson would be the only man she would ever consider having a child with.

But he wasn't ready for that. Neither was she. Not really. She'd only begun to hope again, and she had no idea if that was a fluke, and the all-consuming sadness would return.

She slid the door open and followed Mia to raised garden beds in the corner of the yard. Hannah said the members of Gage's team helped Gage build the beds and fill them with quality garden soil instead of the sandy coastal soil.

What a blessing to be surrounded by this family of coworkers. Maggie could easily imagine living among them. Their different personalities and gifts would make for a lively group. And also for some challenges, she suspected, as there were plenty of egos on this team, too.

Maggie stopped by a tall trellis of peas and looked at Mia's eager face. "Do you want to pick peas?"

Mia looked up at her. "Can I eat some?"

"Of course." Maggie ruffled the sweet child's curls, and the pain lessened. Maggie found that she could interact with Mia without that intense anguish that often made her double over. Sure, the pain was there. It would always be, but it felt more manageable today.

Was it the hope? Was it turning back to God? Was it loving Jackson again, because she had to admit she was in love with him. She couldn't do anything about the feeling, but it was there in her heart.

Between two trellises of peas, she found lettuce growing happily in the shade. She plucked green, red, and purple leaves before moving over to the plump red sun-loving tomatoes. Her tote was getting full, but on the way back to Mia, Maggie grabbed a cucumber. A salad, and any peas that survived Mia's picking, would go well with the salmon.

Maggie sat down on the edge of the garden box to watch Mia open a pea pod and expertly dislodge peas into her mouth. She chewed thoroughly and smiled at Maggie. "Mama says since I love peas, she's going to grow a whole trellis of them just for me next year."

"She seems like a wonderful mother."

Mia frowned, not at all the reaction Maggie expected.

"I love her. She's so nice, but I still miss my real mom. She's in heaven with God. Mama, that's what I call my new mom, says it's okay if I still miss my mom. She says I always will."

Maggie's heart clutched at the thought of this adorable child having to live through the loss of a parent. "Your mama's right. My mother's been in heaven for a lot of years, and I still miss her, too."

Mia gave a serious nod, but then she spied a large pea pod, and her sorrow vanished as she plucked it free and expertly emptied the pod.

Maggie couldn't let the sorrow go quite as quickly. Was she fooling herself to think she could move forward? Find a future with Jackson? Hopefully, their conversation tonight would help her understand that.

"Now, how about we get these peas inside?" she said. "I need to get started on Jackson's dinner."

She nodded and picked up the bowl. "I like Jackson."

"Me too."

"But you really like him." Mia giggled.

Maggie didn't want to encourage Mia, but she couldn't hold her laughter in and giggled right along with the little girl, loving the feel of the simple pleasure of having fun again. Her phone rang, and at the sight of Nate's name on her screen, her laughter evaporated.

"You know," Maggie said to Mia. "Jackson's kind of a big guy, and he eats a lot. Go ahead and pick more peas while I answer this call."

She stepped out of earshot. "Nate."

"We hit the jackpot in CODIS," he said. "The DNA profile matched an Andre Gamblin."

Gamblin. She didn't recognize his name, and he wasn't one of the missing men. So who was he? "If he's in CODIS, he's either suspected of a crime or a victim of one."

"Convicted felon."

Maggie stifled a gasp. "What did he do?"

"He went away for obstructing an investigation, and as an accessory to rape." Nate paused and drew in a long breath. "His brother Ozzie raped a woman. Andre sat by and did nothing to stop it and even helped cover it up. Ozzie's still in prison, but Andre got out a few weeks ago."

"And now someone killed him," Maggie said making sure to keep her voice down. "Do you think it's related to the rape?"

"Could be. Hopefully the homeowners can shed some light on why he was on their property. They're back in town, and I'm scheduled to interview them in an hour. Until then, I have my detectives running a background check on both of the Gamblin brothers."

"Thanks for letting me know. And keep me updated if you can."

"Will do."

Maggie disconnected and stood still for a moment, thinking about the victim. He was a felon—a convicted felon. But just because he'd done something terrible, she shouldn't feel any less inclined to help find his killer. She wished it was that simple. Deep down she suspected she held some prejudice against the man who covered up a rape. Which meant if Nate needed her help to find the killer, she'd do even more to help to compensate for her emotions.

She stowed her phone and put the murder out of her mind so when she reached Mia again she could smile at the child. Not that it was difficult to find a smile when she found the little imp sitting near a pile of empty pods, contentment on her face.

Maggie hoped she hadn't eaten too many peas and got a stomachache. "I think it's time for us to go back inside."

Mia grabbed her bowl and skipped toward the door. How wonderful it would be to have a child's perspective on life again. To be this carefree. Yet, even as a child, Mia already endured her share of tragedies. But she lived happily in the moment, and Maggie vowed to live more like Mia going forward.

Back inside, Hannah had lined up the marinade ingredients on the countertop along with a boxed rice dish. "Anything I can help with?"

"I'll need a zipper bag for the marinade and some measuring cups."

Hannah pulled out a drawer. "Cups are here, and I'll grab a bag."

Maggie took a bowl from the shelf and made quick work of mixing all the ingredients in the marinade. Thankfully, she cooked salmon often enough that she remembered the proportions. She took the bag from Hannah, poured the teriyaki marinade inside, and added the fresh pink filet.

Hannah looked across the island at her. "That's it, huh? Seems easy enough."

"And it's really tasty on the grill." Maggie zipped the bag closed.

"You'll have to give me this recipe."

"Glad to." She smiled at Hannah. "I should get going and get that salad ready before Jackson gets back."

Hannah helped her load everything into the tote with the fresh veggies and looked at her over the top. "We could do this all the time, you know. You and me cooking and sharing. If you'd consider my idea."

Maggie smiled at Hannah but didn't want to mislead her. "It sounds wonderful, but Jackson and I aren't in a place for a relationship, and I don't know if we ever will be."

Hannah frowned. "Is there anything I can do to help?"

Maggie shook her head.

"Then I'll pray that everything works out between you." Hannah scooped Maggie into her arms for a quick hug.

Maggie wished she could talk to her new friend about Alison. She would be a great help in working through grief. Maggie didn't have to know her any better to know she was just that kind of woman.

Maggie pushed free before she got comfortable with the amazing woman's support and told her about Alison. She grabbed the tote and drove Jackson's truck down the winding road to his cabin. She felt so natural driving his vehicle and stepping into his home. How could that be when she'd been here for such a short time? Been in Jackson's company again for such a short time, too?

She clicked on a music station on his TV to distract her traitorous brain. Humming along with the songs, she prepared the salad, shelled the peas, and rushed up to his deck to see if it held a table and chairs for dining. She was overjoyed to see it did and could easily imagine dining with him up there. If the clouds passed over, they would be sitting under a sky blanketed with stars. A perfect, relaxing location to talk to him.

She raced downstairs to the bedroom to change her shirt, run a comb through her hair, and freshen up her makeup. She put the mascara tube back in her travel bag just as a chopper sounded in the distance.

Her stomach filled with butterflies, the lighthearted flutter a welcome feeling to the years of dread and sadness. She grabbed his keys and was soon driving past their small town. With her heart changing, it felt like years passed since she walked this stretch of road with Jackson. She felt the force of the helicopter's rotors above before she reached the heliport and arrived to see it touch down.

She shifted into park and stared at the door, willing it to open. When it finally did and Jackson stepped down, the butterflies took flight in her stomach again. He was wearing a wetsuit, the top folded down around his waist, a body hugging T-shirt underneath displaying his sculpted muscles. He really was a fine-looking man. And a wonderful man. Watching him now, she couldn't believe she ever let him go without a fight.

She couldn't let him go a second time, could she? Or walk away herself?

He waved at her then motioned at the helicopter. She took it to mean he had something to do before he could leave. She wanted to call out that she had big plans for him and that the others should let him go, but he wasn't the kind of guy to walk away from his responsibilities, even if it was just cleaning up from a mission. She appreciated that about him.

She hopped out of the truck and watched the team exit the helicopter. They wore wetsuits like Jackson. All except Coop who slid out of the cockpit. He was dressed in black cargo pants and a black shirt. His hair was also black, making him look darkly dangerous.

Maybe it was time she met him. She approached. He caught sight of her and his grayish-blue eyes locked on hers.

She held out her hand when honestly, his intensity had her wanting to turn and run. "Maggie Turner."

"Good to meet you." He shook her hand with a force that she thought might dislodge her arm.

"I hear I'll be flying you home in the morning," he said.

News to her. "Why not Riley?"

"He has to teach a class," Jackson said as he joined them. "I should have told you to wait a bit before heading down here. We need to dry out the boat and stow equipment."

"Can I help?"

Coop looked like he planned to scoff, but a sharp look from Jackson stopped him.

"You can carry dive jackets and bags to the utility vehicle if you want." Jackson smiled. "Just follow me."

She trailed after his silent footfalls and was fascinated by the unique boots he wore with his suit. He scooted a pair of what she assumed were the dive jackets he mentioned toward the door. They were black and resembled a life jacket with a kind of backpack on the front instead of the back.

She held one up. "Why are these backwards?"

"You mean why do we wear the packs on the front?" he asked as he dug out another pair of them.

She nodded.

"Two reasons. We need a low profile on the back to escape detection on surface ops, and it also puts the tools in front so we can reach them."

She lifted one. "It's heavy."

"Under fifty pounds."

"Still heavy."

"Yeah, they are." Eryn joined them. "You want to try mine on?"

Maggie blushed. "Would it be weird if I said yes?"

"Not at all."

"You two go ahead and play dress up. I'll be right back." Jackson went back to the other side of the chopper to help unload the boat onto a wooden platform with a pallet jack.

"Thanks for asking to try this," Eryn said, lifting the vest toward Maggie. "Gives me a good reason not to have to lug that boat one more time today."

The vest settled in place, and Maggie thought she might topple over. "What makes this so heavy?"

"The equipment, of course, but also the buoyancy device and breathing apparatus."

Maggie was in awe of the many skills she'd seen these team members display in a few days. "How do you even know how to use all the equipment you have here?"

"Everyone had a specialty coming into the group. We shared our knowledge and trained for like a million hours. Gage was a SEAL so anything water-related is his job to teach us and that includes using dive jackets."

Maggie nodded. "Do you like doing all of this stuff?"

She nodded. "You might, too, if you tried it."

Maggie shrugged out of the jacket. "I guess I wouldn't mind jumping out of a helicopter if I knew what I was doing."

"The guys with a military background are far more proficient than I am, but I'm training as often as I can. Maybe someday you can come along on a training mission just to see what it involves."

"Yeah, I'd like to do that." She turned and caught Jackson watching her. He didn't look keen on her joining them on any mission. Maybe more than that, he wasn't keen on her being in his life beyond taking her back to Ashland in the morning.

17

Jackson stepped out of the bedroom. His hair was wet from his shower, and he wore his usual black cargo pants with a knit shirt in the same color. But his feet were bare as he silently moved across the room toward her, reminding her of a stalking panther. And at the same time, his lack of shoes felt so intimate—so personal—that she had to wonder if she made a mistake in planning this dinner under the moonlight.

Sure, she wanted to talk to him about his crazy need to protect others. Talk about Alison. About a possible future. But what if he had no thoughts of a future with her, only dinner tonight and dropping her off at home tomorrow?

She'd have to tread lightly and play things by ear. "You look refreshed."

He nodded and smiled. "Funny how you can spend the afternoon in the water and need to come home and shower it off."

"The salt," she said.

"That was my attempt at making a joke."

"Oh." The tension between them was thick and uncomfortable.

She busied herself with pouring him a tall glass of iced tea.

"You didn't have to cook for me." He took a seat at the island, and she set the glass in front of him. "But I'm starving, so I'm thankful you did."

"You know I love to cook."

"Yeah, and it's your stress reliever, too." He met her gaze. "But Vetter's in custody, so what are you stressed about?"

She couldn't tell him about her plan to talk to him. She wanted the conversation to feel more organic. "I have to admit your mission today was pretty nerve-wracking for me." She looked down at the counter to keep him from seeing the half-truth in her eyes. "What exactly did you do?"

He grabbed his iced tea. "Pretty routine stuff. We dropped the RIB from the chopper and followed it into the water."

She looked at him. "RIB?"

"Sorry, Rigid Inflatable Boat." He took a long drink of the tea, and she could hardly look away from the strong column of his neck as he drank. "We dropped the RIB packed with the motor inside and inflated the boat in the water."

That beautiful neck could have gotten hurt along with the rest of him. "Couldn't Vetter have simply shot the boat, and it would have deflated?"

"Yeah, that's the one problem with RIBs, and why we usually only use them at night."

"But you didn't do that today."

He held his glass midair and watched her for a long moment. "The thing is, in this line of work or in the military, you often have to improvise to complete an op. Sometimes that means taking risks."

She planted her hands on the cool granite counter. "I know that's what has to happen, but I don't like to hear it."

He rested his hand on hers. "You know we'd never do anything that wasn't necessary, right? We perform a risk assessment on every action. If the majority of the team isn't in agreement, we don't do it. You've seen the incredible brain power in this group. How could we go wrong?" He chuckled.

Despite her ongoing concern for his safety, she laughed, too. It felt like the right time to broach her subject. "Why do you do it, Jackson? I know to save and help others, but why do you have such a driving need to help?"

He set down his glass, his gaze pensive. "You've never asked me that before."

"I know. I guess knowing the details of this op and seeing what you've done to protect me made me realize how much you risk."

He stared at his glass and turned it in circles in the condensation ring on the countertop. "Just doing my job. Everyone on the team does the same thing."

"I know, but why do you want to help others this way?" She bent to get him to look at her. "It almost seems like an obsession to you."

A war of emotions battled in his expression. He pushed to his feet and stepped back, looking like he wanted to leave the room. He finally rested his hands on the counter and met her gaze again. "Part of it's losing Alison. But even before then, I knew this is what I had to do in life."

"Why?" she asked, more insistent this time.

He took a long breath and let it out. "You know my granddad died when I was a kid. I was eight. He'd taken me out in his boat to go fishing. We did that all the time, but that day changed everything. He was casting out a line, and he suddenly keeled over and was unconscious. I didn't know what to do. I tried to wake him up, but he didn't move. I rowed back to shore and ran to the house to get my grandma. By the time we got back to the boat, he was dead. He had a massive coronary."

She could imagine him in that situation as a young boy and wished she could take away his pain, but she couldn't. "I'm so sorry, Jackson. That must've been really hard for a boy to take."

"It was. My dad was always traveling, and Grandpa did everything with me. Baseball, hiking, camping, fishing. He was always there for me, but when he needed me, I couldn't help." He pushed off the counter and clamped a hand on the back of his neck. "At the funeral, I swore I'd find a way to help others. That I would never be responsible for someone dying again."

She went around the island and freed that hand from his neck to hold it close. "But you weren't responsible. You can't be responsible for others in this way."

"Really? Then why do you feel responsible for Alison?"

"I don't anymore."

"You did just a few days ago."

"I know, but a lot has changed for me. You've helped me see things differently and so has Hannah. Even Eryn helped. I truly want to believe that God doesn't get things wrong and hope I've made enough peace with losing Alison that I can move forward now."

He pulled his hand free and eyed her with surprise, suspicion. Maybe even disbelief.

She felt tears pricking her eyes. This conversation hadn't gone the way she hoped. Not at all.

~

Jackson gaped at Maggie. He couldn't believe she was moving on. He was glad for her—really, he was—but part of him resented it. Moving on meant letting go of their baby girl, and he couldn't do that. He didn't want to let go of her. Even if it meant a life of unhappiness. He needed to cling to her so he didn't forget her. Her short life had to have purpose and meaning. And apparently, he was now the only one who would keep her alive that way.

He'd tell Maggie how he felt, but honestly, he couldn't talk about this tonight. He was spent. The lack of sleep the last few nights coupled with the crazy emotions he felt when he came face to face with the man who hurt Maggie, and the residual adrenaline from the mission had exhausted him, and he needed a stress-free night.

"Is there anything I can do to help with dinner?" he asked.

Disappointment flooded her eyes, but she blinked it away. "Do you still like to grill?"

He nodded but couldn't continue to see the sadness in her face. He looked away. Maybe she didn't want him to drop the subject of Alison, or maybe she thought he would move past the loss of their daughter. Either way, he would only hurt Maggie more by telling her how he felt, so he kept quiet.

"Then you can cook the salmon." She picked up a cookie sheet holding a grilling basket with a large salmon filet and handed it to him.

He took one last look at her and stepped out on the deck before he changed his mind and continued with the conversation. She'd already lit the grill, and he opened the lid, the heat hitting him full on, much the way her talk about Alison had smacked him in the face. He felt like he was under fire. Maybe like the enemy was approaching. The enemy in this situation was his own mind and emotions, and he honestly was too tired to even know for sure what he felt.

He laid the basket on the grill, and the salmon sizzled. He closed the lid and sat down to set an alarm on his phone to remind him to turn the basket. He probably should go back inside and spend time with Maggie. After all, she'd gone to all of this trouble for him. And soon, she would be out of his life.

The thought was like a knife to the gut. Cutting and twisting. But he could do nothing about it, so he laid his head back against the chair. Cleared his mind as he did before every mission. Focused solely on what needed to be done.

Tomorrow he would meet with Blake and Garrett. Look Garrett in the eye and tell him what he thought of him. After that he would call Scott's father and tell him about Garrett and Vetter to help give him some closure in his loss.

Don't you deserve the same closure? The thought had him sitting up straight. If Maggie was right, he wasn't to blame for the accident that killed Alison. Maybe he did deserve the closure, but he didn't want it. Not if it meant letting go of his precious child.

The alarm dinged, and he got up to turn the salmon. He stood waiting for it to finish and when it was pink with tantalizing brown marks from the sizzling flame, he took the basket into the kitchen.

Maggie had placed big bowls of salad at the table along with bottles of dressing. She mentioned in the truck that she wanted to eat on the rooftop deck, but obviously she changed her mind. A good thing. The last thing they needed was a romantic night under the stars and moonlight.

They plated their salmon, a long grain and wild rice dish, and peas. At the table, Maggie gave a blessing for the food, and Jackson prayed with her. He believed every word she said. Believed God gave him every blessing in his life, just like Maggie had said. But he just couldn't let go of his anger at God and himself for Alison's death.

He forked a bite of the salmon. He knew it should taste amazing, but it felt like putty in his mouth. Bland and chewy.

"You cooked this to perfection," Maggie said.

"Easy enough, but it's the prep that makes it so good." At least he assumed from Maggie's delight that the fish was tasty.

He ate his dinner, and they talked about the compound. The team. His role there. She mentioned more about her life, too, and he was honestly eager to hear about it.

"My love is still the forensic work," she went on, her eyes alive with the topic. "It's horrible to say that I wish I could do it full time. Not when it means for me to work more, people have to lose their lives under suspicious circumstances."

"Nah, it just means when they do, you want to be the one to help. Just like our team. We don't want people to suffer, but suffering is a given, and when we can help alleviate it, then we're glad to do so."

"What about your own suffering?"

"How's that?" he asked reluctantly.

"You could end that, too, but you're choosing not to."

Right. They were back to the same topic. He just couldn't respond. "Thanks for the amazing meal. Why don't you go put your feet up, and I'll do the dishes?"

Disappointment darkened her eyes just as it had earlier, but she got up and went to the sofa. He made quick work of the few dishes, putting his frustrations into working fast, and almost hated that he finished quickly, as that meant he had no excuse not to join her. Not that he didn't want to sit with her, but he didn't want to bring up anything personal again.

He sat by her side, but she didn't look at him. "So tomorrow, Coop wants to take off by eight."

"Will you come with us?" She continued to stare straight ahead at the fireplace.

He might not be able to offer more to her, but he would do nothing less than see that she was settled back in her home. Sort of like walking her to her door. After all, his granddad said a gentleman always walked a girl to the door. "Nate arrested Garrett. Blake will be there first thing in the morning to question him. I want to meet up with him and talk to Garrett."

"Really?" She shot him a look. "What's the point in that?"

"I need him to know what I think of what he did."

She watched him carefully. "What good will that do?"

"It will get this sick feeling out of my gut over Scott's senseless loss," he said as his dinner churned in his stomach. "And I need that right now. More than you know."

18

Jackson pulled up to Maggie's house and turned off the engine. He planned to walk her to the door, and once she was safely inside, he would leave, but he knew it wouldn't be that easy. He wasn't going to be able to walk away like that. Could have to do with not getting the result he expected in his visit with Garrett. The guy wasn't remorseful in the least, and the ache remained in Jackson's gut. It was probably time to admit it wasn't Garrett putting the pain there, it was the upcoming separation from Maggie.

He took out his keys and walked up the path. They were supposed to leave Cold Harbor at eight, but instead, the entire team had breakfast with Gage and Hannah. She wanted to acknowledge a job well done and say goodbye to Maggie. The meal went on and on as if Hannah was trying to delay the departure. He finally got Coop down to the helipad at ten, but by the time he'd finished his preflight check and repaired some malfunction, it was noon before they took off. Then two hours at the jail and now it was going on midafternoon.

At the front door, his stomach grumbled, protesting the lack of lunch.

"I'm not letting you leave on an empty stomach." She unlocked the door.

"Coop's waiting at the chopper for me."

"You can bring something back to the helicopter for him to eat."

Jackson knew better than to argue with Maggie when she got it in her mind to feed him. There was no getting between her and her cooking.

She stepped inside, and he followed, setting down her suitcase in the foyer. He locked the door. She turned, questions in her eyes.

"You may not have a killer after you, but you should still be security conscious," he said.

"I am." She went to the refrigerator and emerged with turkey slices, Swiss cheese, pickles, and sort of a pinkish sauce.

"Sit," she commanded. "It'll only take me a few minutes to whip up a grilled sandwich."

She took a bag with ciabatta rolls from the cupboard and got out a portable sandwich press. She started heating it, the griddle smoking and smelling hot. She sliced the bread, loaded it with everything she'd taken out of the fridge and put the sandwich on the grill.

His mouth watered at the sight of it, and he decided to forget that he was leaving tonight and enjoy what was likely the last lunch he'd ever have with her.

"I'll grab some plates," he said.

"I've got it." She smiled at him. "Now that the danger is gone, it's my turn to take care of you."

He loved her generous heart. Her kindness. Her willingness to put up with him even when he avoided the subject she most wanted to discuss. Time he admitted it. He loved her.

Had always loved her. Had never stopped. A till-death-do-us-part kind of love.

He sat back, shocked at the truth of it all. Question was, what would he do about it? What could he do about it? They were still at odds, and she didn't deserve to be saddled with him until he figured things out.

His phone rang. He looked at the screen.

"Coop," he answered. "I suppose you want to get going."

"Actually, that's why I'm calling. I figured you'd be here soon so I started my preflight checklist, and I discovered that the problem I fixed at the compound goes a little deeper."

"How long will it take to fix?"

"Depends on if I can find a replacement part. Vince thinks he can help with that, and I'll let you know what I find."

"Roger that." Jackson disconnected to find Maggie watching him. "Coop needs to replace a part on the chopper. I won't be leaving right away. Mind if I hang with you here?"

"I was going to head over to Summit after lunch, but you're welcome to come with me if you want."

"Sure. Now that I don't have to protect you, maybe I can help with the recovery effort. If you show me what to do, that is."

"Of course." She plated his sandwich, sliced it in half, and added carrot and celery sticks to the plate. "The sandwich will be hot."

He had to force himself to wait a minute or two before taking a big bite. His taste buds exploded with the sweet and savory flavor. "It's a good thing I'm not with you every day, or I'd weigh three hundred pounds."

She frowned, and he realized he said it was a good thing he wasn't with her.

"Sorry," he said. "That came out wrong."

"It's okay." She settled the second sandwich on the grill and headed for the refrigerator. He didn't know if she turned away to retrieve something or because she was upset with his thoughtless comment, but when she came back holding a pitcher of iced tea, he relaxed again.

As her sandwich cooked, she cleaned up. When hers was ready, she cut it in half, and without asking him, placed half on his plate. He ate far more than she did, and she always shared her food with him. The simple kindness creased his already bruised heart.

"Thanks," he said, but couldn't add anything else without choking up.

She nodded and took a seat. They finished the meal in silence and made it all the way back to the blighted neighborhood with hardly uttering a word. On the way in, she stopped to talk to supervisor McCall.

"I hear you were able to use DNA to identify the victim," he said.

What? That was news to Jackson. She hadn't mentioned this at all.

"You know the guy was a rapist, right?" McCall looked like he wanted to hit someone.

"Actually, his brother's the rapist. He just helped cover it up."

McCall shook his head. "Just as bad in my book."

Jackson agreed. Anyone who would harm a woman or see one being harmed and do nothing about it was lowlife.

The lowest of the low. Not that it meant the guy deserved to be murdered, though. "What's the victim's name?"

Maggie turned to him. "Oh, right. You were out on the mission when Nate called, and I forgot to tell you when you got back. His name was Andre Gamblin."

"And the brother?" The rapist? The lowlife?

"Ozzie. Same last name." She didn't seem to be appalled by this information, but then she'd had time to come to grips with it. She changed her focus to McCall. "What do you have for me today?"

"Fewer fragments for once. You should easily be able to catch up."

"My..." She glanced at Jackson, her expression held confusion. "My friend, Jackson would like to help."

Ah, she didn't know what to call him, but looks like he'd been firmly put in the "friend" zone and that stung. They weren't friends. Okay maybe they were, but they were more than that, too. He loved her. She seemed to feel the same way.

"I can always use another hand." McCall clapped Jackson on the back. "Let's grab you a vest and mask and get you started."

Jackson nodded, but even as he followed McCall to the truck, Jackson's mind kept chewing over the friend comment, and he knew he had to do something about that. It was the what he didn't know.

Maggie cleaned up from dinner while Jackson lounged in the family room talking to Daria. Maggie was thankful to have a few minutes away from him as he'd been looking at her oddly ever since their conversation with McCall. She didn't know what was up with that, but maybe he would tell her eventually, as he was spending the night in her guest room. He almost refused her offer and said he would sleep on the sofa, but she pointed out that there wasn't any danger, and he didn't have to keep the door in view.

"I'm gonna take a quick walk," she heard him tell Daria.

She watched him walk to the windows and check the lock before disappearing down the hallway. She wasn't surprised that he was being overly cautious. He kept checking in with her at Summit, too, distracting her from her work and making it take longer.

He stepped into the kitchen, checked the window locks and the back door lock, and headed down the stairs. She appreciated his care, but he would have to find a way to relax or he would burn out. It wasn't her business to help him do so, but when he came back upstairs she would try one more time.

She hung the dishtowel to dry and went to the family room. Daria looked up from her phone.

"When Jackson gets back upstairs," Maggie said. "I'm going to suggest we go for a walk."

"And you don't want me to tag along." She grinned. "What's his deal anyway? I mean I know he's like this security bodyguard kind of guy, but you're not in danger. Does he ever relax?"

"That's what I plan to ask him on the walk."

Daria got up. "Good luck with that. He's so fierce he kind of scares me."

Maggie could see that. She felt that way in Coop's presence, but only because she didn't know him. If Daria got to know Jackson better, she wouldn't be afraid of him.

He entered the room, and Daria skittered away.

He stopped abruptly and watched her leave. "I didn't mean to scare her off."

"I know you didn't do anything, but she's afraid of you."

He shot her a look. "For real?"

"You're kind of intense, Jackson."

He scratched his jaw. "I suppose I can be."

"More than you used to be. You don't seem to relax at all anymore."

She expected him to offer a reason, but he simply shrugged.

"You want to take a walk with me?" She patted her stomach. "I need to wear off the stroganoff we had for dinner."

"Sure," he said, but it was followed by a deep frown.

"You're worried about going on a walk? I'm not in any danger."

"It's not you I'm worried about." He didn't elaborate but headed for the door and held it open for her.

The moon hung like a giant orb in the sky, lighting the area, and she decided to take one of her favorite trails that led to a small waterfall. A perfect place to have that conversation with him. She started in that direction, and he followed close behind. She didn't speak but listened to his sure footfalls behind her. He was a big guy, but he walked with grace. Likely from years of exercising stealth on his missions.

She strolled past tall pines. A soft breeze blew through the area, cooling the night and perfuming the area with pine. She shivered and soon felt Jackson settle his outer long-sleeved shirt on her shoulders.

"Thank you," she said, looking back at him.

The chiseled planes of his face were emphasized in the moonlight, and his eyes were even a darker gray in the subdued light. He looked so handsome she had to concentrate on breathing and holding herself in check before she ran a finger along his full lower lip accented in the light and then kissed him.

She started foreword, almost running from him on the path that wound down to the waterfall. The sound of rushing water matched the pounding of her heart. At the overlook, she stepped behind a large boulder and hoped Jackson would remain on the other side. She needed something between them to keep her from foolishly kissing him.

He moved closer to the edge of the cliff than she liked, but he didn't fear much. At least not physical things.

"When I was a young, this was my favorite spot on the property," she said. "I always felt like God was closer here somehow."

"It's beautiful." He didn't look at her but kept his focus on the falling water.

"I'm ashamed to say I've avoided it since Alison died. Since I was mad at God, I didn't want to be here."

"Then I should be ashamed, too, because I'm still mad."

"I know I'm not one to talk. It's taken me years to deal with this, but I hope you can, too."

He turned to face her then, the light falling on his back, leaving his face shadowed when she desperately wanted to see his expression.

"See, here's the thing," he said, his voice barely loud enough for her to hear. "I feel like if I let go of the pain, it's like giving up on Alison and letting her go."

"What if you do the opposite?"

"What do you mean?"

"What if you started talking about her? Sharing about her." Maggie's need to see his face had her coming around the rock. She took his hand.

He looked down at it, then back up, but said nothing.

"You could start with Hannah or the team. Tell them about our child."

"To what end?"

"To let them see your pain and help you."

He frowned. "I don't need their pity."

"It wouldn't be like that, and you know it. They've all experienced loss in life. Maybe not a child, but someone they cared about. They won't pity you, they'll love you more for sharing."

"I'm not sure that's the answer."

"Then what about sharing our story with people who need to hear it. To hear that there's life after loss. As you find your own way out of it, you can help them, too."

He lifted her hand to his lips and kissed it. "You're an amazing woman, Maggie. I'm glad you could finally move on. I hated that you had to go through this horrible week, but I'm glad to have reconnected, and I'll think about everything you've said."

"That's all I can ask for." She squeezed his hand, and he turned to leave.

Just like the team's mission to rescue others, she'd had the same mission tonight, and she failed. It was all up to God now.

Maggie shot up in bed. Her heart pounding.

Something was wrong. Very wrong. But what?

She looked around her bedroom. Everything was in the right place. Her chair. Her robe at the foot of the bed. Her covers rumpled, but still intact.

She glanced at the clock. Nearly five a.m. Maybe the noise had come from some animal stirring outside her window. Wouldn't be unusual. The woods were full of them. Maybe the woodland creature was heading back home as the sun would be up in less than an hour.

She listened. Heard nothing. Sat there in the dark, the moonlight streaming through the rivets of her blinds and falling on her bed.

Had she dreamt it, whatever it was? She tried to remember her dreams. She'd fallen asleep thinking about the way Jackson had tenderly kissed her hand. How it sent tingles running up her arm. Through her body. And how broken her heart felt when she failed to help him.

Maybe he wasn't sleeping, and she'd heard him moving around.

She got up, slipped on her robe, and stepped into the hallway. The house was dark. The family room was dark and empty, too. She checked the kitchen. He wasn't awake. Or at least he wasn't out of the guest room. She started back down the hallway and stood to listen outside his door.

Nothing. No sound of movement from his room.

Okay, fine, she imagined it, or dreamt it, and she should just go back to bed.

She slipped into her room and quietly closed the door so the latch didn't wake him. She wasn't worried about waking Daria. She was a sound sleeper and not much woke her. Not even her alarm clock, so she had to set two of them every night.

Maggie shed her robe and went to grab a glass of water from her bathroom. She passed her walk-in closet and heard it then. The noise. A creaking in the ceiling.

What in the world?

Was the house just groaning in the wind?

Doubtful, as wind wasn't buffeting the windows.

She stepped to the closet. Reached for the light switch and looked up.

Movement above caught her attention. Something big. Body-sized.

She flipped on the light.

A large person all in black—including a ski mask— tumbled from the attic crawl space.

She screamed, her voice spiraling up and echoing through the house like a banshee cry.

19

Jackson flew from his bed. Did he dream the scream or did Maggie actually scream?

He raced to her room and didn't bother knocking but pushed through the doorway. He stopped and raised his hands when he saw a masked man with a gun to Maggie's temple.

The creep had his other arm clamped around her neck, his finger already on the gun's trigger. Panic assaulted Jackson. With a finger on the trigger, this guy could accidentally discharge his weapon. Maggie wouldn't stand a chance.

"Who are you?" Jackson asked while thoughts pinged around in his brain.

"No concern of yours. We'll be going now." The man tightened his hold on her neck.

Her gaze darted around, and she lifted her hands as if planning to pull the arm away, but then let them fall helplessly to her side.

Jackson's stomach cramped hard. She looked so panicked he could hardly keep from leaping at the man and taking him down.

"Move to the window," her assailant said to Jackson, likely wanting to get him out of the way of the door

Jackson stared at the guy and wished he could figure out this man's identity. Had Vetter or Garrett hired this man in a desperate attempt at revenge?

"Did Vetter or Garrett send you?" he asked.

"As I said. It doesn't matter who I am." He tipped his head at the window. "Now move out of our way."

Jackson took a few slow steps, his mind racing to find a way to stop this man from taking Maggie.

"How did you get in the house?" Jackson asked to buy time.

"Picked the lock and walked in the front door while you were all out playing search and rescue at Summit." He grinned, a self-satisfied number that showed uneven teeth. "I hid in the attic until you all were snoozing. But this one had to go and get curious. Who knew she was such a light sleeper?"

Jackson knew that, but it hadn't ever been important before this very moment. He kept staring at the guy, when suddenly something Maggie said on the first day came back to him. Crooked teeth. The man she talked to at the Summit neighborhood had crooked teeth.

"You're the guy," Jackson said, realizing he'd been wrong about Vetter. He never actually admitted to attacking Maggie. Just that he needed to do something about her seeing him. "The one who tried to kill Maggie at Summit the other night."

"You're a regular Sherlock." He chuckled.

"Why are you doing this to her?"

"Why? Because she saw me that night. I came by to see if they'd found Gamblin's body yet. Now she can identify me. I'm not going to prison for murdering that lowlife scumbag.

He deserved it. Every bit of it." His eyes were inflamed with anger. "Now move or I swear I'll kill you both right here."

Jackson knew it was time to get out of the way, but he also knew what that meant. This man was going to walk out the door with Maggie, and Jackson needed a clue of the man's identity in order to hunt him down.

Jackson started moving toward the window and locked gazes with Maggie. "I'm sorry, honey. But don't worry. You know I'll be right behind you."

The man shoved the gun into her temple so hard her head jerked. Jackson saw red and could barely stand by and let this man abuse her this way.

"You follow us and she dies." The guy pivoted Maggie as he moved them across her bedroom, his gaze following Jackson.

Jackson kept his focus on Maggie, his insides screaming to find a way to stop this.

The man backed to the door. Maggie opened her mouth as if to speak, then closed it before they disappeared into the hallway.

What was she about to say? Did it really matter?

Jackson's worst nightmare had come true. He failed her again, and this time, his error could very well cost her life.

Maggie could hardly breathe. Not only from the arm clamped tight against her throat, but also from the fear that was stealing the little breath she could gain. It felt like a big fist grabbed hold of her stomach, squeezing it into a tight ball of panic. She still didn't know who this man was, but she did know he was a killer, and right now, that was all that mattered. If he killed once, he would kill again. This time it would be her as she couldn't see how Jackson could follow them without endangering her life.

She wanted to look back to see if he was coming down the driveway behind them, but her abductor held her too tightly for her to take a look. She didn't hear Jackson, but that didn't mean he wasn't there. He could tail them, and this man would never know it. At least Jackson could follow them until they got into a vehicle and drove away. Jackson couldn't very well follow then. Just starting a car engine would alert this man. And on these twisty remote roads, her abductor could turn off anywhere, and they could be long gone before it was safe for Jackson to come after them.

Near the end of the drive, the man veered into the woods, the shadowed area extinguishing the wavering light of dawn. He kept up his pace, the gun still planted at her head. But as they walked, his arm slackened around her neck a fraction, allowing her to breathe a bit easier.

"Where are you taking me?" she got up her aching throat.

"You'll find out soon enough."

"I don't get it. If you're planning to kill me why not just do it now?" she asked and hoped he wouldn't take her up on the suggestion.

"And let your bodyguard take me out right after I do? No way." He took her on a crazy zigzagging path through the woods as if trying to confuse Jackson. But this creep didn't know Jackson. He wouldn't be confused. He could track them. Of that she was sure. Of course, when the guy got her in a car, that would change. Jackson's team didn't have a dog, but she knew the sheriff's department did, and Jackson would call in all resources to find her.

They came out of the woods a few miles down the road from her property, and she spotted an older model gray

Camry parked on the side of the road without license plates. Even if Jackson was right behind them, he couldn't track them that way.

"We'll climb in on the passenger side together." He pressed her body against the car and released her neck. He fumbled in his pocket and held out a key fob to unlock the door. "Here are the keys. You're driving."

He pressed them into her hand. She thought to refuse, but she knew he would simply force her to take them, so she curled her fingers around the metal. He opened the door. Keeping the gun at her head, he maneuvered them into the car until she was settled behind the wheel.

"Get it going," he said.

She cranked the engine and reached for her seat belt. He might be planning to kill her soon, but she wasn't going to let that happen, and she also wasn't going to risk her life by not wearing her seat belt.

She got them on the road. "Where to?"

"Keep driving, and I'll give you instructions."

She glanced in the rearview mirror and spotted Jackson jogging behind the car. She let up on the gas.

The man glanced in the side mirror. "Go faster or I'll turn and shoot him."

She didn't want anything bad to happen to Jackson. She pressed on the gas, and before long, she could no longer see Jackson.

She felt so empty. So alone. So afraid.

Jackson stopped on the side of the road and panted for air. His heart pounded against his chest, and his gut was tied in a rock-solid knot. He failed Maggie. Really failed her. Panic assaulted him, and he didn't know what to do. Running after the car was foolish. There was no hope of catching it, but having no idea of the abductor's identity, Jackson couldn't just let them disappear.

But disappear they had. Into the cool light of dawn. He had to do something. Now! But what?

Think, man, think!

He needed the team, but they, minus Coop, were in Cold Harbor. Somehow, they needed to get here. How, with the chopper out of commission? Maybe Coop could borrow Vince's helicopter.

Yeah, that was it. Jackson hoped, anyway. He dug out his phone and dialed Coop. It took five rings before he answered.

"I need help, now!" Jackson blurted out and explained Maggie's abduction, the panic welling up inside his body scaring him. He never felt this out of control before, and he needed to be in control to run the op to find Maggie. She needed him to keep it together. Needed him to figure this out.

He took a long breath. Blew it out and forced a calm to his tone that he still didn't feel. "We need to get eyes in the sky right away to find the vehicle. Can you fly Vince's chopper or maybe take the part you need from his helicopter?"

"Part won't work, and he's gone home for the day. Let me see if I can roust him."

"No. Not see. Do it," Jackson demanded.

"You need to calm down, man. You aren't doing anyone any good like this."

"Easy for you to say."

"Hey, I get it. I was there not too long ago. You have to trust that God will protect her, and she'll be okay so you can move forward in making a logical plan to find her. If you can't do that, then step down, and I'll take over."

Jackson ground his jaw, resolving to do what Maggie needed from him. He wasn't going to fail her again. "I've got this."

"Then let me get ahold of Vince."

"Call me the minute you hang up." Jackson disconnected and started for Maggie's house. He didn't have a good relationship with God right now, but he did know God was there and would hear his prayer and answer it.

Problem was, Jackson knew he might not like the answer. Still, he prayed. Hard. Each step down the deserted road, he pled with God to spare Maggie's life and bring her back to him. To give him the plan he needed to find her and save her.

He took a few more calming breaths and set his mind on finding the next logical step. If he couldn't get up in the air himself, he needed help in looking for the car. The local sheriff likely didn't have a chopper, but state police might. Worst case, Nate had deputies patrolling on the ground.

He dialed the sheriff's cell.

"Sheriff Ryder." His sleepy answer told Jackson he woke him.

"Sorry to wake you, Sheriff. Jackson Lockhart, here. I need to report an abduction." He shoved down the panic and concisely reported the incident.

"Man, oh, man," Nate said. "The creep killed Gamblin, huh? Poor Maggie. She was just in the wrong place at the wrong time and doesn't deserve this."

Jackson more than agreed with Nate's statement. "Our chopper's out of service or I'd be in the air tracking them. I need your help until we can get eyes in the sky."

"You do know we're a small agency, and we don't have a helicopter, right?"

"I figured as much but thought maybe the state police do."

"That's a negative."

"Can you set up a roadblock, Sheriff?" Jackson reached Maggie's house and jogged up the steps.

Daria stood in the doorway, clasping her hands together. "Is she—"

Jackson held up a finger and gestured for her to go inside. He followed and closed the door.

"It's Nate," he said. "And yeah, I can set up the roadblock, but you're in the far reaches of my county. You should know it's likely the suspect will have turned off long before I can get a deputy out there."

"Understood," Jackson replied but hated to have to admit it. "If we're going to find her, I need more information on Andre Gamblin's murder." Jackson twisted the deadbolt and felt as if he was somehow cementing Maggie's fate by locking her out.

The knot in his gut tightened when he didn't think that was even possible.

"You at Maggie's house?" Nate asked.

"Yes."

"I'll head over with the file as soon as possible."

"Thanks." Jackson disconnected and shoved his phone into his pocket.

"Is Maggie okay?" Daria cried out, her eyes wide with concern.

Jackson didn't want to scare Daria even more, but it couldn't be helped. "Last I saw Maggie she was fine." He gave her an abbreviated version of Maggie's abduction.

Daria clutched her chest. "Are we safe here?"

"This wasn't random. Maggie was the target, and you should be fine. Still, you may want to go back to your friend's house."

"Yes. Yes." Her head kept bobbing. "I'll get ready and leave now."

At the door, she turned back. "You'll find her, right? I mean you guys are like this amazing team, and if anyone can find her it will be you."

"You can be assured I will find Maggie." Jackson ground the words out between his teeth.

Daria nodded and fled down the hallway. He grabbed his laptop from his tote bag and took it to the kitchen. After placing it on the counter, he made a pot of coffee. He left it to perk and turned to his computer.

He entered Ozzie and Andre Gamblin's names in an Internet search box. A long list of news articles about the rape filled the page. He clicked on the first one from the local newspaper. Their mugshots flashed on the screen. Both were snarling, their heads cocked in a look of superiority. Jackson's fists curled.

He started reading the story, and it confirmed what Maggie had told him about the rape. The story went on to say the journalist tried to interview the victim, but she refused. Jackson couldn't believe this writer even tried to interview the woman. She'd already been through so much, why make her relive it just to sell papers?

Jackson's phone chimed a text from Coop. Vince was going to send his pilot and chopper back to pick up the team while Coop stayed to wait for the part and fix the team chopper.

Jackson's heart lifted a notch. At least his teammates—the people he counted on to have his six and Maggie's, too—

would be here soon. Together, Jackson was confident they could bring Maggie home.

He turned his attention back to his computer and read every article about Ozzie and Andre. Jackson was just about to enter the victim's name in the search engine when the doorbell rang. He glanced up, surprised to see two hours had passed. Maggie, his sweet Maggie, had been missing for more than two hours now. He could hardly fathom it. He vaguely remembered Daria saying goodbye, but he didn't know how long ago.

He went to the door and opened it. The sheriff stood strong in the morning sun, casting a long shadow into the room. He held a thick folder in his hand.

"Anything from the roadblock?" Jackson asked.

Nate shook his head, and he already looked exhausted when the search had only just begun.

"Would you like some coffee?" Jackson offered.

"That'd be great."

Jackson led Nate into the kitchen. "I've been researching the Gamblin brothers online. I haven't found much of anything that I didn't already know."

Jackson's phone rang, and seeing Eryn was calling, he quickly answered.

"Tell me you and the team are on your way," he said.

"Vince's chopper just landed."

"Then I'll see you soon."

"Yeah, but I wanted to tell you we just received information on that shoeprint Riley cast outside Maggie's house."

"And?"

"And the shoe's not from a traditional manufacturer. It's a 3-D custom-printed shoe."

"Say what? I've never heard of such a thing."

"The company's a web-based business. Customers use a

smart phone app to send a digital photo of their foot. This allows the company to see about five thousand data points on an individual's foot. They then produce a shoe within a couple of millimeters of the person's foot size."

"Do you think if we send this casting to them, they could ID the buyer?" he asked, though he knew it would take a full day before they would receive the cast, and he couldn't believe he wouldn't have brought Maggie home by then.

"Better yet, the lab took precise high-resolution 3-D images of the print, and I'm forwarding those shots to you along with the company contact information. If you can get them to agree to work with you without a warrant, you could forward the photos, and they might be able to provide the customer's name."

"The sheriff is here, and he could get the owner to work with us."

"Good. I'm sending the files and will be boarding the chopper after I do."

"Roger that." Jackson ended the call and told Nate about the shoeprint.

"I'll call them the minute you receive the information. If they won't play ball, I can have a warrant in an hour or so."

Jackson's phone dinged, and he quickly opened the text from Eryn with a shaking finger. He hated the way his nerves were impacting his body, but at least now they were nerves of excitement over the lead and not solely the fear of losing Maggie.

20

A bus. Maggie's abductor planned to flee in a big old Greyhound bus. The last vehicle she expected a criminal who wanted to stay under the radar to use, but he said he had hoped to take her without anyone seeing him and no one would have even known what had become of her, much less look for a vehicle of any sort.

She parked the Camry as he directed. The big silver bus with a faded Greyhound on the side sat on a narrow drive deep in the woods. It explained the keychain she found next to Andre's body. This creep had dropped it.

She couldn't help but shake her head over his choice of vehicle. "Why a bus?"

"Why not?" He grabbed the keys from the ignition.

He opened his door, the infernal gun still pointed at her. "I'm going to back out slowly, and you're going to crawl over here and get out, too. If you try anything—and I mean anything—I don't need you anymore, and I won't hesitate to shoot."

"If you don't need me, then why not do it now?" she

asked and hoped she wasn't encouraging him to kill her sooner rather than later.

"I may not need you, but I still want to carry out my plan." He inched backward and settled his feet on the ground, keeping the gun aimed at her.

She'd known on the drive that he wouldn't kill her while she was behind the wheel, but now? Now his life didn't depend on hers as he just confirmed, and he was free to shoot at any time.

Fear rushed through her veins feeling like cold water, and she couldn't move.

"Get out now or I shoot. You have to the count of five." His angry eyes locked on hers. "One. Two."

"Stop. I'm coming." She climbed over the middle hump, making sure to keep her focus on him and not make any unnecessary movements. The moment she stood on the ground littered with pine needles, his arm went around her neck, and he planted the gun on her temple again. He pushed her up against the bus and unlocked the door.

"Inside—now." He gave her a shove toward the door, the gun not leaving her head.

Was he going to kill her in this bus?

She feared so, but there was no choice but to climb up the steps. She shot a look down what would've once been an aisle lined with seats, but he converted the bus into a home on wheels.

On the right was a sofa in a hideous blue floral pattern, and the same fabric served as curtains for the many bus windows. To her left an orange swivel chair and tiny table butted up to a small galley kitchen and a bedroom filled the back wall. The whole place gave off a retro sixties vibe—when she suspected he'd converted it.

"In the chair." He gave her a push down the aisle

She dropped onto the worn vinyl chair.

"Hands behind the chair."

She leaned back and extended her arms.

He reached back to the counter holding a pile of thick zip ties. The gun lifted from her head. She seized the moment and shot to her feet. He spun and cracked the gun across her skull.

Pain razored into her head. Stars danced in front of her eyes. She blinked hard and dropped to the chair before she hit the ground.

He poked the gun into her forehead and got in her face, his breath stale and nauseating. "Try that again, and I'll shoot you in the back as you run."

He jammed the gun harder. "You hear me?"

"Yes," she got the word out, though she felt like she might throw up.

He backed up and grabbed a zip tie, the gun never leaving her head. "Hands behind your back."

She followed his direction, and he moved behind her. She braced herself for another poke of the gun to her head, but it didn't happen. He fastened one end of a zip tie around her wrist, cinching it so tight that she cried out.

"I might've been nicer to you if you didn't try to run." He secured her other wrist and came around front again. He glared at her, then backed away, the gun pointed in her direction. He stooped to retrieve a thick rope from the sofa and moved behind her again.

The rope came around her chest, and he jerked it tight. She could still breathe, but it was a struggle. He wound it around her several times and tied it off.

"Okay," he said as he stepped back to survey his work. "Sit back and enjoy the ride."

She fought through the pain in her head and the rope

constricting her body to find the courage to stay alert. "Where are we going?"

"Where?" he asked, a sick smile sliding across his face. "A place where your body will never be found."

~

Nate hung up from his call to the shoe company and faced Jackson. "Guy's name is Tyson Fenwick."

Jackson was overjoyed to finally have the identity of the jerk who'd taken Maggie six hours ago. "I know that name. He was mentioned in the stories I just read. Ozzie raped his sister."

Nate nodded. "I have his address. It's a trailer park near Medford."

Perfect. "The team should have boots on the ground in a few minutes. Give me the address, and I'll send them over there to do recon while we head that way."

"I'll share it on one condition."

"Name it."

"They can only do recon and can't take the law into their own hands unless her life is in imminent danger."

Jackson nodded. "I'm good with that. We'll likely be there before they finish recon anyway."

Nate rattled off an address. Jackson dialed Gage and quickly relayed the information along with Nate's instructions.

"We're just touching down now," Gage said. "We'll need to load the necessary equipment in our vehicle first. I estimate our ETA for that address at eight minutes."

"Roger that. I'm on my way." Jackson grabbed his pack from the sofa and headed for the door. He heard Nate's footsteps right behind him.

On the porch, he stopped to lock the door, thankful that Daria had gone and he wasn't leaving her alone. Nate rushed past Jackson and jogged down the stairs to climb into his county vehicle.

Jackson jumped into the passenger seat. He would rather take control and drive, but Nate could run lights and siren and get them to the trailer park faster.

Nate soon had them racing down the road with the lights and siren running just as Jackson hoped. They'd only traveled about ten miles when Jackson's phone rang.

"It's Gage," he told Nate and answered.

"Bus is gone," Gage said.

"Say that again." Jackson plugged his free ear to block the siren's wail.

"Fenwick lives in an old converted Greyhound bus, and it's gone. I talked to the neighbor, and he said Fenwick was taking a short trip and would be back in a day or two."

Jackson let the comments filter through his brain for a moment. "You think he ditched the car and has Maggie in this bus?"

"Would be my guess."

"Then we need to get back up in the air. A bus will be easy to spot."

"Coop has the helo fixed and ready to go."

"Perfect." Jackson glanced at Nate. "We have a change in plans. We need to get to our chopper." Jackson shared the location. "What's our ETA for that?"

"At this speed, ten minutes."

"Can you go any faster?"

"Sure." He grinned and punched the gas.

Jackson turned his attention back to the call. "I'm going up with you. We'll be at Vince's place in less than ten minutes." Jackson hung up before Gage argued that it would be better for them to go up now.

Jackson couldn't let that happen. If the team took off and spotted the bus, they wouldn't come back for him, and he planned to be in on every step of Maggie's rescue.

Jackson told Nate about the call, speaking loudly to be heard above the siren.

Nate reached for his radio. "Dispatch, issue an alert for a '64 silver bus with blue accents and greyhound emblem on the side." He added the Oregon plate number and the general location where they believed the bus to be located. "Driver is armed with hostage. Detain, but do not approach. Repeat. Detain, but do not approach."

Jackson went straight to his phone to pull up pictures of a 1964 Greyhound bus. He and the team would soon be breaching this vehicle, and he wanted to learn every detail possible to guarantee a safe breach.

Several pictures of the older bus filled the screen, and he studied each one. Their actions when approaching the vehicle would depend on Fenwick's location in the bus at the time, but assuming they stopped the bus on the road and he was in the driver's seat, they could easily take him down before he could harm Maggie.

Nate finished his call and glanced at Jackson. "Is the bus you're looking at the right year?"

Jackson nodded and held it out, allowing Nate to get a better look without having to take his focus from the windshield while they were speeding down the road.

Jackson lowered his arm. "From what I've seen in my search, we're lucky Fenwick didn't choose an older model. Those buses have smaller windows and would've been too little to breach."

Nate raised an eyebrow. "You're assuming that you'll be doing the breaching."

Jackson eyed Nate. "You think your team would do a better job?"

"Likely not, but I can't just turn my back and let you all have free reign in my county. The legal repercussions are too great."

"First, you're assuming the bus is still in your county. They could be far away from here by now."

"True. And second?"

"Second, once we're up in the air you won't know what we're planning to do, and you wouldn't be culpable for our actions."

"I don't know, man." He let up on the gas as if he was rethinking things.

"Let's just get to the chopper as fast as we can, and then we can hash out the plan."

Nate's brow furrowed, but the car sped up again. They reached Medford, and fortunately for them, the logging company was on the near side of the city. As Nate had said, in less than ten minutes they pulled up to the helo that was fired up and waiting.

Jackson was out of the vehicle before Nate came to a complete stop. Jackson raced to Gage who stood talking to Alex out of rotor range.

Nate moved quickly, too, impressing Jackson that he joined them before Jackson could utter a word to Gage. Jackson introduced him to Gage.

"I'm going with you," Nate demanded.

Gage eyed him.

"Look," Nate said. "We can either stand here arguing or we can get moving."

Gage shot Jackson a questioning look.

Jackson eyed Nate. "We're a well-oiled machine, and we can't mess this up by having a stranger interfere."

"Don't worry. I'll hang back, but if you do find Fenwick in my county and put down, you might need ground transportation to get to him, and I can arrange that."

"Then we're a go." Jackson bent forward and jogged to the helo. He took a seat by the door. So what if the others had to climb over him to take their seats. He would be the first one out of the helo when they located that bus, and he would do whatever he needed to do to make that happen.

Maggie's abductor nodded off. The bus hit the gravel on the side of the road.

"Wake up!" she cried out before he ran them into the steep ravine abutting the narrow road.

He jerked the bus back onto the pavement. The rear-end fishtailed, sending her chair tilting. He gained control and got the vehicle pointed down the road.

She released a long breath. "You need to stay awake."

He eyed her in the rearview mirror. "What difference is it to you?"

She didn't bother to respond but kept her eyes on him to watch for his head to droop again. With each mile that had passed under the bus, she'd tried to come up with a way to escape his clutches but thought of nothing.

She only hoped Jackson figured out how to find her. But she feared the only way he could was if he figured out who killed Andre Gamblin. That way Jackson would have this man's ID and might be able to find the bus.

They rounded a bend, and the bus slowed. He eased it onto a wayside stop where she suspected logging trucks traveled. She glanced out the window. Large trees and plenty of scrub filled the area, so they were well hidden. He parked, killed the engine, and swiveled to the side to rest his head against the window behind him.

"Why are we stopping?" she asked, but dreaded the answer.

"Need a quick nap."

She wanted him rested so he didn't crash the bus, but she also wanted answers. She hoped knowing something about him might help her figure out a way to escape. "You never said your name."

"I didn't." He remained in place, not bothering to look at her.

"Don't you want me to know who you are?"

"Don't much care."

"But you care enough to kill me. You must want me to know why."

He shrugged.

"I deserve that much."

"Maybe."

"Did you kill Andre Gamblin?"

He sat forward and shot her a look. "You were able to identify him, then. Reporters said you couldn't do it. That his dental records wouldn't help because he was too burned to use DNA."

"I have a friend who's pioneering DNA extraction from burnt bones."

"Shoulda known this would happen. It's the way the world works." He shook his head and got up. "A guy like Gamblin gets off with lesser charges on a technicality, and I do one thing wrong and you have some super technology that will convict me."

"So you did kill Andre?"

"Didn't say I did."

"You all but admitted it. You're going to kill me. Why not tell the truth?"

"Why not indeed." He strolled to the kitchen and grabbed a soda from a small refrigerator.

She stared up at him. "What's your name?"

He held his finger over the can as if he planned to open it but was deciding if he should. Or maybe he was pausing to question if he should share his name.

"C'mon," she said. "You won't let me live so why not tell me who you are."

He popped the soda top, and it hissed into the air. "Tyson Fenwick."

Tyson Fenwick. His name didn't sound familiar. She was sure she'd never heard it before. "And how do you know Andre?"

"How? How?" His voice climbed up an octave. "He sat by watching as his brother raped my sister."

"Oh...oh, no. That's horrible." She looked at him, and his expression hardened even more. "I'm sorry to hear about your sister."

He took a long drink of the soda and swiped the back of his hand across his mouth. "Yeah, like that was the worst of it, but it wasn't. She never recovered and lived in fear every second of every day. Got so bad, she couldn't leave the house. She even lost her job. Her life was basically over. So one night," he paused and seemed to struggle to take in enough air. "One night, she took a bottle of sleeping pills."

He clenched his jaw, set the soda on the counter, and laid his hands on it, his head down. "I vowed that night when the Gamblin brothers got out of prison, I would make them pay. So I started with Andre. Seized the opportunity to shoot near a dive bar when he was drunk. My buddy was in

Florida so I hid Andre's body in my friend's shed until I could prepare Andre's final resting place. Then the fire broke out. Of all the bad luck."

"I can understand your anger and grief, but murder? Doesn't that make you like them?"

He spun on her. "You don't know a thing, lady."

"You're right I don't, and I can even understand your desire to kill these brothers but taking me hostage makes you just like them."

"No. It. Doesn't," he ground out between his teeth. "I'm not violating you like they did my sister."

"You're going to kill me. Isn't that even worse?"

He stepped to her then, his face ablaze with anger, and his eyes unfocused. His crazed look told her he'd lost touch with reality and couldn't understand what he was doing was as bad as the Gamblin brothers' actions.

He got in her face. "When you live through what I've been through, then you can judge me. Until then, keep your mouth shut."

Maggie turned her face away. She didn't want to anger him any further, so she would change the subject. "You also never said where we're going."

He backed up and leaned against the counter. "Far away from everyone and everything so no one knows I was involved in this."

"Right. You need to get away with killing me to keep from going to prison."

"Gotta make it five years until Ozzie gets out of jail. I have a bullet with his name on it, too. Then I don't care about myself. Justice will have been served."

She met his gaze. "You're so bent on getting justice for your sister, but how can you kill me? I have a family, too, you know."

"Had a family." He moved the can of soda to the sink. "I did my research. Your mother has been dead for fifteen years, your dad a year ago, and you don't have any brothers or sisters."

"What about my grandparents? Don't you think they'll mourn my loss?"

His eyes flickered for a moment. "It can't be helped."

"Actually, it can," she said leveling her gaze on him. "You can turn around and take me home."

"That's not going to happen no matter how much you plead or try to reason with me." He took the gun from his belt and pressed the cold steel against her forehead. "So just shut up until I tell you to talk."

21

Jackson brought up the image of the bus on his phone and passed it around the group. "Right now, the plan is for Coop to put down on the road ahead of the bus to stop it. But if that's not possible, we'll have to play things by ear once we locate the bus."

Jackson could see the thought *if we locate the bus* in everyone's eyes, but he wouldn't let himself think that way. "Once we have the vehicle stopped, we'll approach with tactical ladders. Bust out the window near the driver and board. I'll take the driver."

"You sure that's a good idea?" Alex asked. "One of us might be more levelheaded about this rescue and should take the lead."

Jackson felt Gage eye him, but he didn't change his focus from Alex. "I'm taking Fenwick out. End of discussion."

Jackson waited for someone to speak, but when no one uttered a sound, he faced Riley. "You'll be on overwatch as usual. This guy even blinks wrong, I want you to take him out."

"I can't allow that to happen," Nate said. "No one takes anyone out."

Jackson fired Nate a frustrated look. "We're not a trigger-happy bunch. If it's a choice between Maggie or this creep's life, you can be sure we'll do what needs to be done."

"Only way I'll let this go forward is if I'm taking a stand next to your sniper." Nate looked at Riley. "I assume you have a scope I can use to watch the action and an extra comm unit."

Riley nodded.

"Good, then if a shot needs to be fired, I'll give the official word." He shifted to lock eyes with Jackson.

He wanted to stare the sheriff down until he caved, but Jackson could tell he wasn't going to give in. He was a good sheriff, a strong one, and Jackson admired that.

"Okay. Nate will give the go ahead." Jackson met and held Nate's gaze. "But you better be watching and listening. If anything happens to Maggie, it's on your head."

"I can handle it." Nate sat back and crossed his ankles like they were discussing sports instead of the tactical taking of a life.

Jackson glanced around the group and saw the look of respect for Nate on his teammates' faces.

"Approaching target area," Coop's voice came over the headsets.

Jackson lifted his binoculars and scanned below as did everyone except Coop.

Jackson spotted what looked like a large silver Twinkie parked off a logging road. "You all see what I'm seeing?"

"Affirmative," Gage said and the others agreed.

"Coop, can you put down nearby?"

"I could set down behind him, but that wouldn't help. I'll need to do a flyover to get a better view from the north."

278

He moved them west of the target, and Jackson knew he was trying not to let Fenwick get antsy over hearing the chopper. Good news was if he did have binoculars and spotted the chopper, the lack of markings would tell him they weren't military or law enforcement, and hopefully he'd let his guard down the way Lyle Vetter did on the ocean.

Jackson watched the forested area pass below. When they were a good distance north of the target, Coop swooped the chopper down toward the road. "We're good to land."

"Then let's do it now before Fenwick gets antsy," Jackson said, and his stomach filled with butterflies.

He always got them before an op, but this one was especially important and risky, and he had to admit to being afraid it would go wrong. Being an elite operative didn't mean you never had any fear. Just meant you'd learned how to control the fear and could still perform at a higher-than-normal level.

"Looks like I'll have a clear shot once we round that bend," Riley said. "You'll have to give me a few minutes to shimmy up a tree, though."

Riley handed a spotting scope to Nate.

"You good to climb a tree?" Jackson asked Nate.

"Can't say as I've done it lately, but yeah, I'll manage." Nate studied the scope.

Jackson gave the guy credit for not letting anything seem to discourage him. He fit in very well with the team.

The chopper dropped, the road coming up to meet them. Jackson mentally prepared himself to take action. They hit with a soft bounce, and he had the door open in a flash. The team poured out of the helo like ants at a picnic, and he led them south, moving double-time. They reached the bend in the road, and he raised his fist and signaled for the team to move to cover provided by trees. When they hit their positions by the bus, and Riley with Nate in tow took their stand, each person would report in, and Jackson would give the signal to breach the bus.

He stepped off the road and had to focus not to plunge down the steep ravine or make noise to alert Fenwick. He would likely have heard the helo land and could already be spooked. Jackson found his way through the trees and scrub until the bus came into view. He paused to assess with his binoculars. He spotted Fenwick sitting behind the wheel but facing the door. He wasn't moving at all.

Maybe he hadn't heard the thump of rotors or felt the rumble. If not, he must be dead or sound asleep. Had he stopped to take a nap?

Jackson started moving again and reached the bus. From his angle below the vehicle he couldn't see into any window, and he wasn't about to pop up and give away their location just to check. He squatted and waited. Alex took his position ahead of him where he'd be ready to pry the door open.

"In place." Riley's voice came over Jackson's earbud. "Looks like Fenwick is sleeping behind the wheel. No sign of hostage. Must be deeper in bus."

"Roger that."

So the guy was asleep. They couldn't ask for a better scenario. Now Jackson just needed to hear from Eryn and Gage, and they'd be a go. Adrenaline flooded Jackson's body in a rush that left him eager to move. He breathed deep. Let it out.

Please don't let me fail her. Please don't let her be injured. Anyone on the team be injured.

"We're set." Gage's voice startled Jackson, but he recovered in a flash.

"We're a go in five." Jackson counted down to one. "Go. Go. Go."

He plunged out of the scrub behind Alex and powered up the steep hill. The muscles in his legs burned, but he felt so alive he could hardly contain his eagerness and keep his focus.

Alex reached the door, inserted a pry bar, and held his position. Jackson stacked behind him, waiting for the sound of breaking glass on the other side of the bus. The punch wouldn't make an earth-shattering noise, but they'd hear the driver's window break, and they'd definitely hear Eryn and Gage clearing the glass.

A short pop sounded, and Alex split the door from the frame. He jerked it open. Rifle out, Jackson bounded up the steps. Fenwick was on his feet. His handgun was out and pointing at Maggie—bound to a chair.

Jackson's heart split. "Don't do it, Fenwick!"

Fenwick's eyes were wide with panic. "Then you all get out of here and leave us be."

Jackson wanted to look at Maggie but he couldn't take his focus from Fenwick. "I can't do that."

"Then your friend dies," he said, his voice cold and calculating.

Jackson's heart sank, but he didn't let Fenwick see the fear that was clutching his heart. "Or does she?"

Fenwick sneered. "What do you mean by that?"

"You have a red dot on your head. A laser from our sniper's rifle."

"You're bluffing."

"Look in the mirror."

He turned his head slightly to look in the big rearview mirror, his face blanching, but when he looked back at Jackson, he jutted out a defiant chin. "So there's a dot. Doesn't mean it's attached to a rifle."

Riley spoke in Jackson's earbud. "If Maggie's on the left side of Fenwick I can demonstrate."

"She is. Go for it."

"What?" Fenwick asked.

"Our sniper is going to give you a little demonstration. Be sure you don't move."

A bullet pierced the front window and lodged in one of the kitchen cabinets behind Fenwick.

"Seen enough?" Jackson asked and tried not to gloat.

Fenwick gnawed on his lip, his gaze darting around. He spun on Jackson. "So what if your sniper gets me? I could shoot Maggie first."

"Actually, you couldn't. Our sniper will sever your brainstem, and you won't have a chance to even flinch, much less get off a shot." Jackson paused for a long moment. "What's it going to be? You put down the gun or our sniper takes you out?"

Fenwick thought for a minute, his gaze traveling around the bus again. He sighed. "Fine. You win."

"Place your weapon on the floor. Slowly."

He bent forward and lowered the gun to the floor. Jackson wanted to lunge at him and take him down, but he kept his rifle trained on him and stepped aside to let Alex kick the gun out of reach and zip tie Fenwick's wrists. Alex dragged Fenwick to the door, and Jackson had to hold himself in check to keep from ramming the butt of his rifle into the guy's face.

Maggie moved in his peripheral vision, drawing his attention, and he forgot everything else to go to her. He squatted in front of her and ran his gaze over her. At the sight of a big knot on her forehead, his gut clenched, and he wanted to take off and beat Fenwick within an inch of his life.

"Thank you." She exhaled heavily and smiled at him. "I hoped you'd come. I thought you would, but I couldn't be sure you'd figure out where he took me."

"I promise you," he said looking into her eyes. "I will never fail you again. Never."

~

Maggie didn't know how to respond to Jackson's statement. He said what she wanted to hear. It sounded like he was planning to be there for her in the future. But what did that mean exactly?

She wanted to accept his words as something uttered in the heat of the moment and let it go, but she couldn't. "You can't make a promise like that."

"I can and I did." He retrieved a switchblade from his pocket.

"But you're only human, Jackson. You're bound to make a mistake again."

"I won't. Not when it comes to you." He clamped down on his jaw and worked the muscles hard.

She looked deep into his eyes. "And at what cost will you hold that promise?"

"I don't understand." He flipped open his knife and quickly sliced through the rope circling her body.

"You're already stressed out about not wanting to fail others. The stress from this promise will paralyze you, and your quality of life will be horrible. I couldn't bear to see that happen."

He didn't answer, but moved behind her, gently took her hands, and cut the zip ties. She wanted to rub her wrists, but the muscles in her upper arms ached from holding them in such an unnatural position that all she could do was let them drop to her sides for now.

Jackson came back around. He snapped his switchblade closed and shoved it into his pocket. His expression reminded her how fierce he looked holding his rifle and staring down Fenwick. He'd been in his element. In command and someone who would in all situations do his best to take care of others around him.

When he didn't say anything, she stood up and lifted her hand to caress the side of his face. Pain shot down her arm, but she didn't care. "You're an amazing man, Jackson. I am so blessed to know you. Thank you for coming for me."

His eyes lingered on her in a tender expression, and she knew she had to kiss him. What was to become of them after that she didn't know, but right now it felt like the right thing to do.

She put her arms around his neck and raised up on her tiptoes. He met her halfway and crushed her to him as his lips settled on hers. Fireworks exploded in her brain, and she felt as if she might melt in his arms. She returned the kiss, deepening it, clinging to him. Willing him to see how much she cared for him. How much she wanted to be with him.

"Um...excuse me," Alex's voice cut through her brain fog.

She withdrew from the kiss but remained in Jackson's arms. Breathing hard, he rested his forehead on hers, and she was surprised he didn't step back.

"Sorry," Alex continued. "But Nate wants to get Fenwick transported to jail, and he wants to talk to Jackson first."

"Roger that," Jackson said.

Alex nodded and jogged down the stairs.

She extricated herself from Jackson's arms and instantly felt alone.

His expression tightened again, but he kept his focus on her. "I'll be right back, and we can continue this."

"Actually," she said, knowing he wasn't ready to continue with her in any capacity right now, "I don't think that's a good idea for either of us."

"What are you saying?"

"I'm saying no matter what our feelings are for each other, you aren't ready to offer anything more than a kiss right now. Not until you accept that you aren't perfect and don't make promises you can't keep. It's time to end this before we both get hurt again."

"So that's it then," he said, his hands clenched.

She nodded, her heart already aching at the thought of being without him.

His disappointed gaze lingered on her for a long moment, then he spun to walk out the door.

22

The Fourth of July in Cold Harbor. Maggie never thought she would be there, but Hannah begged and begged until Maggie accepted Hannah's invitation to the picnic and fireworks. Maggie wanted a chance to properly thank the team for their help, even though she knew Hannah was trying to get her and Jackson together. She also knew Hannah's plan would fail.

The shared kiss after he rescued her told her he wanted her. But he obviously hadn't worked things out as she hadn't heard from him since that day. If he found a way to live with his fears and not exist in a desperate kind of agony, he would have called. His quiet mood tonight at the beach when everyone was loud and boisterous confirmed her assessment.

How could he not enjoy this night? It was magical. A cool seventy degrees, a gentle wind blew as the ocean waves rolled in to lap the shore. The fireworks would soon be launched from a ship in the ocean where there was no danger of sparks starting a forest fire, and Maggie could already feel the excitement in the group.

She rested her bare feet in the sand still warm from the day. Riley and Alex had built a roaring bonfire. To the delight of everyone else, they razzed each other on their caveman fire building skills as they did so, making Maggie and the others laugh. Except Jackson.

She relaxed back in the lawn chair and glanced around the fire pit at his friends. His family really. Coop, the guy she'd been so leery of, sat on a log, his fiancé Kiera on his lap. The ferocity in his gaze had long ago disappeared, and his love for Kiera was unmistakable. She obviously felt the same way. Her brother, Kevin sat next to them, his face in his phone, oblivious to everything around him.

Eryn sat in a beach chair that hugged the sand. She held her sweet little Bekah who'd plugged her thumb into her mouth, her eyelids heavy. Her ponytail was the same rich black as Eryn's hair, and her eyes when they were open, were big and round like Eryn's. Bekah really was the spitting image of her mother. A rough and tumble little girl, she'd been playing tag with David and Mia, but was too little to keep up with them, and they'd soon worn her out.

Across the fire from Maggie and near Jackson, Hannah opened a tote bag and took out marshmallows, chocolate, and graham crackers along with long roasting sticks.

"S'mores," David shouted.

Mia tottered over to the fire, and Maggie glanced at Bekah to see her reaction, but her eyes remained closed.

"Bekah's like you, Eryn," Riley said. "Can and will sleep just about anywhere."

"And," Alex said, a twinkle in his eyes. "She's wiped out from trying to keep up with the big guys just like you, too."

Eryn rolled her eyes as the team chuckled, and Alex playfully jabbed her in the arm. Maggie loved the team's good-natured teasing and could really imagine settling down in Cold Harbor with Jackson and being a part of the group. She glanced at him again to see if he was going to join in, but he hadn't moved an inch, nor was he smiling.

What was up with him? Did he not want her here? Likely not. Even if he didn't, she wasn't going to let it ruin her night.

Hannah knelt by the fire, and Gage joined her. He gave her shoulders a quick squeeze, and together they helped Mia and David settle their marshmallows in the glowing fire.

What a sight they made, the little family. Flames licked toward the sky, flickering on their joyful faces. Mia was especially a sight to behold with her face rapt with wonder. Maybe it had to do with her brain injury, or she just plain loved roasting marshmallows. Either way, Maggie doubted the precious little girl could be having any more fun.

Maggie thought of Alison and waited for the usual pain to come, but instead it didn't cut her like a knife. It was only a dull ache. She glanced at Jackson to see what he was thinking, but his expression was as blank as it had been since she arrived in Cold Harbor. He was watching Mia and David, but if he was feeling any pain, he wasn't letting on.

Maggie wished she could read his mind. Was it possible when she nearly died at Fenwick's hand that Jackson had bottled up his emotions even more? She could see that happening. Or did he come to realize she was right that if they were together he would always be on edge, and he didn't want to live like that?

Riley moved closer to the fire, held out his hand to Hannah, and looked at her with a little-boy pout. "Marshmallow, please."

Hannah chuckled, likely from the face he was making, and handed him a stick and the bag. Some woman was going to have a very hard time saying no to that handsome pouting face someday.

"Hey, me, too." Alex dropped down next to them. He smiled, but it wasn't as easygoing as Riley's, surprising her as Alex was clearly the team jokester. Maybe he had something on his mind tonight just like Jackson.

"Mine's done." Mia pulled her stick back from the fire and reached for her marshmallow.

"It's hot, honey. Let me help." Hannah assisted Mia with pressing the gooey mess between the crackers and chocolate. Hannah smiled, and at the same time, looked leery. "You need to sit down to eat it, sweetie, or you're going to make a big mess."

Mia eased backward, bumping into Jackson's legs. She glanced at him then back at her s'more.

"Lap," she said and started licking the gooey white fluff oozing from the middle of her s'more.

Jackson didn't hesitate but scooped her up and settled her in place on his knee.

"You're a brave man, Jackson," Hannah said. "You're soon going to be a sticky mess."

"It's okay as long as Mia shares a bite."

Mia looked horrified at the thought.

He smiled at her. "I was just kidding, sweetheart."

She relaxed against him and took a big bite. Chocolate dripped down her chin to her purple sweatshirt with a sparkling unicorn on the chest. She swiped the gooey mess away with her fingers and rested that hand on Jackson's arm.

Maggie waited for his reaction. He smiled, a look of utter and pure contentment on his face and didn't even try to clean off the stickiness.

Did this mean Maggie was wrong and he'd reached a place where he could move past the loss of Alison? That he might be able to relax and enjoy life now? Dare she hope they might be together? She could hardly breathe for the thought of it.

~

With the way Maggie was looking at him, Jackson almost set Mia down and dropped to his knees to ask Maggie to marry him right here in the middle of the action. But after the way she reacted to his kiss on the bus, he didn't know what she would say and couldn't put her on the spot like that. Not in front of the team and their significant others.

Sure, she'd come tonight, but only because Hannah invited and cajoled her into agreeing. When Hannah made up her mind, she was a hard woman to say no to.

"Fireworks in thirty minutes," Alex announced. He put himself in charge of making sure they were all ready for the event, though how could they not be? A simple turning of a few chairs and they'd have a perfect view of the annual fireworks out over the ocean.

Jackson and the team had come to the fireworks last year, too, but there wasn't one woman in the bunch. Eryn stayed home with Bekah, claiming her daughter was too young to be up this late. By the looks of things, she was still a bit too young. Back then, Gage wasn't married and Coop not engaged. And Jackson? He wasn't even thinking about a relationship with a woman back then. Making it even odder that he wanted to propose marriage tonight.

He shook his head.

They'd all come so far in such a short time. Next thing he knew, Hannah would be expecting a child, and Coop married. And where would that leave Jackson? Holding a friend's sticky child again, instead of his own?

Why? When he had a woman he loved, and who he believed loved him? All because of this irrational fear that she might get hurt, and he would be to blame? He couldn't let that control him anymore. He needed to move on, or he would never really live. Watching everyone tonight confirmed just how much he wanted to find that happiness, and he would. When the time was right he would whisk Maggie down to the beach for some privacy, explain where his head was at, and ask her to marry him.

"Okay, Mia and David," Gage said. "Let's get you cleaned up in the restroom before the fireworks."

Mia pushed off Jackson's lap, planting a hand on his knee and leaving a sticky mess behind. His arm was already dripping in goop, what was one more spot? She took Gage's hand and Jackson saw him wince at the tacky mess, but he held firm and they started off down the beach to the restrooms.

Hannah held out a travel packet of baby wipes. "You can use these, unless you want Gage to take you down to the restroom to clean you up, too."

He laughed and accepted the wipes. He ran one over his arm first and then his knee. He wanted to take Maggie's hand and lead her down to the shore, but before he did, he wanted her to see that he was on the mend and really could follow through on letting go of the past and marry her.

He cleared his throat to grab everyone's attention. "There's something I think you guys should know about Maggie and me."

She sat forward in her chair, her eyes wide and confused.

"I don't mean to bring everyone down, but I wanted to tell you this when everyone was together."

"What about Gage?" Riley asked.

"You all know Hannah will fill him in." Jackson smiled at Hannah.

She swatted his leg.

"Careful, you might end up sticky." He chuckled but then thoughts of Alison sobered him up. "Maggie and I were once expecting a baby. A girl. Alison." Emotions swelled in his chest and tears wet his eyes, but he would go on. For Alison. To keep her memory alive. "We were in a car accident at the beginning of Maggie's eighth month. She was pinned in the car. By the time the firefighters got her out..."

His voice cracked, and he shook his head to ward off tears that accompanied it. "Well...Alison. She didn't...she didn't make it."

He heard the women gasp.

"Oh, Jackson." Hannah met his gaze and then turned to Maggie. "That must've been so hard to handle."

Jackson nodded. "Took us both six years to get to the point where we can truly move on."

"I can't even imagine what I'd do if I lost David," Hannah said. "And now Mia, too."

"Me, too," Eryn said. "Bekah, I mean."

"It was tough, and I'm not telling you this to bring you down or to get sympathy. But Maggie finally got it through my thick skull that if I let go of the loss, I wasn't being disloyal to Alison. That she wouldn't be forgotten. In fact, if I talked about her like this, it would keep her memory alive."

Maggie got up and knelt by his chair to take his hand and peer up at him. "I'm sure our little angel is smiling right now."

Jackson nodded. "I just wanted to tell you all so I could talk about her in the future, you know?"

"Yeah, man," Alex said. "We totally get it."

"We do," Coop added, and Riley nodded.

"Okay." Jackson released his anxiety on one long exhale. "It's almost time for the fireworks, and we should get the chairs set up before Alex decks us."

The good mood was once again restored, and Jackson felt lighter than he had in years. He didn't feel any less pain at mentioning his sweet child, but he felt more at peace. He looked down at Maggie. She was still staring at him, her eyes glowing with pride and something else. Love?

He smiled at her. "At the risk of incurring Alex's wrath, do you want to take a walk down to the water for some privacy?"

"You know I do." She got up quickly and tugged him to his feet.

Hand in hand, they walked toward the surging ocean, and he knew without a doubt in his mind that everything was going to be okay for them, and he could hope for a future together.

Maggie strolled next to Jackson toward the water and relished the feel of his hand cupping hers. She wanted to race down to the waves, but she didn't want to draw attention from their friends or the others gathered on the beach for the fireworks. So she maintained a deliberate pace, the sand squishing between her toes. The closer they came to the water, the colder the sand turned, and she stopped shy of the actual waves. There was no way she could handle the water's frigid temperature.

Jackson faced her. "I wanted to—"

She pressed her finger on that full lower lip, thankful to be able to do so with hope in her heart. She waited six long years to kiss him with that hope—to love him again—and she didn't want to wait another second. "There's just one thing before you say what you want to say."

"What?" he asked barely above a whisper.

"This." She rose up on her tiptoes and settled her lips on his. She kissed him hard. Passionately, making sure he could feel her unconditional love for him. Feel her joy in the brave way he'd spoken about their daughter. Know her hope for their future.

He swept his arm around her back and jerked her against his solid chest as if he was afraid he would lose her again. She raised her arms around his neck and tried to get even closer, kissing him back with everything she had. She lost track of time, of everything but the feel of his lips on hers.

An explosion sounded over the water. Jackson lifted his head, his gaze languid and dazed. She smiled at him and saw a red explosion of color behind his head. "Guess we're not the only fireworks tonight."

He smiled and caressed her hair. "Something I hope we'll still be saying when we're eighty."

"Why Jackson Lockhart, are you asking me to marry you?" she joked.

His smile evaporated, and he looked uncertain.

Had she said the wrong thing? Was he really not as ready as she thought?

"The thing is," he said, his gaze locked on hers. "I'm just starting to figure out how to deal with losing Alison. And how to let go of this unreasonable need I have to make sure others are okay. I know I can move forward with God's help. Your help, too, but I'm sure there will be setbacks along the way. Can you put up with that?"

She sighed out her relief. "I'm in the same situation with

losing Alison. As long as we keep the lines of communication open, I'm sure we can work it out."

He raked a hand over his hair. "Could you...would you...consider a life here in Cold Harbor? Maybe a position on our team as a forensic anthropologist?"

She blinked, then beamed at him. "I could. I would like that very much."

He exhaled loudly. "Then, yes." He got down on one knee and drew a ring box from his pocket.

"You planned this?"

He nodded and opened the box to reveal a solitaire diamond.

She loved that he chose a different ring for this new beginning together. "It's beautiful, Jackson."

He gazed up at her, love shining from his eyes. She remembered his proposal six years ago and everything they'd been through together rolled through her brain like a video of their past.

She got it then. Saw the good that had come from losing Alison. They were both stronger people now and were also more able to appreciate their love for each other because they knew how precious it was and how easily it could be lost.

Jackson lifted the ring from the velvet bed. "Maggie Turner, will you make me the happiest man in the world and marry me?"

"Yes!" The word burst from her mouth like the fireworks exploding over the ocean in electrifying colors.

He slid the ring on her finger. She dropped to the sand in front of him and flung her arms around his neck. "Yes. Yes. Yes."

He leaned back and caressed the side of her face. "What did I ever do to deserve you?"

"I feel the same way." She kept smiling at him and couldn't seem to stop.

Her heart was filled to capacity. They would have their happily ever after—that was certain now—and together after a lifetime of shared love, they would one day hold their precious Alison in their arms again, too.

Want to read other books in the Cold Harbor Series? Read on for a sneak peek of the next book in the Cold Harbor Series!

Dear Reader:

Thank you so much for reading COLD FURY, book 3 in my Cold Harbor series featuring Blackwell Tactical. You'll be happy to hear that there are additional books in this series!

Book 1 - COLD TERROR
Book 2 - COLD TRUTH
Book 3 - COLD FURY
Book 4 - COLD CASE
BOOK 5 - COLD FEAR
BOOK 6 - COLD PURSUIT

I'd like to invite you to learn more about the books in my Cold Harbor series as they release and about my other books by signing up for my newsletter. You'll also receive a FREE sneak peek of my latest book. I love to interact with and hear from readers, so hop on over to the link below and let's connect.

https://www.susansleeman.com/connect/

Susan Sleeman

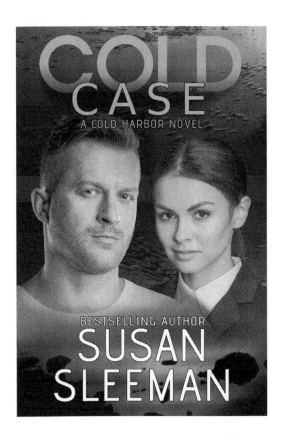

When her past comes back to haunt her...

Former FBI cyber security agent Eryn Calloway worked many cyber investigations during her career as an FBI agent and while serving as Blackwell Tactical's cyber expert. But when her computer is locked with ransomware, she suddenly finds herself facing the biggest investigation of all. Failure to solve the case and find the hacker could result in the loss of her very life.

**Can she let the one man who can protect her get close
enough to do so?**

Enter former Green Beret, deputy Trey Sawyer who offers to
serve as her bodyguard. Trey has been in love with Eryn for
a year, but she lost her husband several years ago and isn't
ready to open herself to the potential for pain again. She's
kept Trey at arm's length and wants to do so now—after all,
she can take care of herself. But she has a four-year-old
daughter to protect, so Eryn reluctantly agrees to let Trey
into her world. But when they're thrown together in a race
for her life, she has to combat both a vicious enemy—and
the pain from her past. Is Trey trustworthy enough to let
him into every area of her life, or is the risk too great?

∽

Chapter One

*Cancel your classes or your computer isn't the only thing that
will be DOA.*

Eryn Calloway couldn't look away from her computer.
Away from the blue screen—the visual known in the
computer world as the "blue screen of death," warning of a
fatal system error.

But this warning was different. Very different.

It wasn't a Windows error. Not a virus. Her machine
hadn't crashed.

Someone was threatening her life. Here. Now. At the
annual Policing in the Modern World Conference where
she was teaching computer courses as a representative of
her team, Blackwell Tactical.

How could this be?

She was smack dab in the middle of a crowd of law enforcement officers mingling in the lobby of The Dunes Resort and someone wanted her dead.

Craziness. She shook her head at the absurdity, but fear had a hold of her stomach and it wouldn't let go.

"Eryn?" Deputy Trey Sawyer's deep voice jolted her.

She whipped around to see him approaching her, weaving through the crowd.

If she hadn't recognized his voice, his red hair would make him easy to find in a crowd. But his voice stood out to her much like a mother instantly picked out her child's voice in a group. Not that Eryn's feelings for him were motherly. Not by any stretch of the imagination.

She filled her lungs with air and connected with his grayish-blue eyes that were often calm and reflective of his easygoing personality. But not today. He looked darkly dangerous and very intimidating.

Every bit of air she'd drawn in whooshed out. She'd never seen this side of him, but man, she liked it equally as well as the laid-back guy.

He ran his gaze over her. "You're as white as a sheet. What's wrong?"

No way she was telling him anything. He was the last guy she wanted to share her problem with.

She reached for the laptop screen to lower it. He shot out a hand and pressed it over hers, halting her movement. His touch amplified the usual tingle of excitement she felt in his presence, and her already stressed-out mind whirled.

She swallowed hard and did her best not to reveal her unease about the hack *and* about seeing him again. They'd danced around their mutual attraction for a year now, and she found him almost impossible to resist. *Almost.* But she managed it so far. The key was to eliminate the time they spent together.

Today was no exception. She would move on as soon as possible, and while he was here, she wouldn't display even a hint of her feelings. Not when she would never let things develop with him. Or any other man for that matter.

He bent forward to stare at the screen and released her hand. He worked the muscles in his strong jaw for a moment then turned his gaze on her, the intensity there making her gasp. "What in the world is going on, Eryn?"

"It's nothing." She tried to sound casual, but she didn't manage it.

"Right. *Nothing* made all the color drain from your face." He grabbed a chair and turned it to face her. He straddled the seat and rested powerful arms on the chair back.

She took a moment to look at him. Not a good idea, but then she didn't have good ideas around him. He wore black tactical pants much like hers, and an Under Armour tactical shirt in an army green color that fit him like a second set of skin, accentuating his muscular build and broad shoulders.

Her gaze wanted to linger there, but she forced it back to his face. She steeled her expression and her voice. "It's nothing. Leave it alone."

She closed her computer and started to get up.

He rested a hand on her shoulder, effectively stopping her from rising. She held there, midair, and refused to look at him.

"I can't let this go, and you know it." The vehemence in his tone surprised her. Where was the laid-back guy she knew? "Someone is threatening you, and you need help."

Right. *His* help. She shook his hand off and stood up. He was acting like most guys—assuming she wasn't capable of taking care of herself. But as a former FBI agent and cyber-security expert, she was capable. Very capable. She turned to glare at him and walk away, but his eyes were locked on her like a sniper eyeing his target. Leaving without discussing this was pointless. He would trail her and corner her in another location.

She sat back down and lifted her chin. "I can handle this."

His gaze softened, his eyes bluer now, a striking contrast to his rich red hair. "Why do you always think you need to be so tough?"

She *did* have to be tough in the law enforcement world to ensure that men took her seriously. Fortunately, her male teammates at Blackwell Tactical respected her skills and abilities.

She deflected his question with a wave of her hand. "Why do you have to interrogate me? I said I can handle it."

He eyed her but didn't budge.

"Look. I'm a cyber professional and know how to deal with this hack." She leaned closer so they wouldn't be overheard in the crowded lobby. "The guy deployed ransomware. You've likely heard of the software that locks a computer until the owner pays ransom to have it released. Well in this case, he doesn't want money. He probably did it to show off. It likely happened when I logged into the unsecured resort network. I'll restore my machine, trace the hack back to the offender, and turn him over to the authorities. End of story."

Trey shook his head. "That doesn't explain why this hacker wants you to cancel your classes, and he's threatening your life if you don't."

Her gut was twisted in a knot over that very thing, but she ignored Trey's concern. "He's likely just testing my competency."

Trey's eyes hardened to steel. "Or this person really does want you to stop teaching and is going to kill you if you don't."

Eryn sat back, putting a wall up between them. "You've been in law enforcement too long for your own good— seeing a problem where one doesn't exist."

"No." He planted his hands on the table. "I'm seeing what was right in front of my face before you closed your computer."

She didn't know how to respond, so she said nothing.

He made a low sound in his throat like a growl, then shook his head. "Tell me about your classes."

She wanted to rush up to her room to take care of the computer issue. But Trey was tenacious and wouldn't let it go until she explained, so she would get it over as quickly as possible. "I'm teaching two classes. One is about how every cell phone is unique and pictures taken on a cell can be traced back to an individual phone due to these unique characteristics."

He sat up a little higher. "I've never heard of that."

"It's a new discovery and not readily used yet, but I want detectives to start thinking about the possibilities of how to utilize this element in their investigations."

"Explain," he demanded.

At his tone, she thought about refusing, but again, he would keep badgering her until she answered. "Digital cameras are built identically, but manufacturing imperfections create tiny variations in the camera sensors. The variations cause some of the sensors' pixels to project slightly brighter or darker colors than they should—called pattern noise. It's not visible to the naked eye but can be found with deeper examination."

"Very interesting, but worth killing you over?" He shook his head. "I don't get that."

"I agree, which is why it's likely just an attention-grabbing measure."

"Don't be so quick to dismiss it without further thought."

She should've known he would keep after it. She would, too. The minute she reached her room. She shifted to stand.

"And the other class?" he asked, stilling her.

She had to appease him. "It's about the Internet of Things."

"Is that a new term? I've never heard of it."

"Not new, but fairly recent, I guess. IoT devices are those with on and off switches and connect to the Internet and/or to each other. Things like cars, televisions, phones, and refrigerators."

"Yeah, I can see that. Computers have invaded our world. There's a 'smart' *everything* these days."

"I know, isn't it great?" She chuckled.

He frowned. If he couldn't laugh at her joke then he really was upset.

"What are you going to do about the hack?" he asked.

"First, I need to get my PowerPoint presentations up and running on my computer so I can teach my next class."

"Now wait a minute." He sat forward. "You're not going to ignore the warning."

"Wouldn't you?"

He blinked. "Yeah, likely, but—"

"But you're not a helpless girl like me and can protect yourself," she finished for him and crossed her arms.

"Wait, no. I don't think you're helpless."

"But I *do* need protecting."

He rolled his eyes and ran his fingers through his fiery red hair, leaving it in disarray. "I can't win here, can I?"

"Honestly, no. I get tired of the double standards in law enforcement. Either I'm as capable as you are or I'm not."

He clenched his jaw. "You know that's not all it is. I care about you, and when I care about someone I do my best to make sure they're safe. Just like you and the rest of your team have each other's backs. If one of the team members is in danger, the others step up."

He was right, and she couldn't argue. He knew the team well. He was good friends with Eryn's boss, Gage Blackwell who owned Blackwell Tactical. Their friendship went back to their military days when Gage was a SEAL and Trey served as a Green Beret, and they'd worked on a joint team together. And a year ago, Trey helped Blackwell out when someone threatened Gage's wife. That was when Eryn had met Trey. Since then, he'd attended several of their law enforcement trainings at the team compound an hour up the coast in Cold Harbor.

She didn't mind acknowledging the team dynamics, but she wouldn't respond to his comment of caring about her. That would take them through a rabbit hole she didn't want to go down.

"You're right," she said. "We do look after each other and have a strong bond. Maybe stronger than most teams since injuries took us out of our chosen professions. It's a bond we all share. But we don't overreact, and *you're* overreacting, Trey."

He shot her a testy look. "No. I'm stepping up here like the team would. You're not going to stop me, so you might as well quit wasting your effort trying." He jabbed his finger on the table. "You can't teach the classes."

"See? You *are* overreacting." His behavior made her even

more stubborn. "I'm not going to back down on that. I'll be teaching my scheduled classes."

He jerked his legs back, the muscles rippling against his pant leg as if he was ready to spring from his chair and fight her foe. He grimaced, but it disappeared as fast as it started. He'd been shot in the leg helping Hannah and still hadn't recovered.

He met her gaze and held it. "You're not teaching if I have anything to say about it."

She worked hard to remain calm and not snap at him. "Why would you have anything to say about it?"

"Because someone has to watch out for you."

"Please," she said and resisted rolling her eyes. "There are five big strapping guys on our team. They're all I need."

"So, you're going to tell them about this, then?"

She hadn't planned on bringing it up. Not when there wasn't proof that this was nothing more than an idle threat. But she wouldn't tell Trey that. Lying went against her Christian beliefs, and she wouldn't start now simply to calm Trey down.

He glared at her. "You tell Gage or I will."

Trey wouldn't hesitate to call his buddy Gage. It would be far better coming from her. "Fine. I'll tell him."

"Today."

She stood and stared down on him. "I'll do it the moment I get my computer up and running."

"How long will that take?"

She rubbed her neck to ease the tension. "If all goes well, a few hours or so."

"Okay, I'll cut you some slack and give you three hours. If you haven't told Gage by then, I will."

She eyed him. "You really are a pain, you know that?"

He smiled, his eyes softening. "A pain who cares about you and doesn't want to see anything bad happen to you."

She blew out a breath. "I appreciate that you care, Trey. I just wish you didn't care so stinkin' much."

~

Trey didn't like letting Eryn walk away from him when she was irritated with him. For so many reasons it was hard to count. But most of all, he knew she hated it when guys underestimated her abilities. Was one of her pet peeves actually, and he fell prey to it all the time.

At five-foot-seven, he thought of her as petite compared to his six-foot-four height. A petite and very pretty woman. She had long black glossy hair that she usually wore in a ponytail, but today it was free flowing and swung with each step. She wore her usual black tactical pants and a no-nonsense knit shirt revealing upper body muscles that she worked hard to build and maintain.

She looked tough, but at the same time managed to appear so feminine that the combination did a number on him. Couple that with her big brown eyes, delicate eyebrows, and a full bottom lip that he dreamed of kissing for months now, and he was captivated by her. Smitten—if truth be told.

He got up to keep an eye on her, his right thigh aching with the movement. He'd suffered a gunshot wound to the thigh when he was helping apprehend a thug bent on killing Gage's wife, and Trey had been confined to desk duty since then. He was starting to believe it wasn't going to fully heal, and he would never go back to patrol.

Eryn slowly made her way through the sea of officers lingering between classes, and many of them paused to follow her progress across the room. A stab of jealousy bit into him. Not that he thought she would be any more interested in one of them than she was in him.

She lost her husband four years ago and was solely focused on raising her four-year-old daughter Bekah. Trey had once asked Eryn out, and she said she had no time for a man in her life. But then, there were moments when he caught her looking at him with such longing, he couldn't help but hope she would change her mind if he was just persistent. So he had been. Very persistent because she was so worth it.

But now? Now he needed to lay back. His leg wasn't one hundred percent, making his future employment uncertain. Not a good time to start dating, and he wouldn't want to lead her on. He had to get his mind right about his future job before embarking on a relationship.

He sighed out a long breath. Life was so complicated at times, even with God's guidance. He knew God heard his pleas since the injury and would point him in the right direction, but Trey had never been faced with such a big U-turn in life. God would show Trey the way as long as he kept the lines of communication open and didn't step out before the timing was right. But man, he wanted to step out. Wanted to get back to work. Forget the mounds of paperwork and get back to actively helping others.

He shook his head, clearing his mind, and started through the lobby toward the coffee stand in the corner. His leg throbbed with each step, but he tried to ignore it to smile at the barista as he ordered a black cup of coffee. None of that fancy stuff for him.

"Trey," Gage Blackwell's voice came from over Trey's shoulder.

He turned and schooled his expression so he didn't let

on about his worry for Eryn. As much as he'd pushed her, he wanted her to have a chance to explain the situation to Gage.

"What's up?" Trey asked.

"I was hoping I'd run into you." Gage clapped Trey on the back. "How about we sit down for a minute?"

"If this is about the job offer, I'm not ready to go there yet." When Trey had been shot, Gage offered Trey a job on the team. Trey wouldn't mind joining Blackwell, but he couldn't be around Eryn every day. Not with the way he felt about her when she didn't return the feelings.

"Leg's getting better then?" Gage asked.

"Nah, but after the latest surgery, I still have a few more weeks of PT so I'm hopeful."

Gage gave him a knowing look, and Trey didn't like it. Gage suffered a permanent arm injury as a SEAL and was faced with riding a desk or leaving the team. Like most men in spec ops, he didn't do desk duty well so he left his team. Everyone on Blackwell Tactical had faced a similar situation. Trey was heading down the same path, but not willingly.

"I hope it works out for you," Gage said. "So this isn't about a job. Got a minute then?"

Trey nodded. "Let's find some place quieter."

He led Gage to the area where he and Eryn had talked. Her face, white against her dark hair, came to mind again, and his gut cramped. He resolved to find a way to get her to agree to let him keep an eye on her until this situation was resolved.

He sat on a plump sofa in a beachy turquoise color and moved around until he eliminated the ache in his leg.

Gage took a seat in a matching plush chair across from

him. "Did I mention that I'm looking for a forensic person for the team?"

Trey shook his head.

"Law enforcement training and protection services are still our main focus, but the number of clients needing us to investigate unsolved crimes has grown rapidly. So we need a forensic expert."

Trey took a sip of the rich black coffee. "Makes sense. Especially since you want to collect the evidence in a manner that would make it usable in court."

Gage nodded. "But you also know one of my main purposes of starting Blackwell is to offer injured soldiers or officers a second chance at a job they love."

"So you're looking for a crime scene investigator who's been injured and benched."

"Exactly. And I'm striking out."

"Yeah, not too many CSI's get injured on the job." Trey rested his cup on his knee. "Did you try the Portland Police Bureau? Their criminalists are required to be sworn officers, and they still work patrol jobs for protests and riots."

Gage shook his head. "Do you have any contacts there?"

"Yeah, I have a buddy on the force. I can give him a call to see if he knows anyone who fits the bill."

"Appreciate it, man." Gage sat back and crossed his feet at the ankles. "I'm a little surprised to see you here."

"Why's that?"

"Didn't think you'd need a lot of training for desk duty." Gage chuckled.

Trey forced a smile. He hadn't reached the point where he could joke about his potential loss of career yet. And besides, Trey thought Gage knew exactly why he was here. Why he always signed up for other trainings at Blackwell's compound, too. Shoot, the whole team probably knew he had it bad for Eryn. He doubted he was very subtle about it.

"Seriously, man, if the leg doesn't improve enough to go back on patrol, let me know. I'll always have a job open for you."

"You don't have to feel guilty, you know. Just because I was helping you out when it happened."

"Actually, I credit you with saving Hannah's life and will always be in your debt, but this is business. I'm smart enough to know you'd be a real asset to the team. But don't go telling anyone that. I won't admit to saying it." Gage grinned, but he looked over Trey's shoulder, and his smile vanished.

Trey pivoted to see what had changed Gage's good mood and spotted Eryn storming their way.

"Wonder what's got Eryn so mad?" Gage mused.

Trey didn't know, but he suspected it had to do with the threat and computer issue. Maybe she failed at restoring her computer.

She locked gazes with Trey and stormed straight ahead. Her muscular legs took her through the crowd in seconds. Breathing hard, she came to a stop in front of him. She looked like a fierce lion planning to defend her cub, and the wild beauty in her expression got Trey's heart pumping hard.

"You couldn't wait, could you?" She locked onto his gaze like a Sidewinder missile. "You had to rat me out."

"I didn't—"

"What happened to giving me three hours? It's been less than thirty minutes."

"Like I said, I—"

"I thought you were a man of your word."

"Eryn," Gage said calmly. "Breathe and give the guy a chance to speak."

She fisted her hands on her hips and glared at him. "Well?"

"I didn't tell Gage anything. He asked to talk to me about finding a forensic person for the team."

"Oh." Her anger evaporated from her expression, and she seemed to melt right in front of them.

"I thought..." She shook her head. "I'm sorry, Trey. There was no call for doubting your word."

Gage looked back and forth between them, his gaze questioning. "But apparently there *is* call for me to wonder what the two of you are keeping from me."

Eryn sank down on the sofa next to Trey. She didn't seem to realize how close she was sitting to him, but he could feel the heat of her leg resting nearby, and he had a hard time focusing on anything but that.

"I got a ransomware notice on my laptop," she said, her breathing under control. "And Trey happened to be passing by and saw it."

"Ransomware?" Gage shook his head. "I can see that happening to others on the team, but you? I can hardly believe it."

"I know, right?" She frowned. "I'm never going to live it down."

"Truer words have never been said." Gage chuckled. "Is that why you didn't want to tell me?"

"Sort of." Eryn glanced at Trey.

He figured her look meant she wanted him to back down about mentioning the warning, but he wasn't about to do so. He opened his mouth to say that when she faced Gage again. "It wasn't your typical ransomware warning."

"How's that?" Gage's eyes widened.

"They didn't ask for payment to release my computer. Not that I would pay it anyway. No point. I back up my machine daily and can restore it with little effort. And this is my travel computer so there's not much on it anyway."

"Travel computer?" Trey asked.

"When I do trainings I often have to access unsecured networks like here at the resort. So I don't want to risk having confidential information on my machine in case I'm hacked."

"But what if you're working an investigation?" Trey asked. "Don't you need access to more information then?"

She nodded. "In that case, I don't access unsecured networks. I use my phone as a hot spot instead."

Trey nodded. He'd heard of using a cell phone like a wireless router, but honestly, he didn't know how it worked.

"I've already traced the ransomware," she continued. "My class files were infected. I was on my way to talk to the conference director about it when I saw you two talking." A sheepish look crossed her face.

"You mentioned this wasn't a typical ransomware warning," Gage said.

She nodded. "The threat actor didn't ask for money or Bitcoins. He wants me to stop teaching my classes."

It often seemed like she spoke another language, and Trey always learned something new when he talked to her. "What's a threat actor?"

"The person or entity responsible for a malicious act. They're often called hackers by laypeople, but in the IT world they're called actors."

"Well this hacker or actor or whatever you want to call him says if you don't cancel your classes he'll kill you," Trey added. "Or at least that's what I thought the warning meant when it said you'd be DOA if you didn't stop."

Gage frowned and locked his gaze on Eryn. "And you didn't want to tell me about this—why?"

"Because of the way you're looking at me."

"And how's that exactly?"

"Like you want to lock me in my room and not let me out until this guy is caught. Or worse, send me back to Cold Harbor for my own protection."

"Neither of those are bad ideas," Trey said.

Eryn fired him an irritated look. "I committed to teaching here, and I *will* follow through on that. The officers only have so much money and time for continuing ed in a year, and I won't make them miss out."

Gage scrunched his dark eyebrows together. "Then we need to be smart about this. I'll assign someone on the team to your protection."

"Who?" she asked. "You, Riley, and Alex are holding classes here. Coop and Jackson are training at the compound. Any change to that would create the same problem."

"I'm free," Trey offered. "And glad to step in."

"Perfect solution," Gage readily agreed.

"No," Eryn said. "No. No way."

"Why not?" Gage asked. "Trey is as capable as anyone on the team."

"It's not that."

"Then what?"

Eryn nipped on her lip, and Trey knew she was trying to come up with anything other than to mention that he had a thing for her.

He could solve that problem for her. "I think she's worried that I've fallen for her and can't keep my hands off her."

"We all know that, but so far you seem to be able to control yourself." Gage grinned.

Eryn frowned. "It's not funny."

"I know," Gage said. "But you've got to admit, it paints a pretty interesting picture."

"Not one I want to paint." She crossed her arms.

"Look," Trey said. "If I promise not to even hint at my interest in you other than to make sure you're safe, will you let me do this for you?"

She frowned and looked like she planned to refuse. Maybe she should. Because even frowning, he wanted to kiss those lips. Still, he couldn't let her off the hook. "If you won't think about yourself, think about Bekah."

She shot him a frustrated look. "Low blow bringing my daughter into this."

"May be low," Gage said. "But he has a point. Your mom and Bekah came along on this trip, so you need to think of them, too."

"I'll send them back to the compound."

"How?" Trey asked. "The compound is an hour down the coast and no one's free to escort them."

"Fine," she said, but crossed her arms, her eyes still locked on Trey. "You can be my bodyguard, but you need to promise to keep things professional between us at all times."

"I promise I'll do my best."

"Glad that's settled." Gage fixed his focus on Eryn. "The guys and I have a three-bedroom suite. We'll move out so you and your family can have it. That way the hacker won't know the exact room where you're staying, and it'll give Trey a room in the same suite, too."

"You're right, *if* the hacker doesn't have her under surveillance," Trey added.

"I can't have you give up such a nice room," Eryn said ignoring Trey's comment.

Gage waved a hand. "I only booked a suite so we'd have a place for the team to meet. We can still meet there, right?"

"Of course."

"Good. Then it's settled. I'll text the others to let them know we're moving."

"Bekah's napping so we'll move our things when she wakes up... if that works for you."

"Sounds good."

She stood. "Thanks, Gage. We can always count on you."

Trey got up, and the jealousy that hit him earlier took a bite again. He wanted Eryn to think the same thing about him. He was dependable and reliable and would be there for her every minute she needed him. She could count on that.

She glanced at him. "I suppose you'll want to come with me now."

He nodded and chose not to comment on the fact that her expression said she would rather go a few rounds with a rattlesnake than have him accompany her. He would have his work cut out for him, but he was always up for a challenge.

Especially when that challenge was someone as beautiful and captivating as Eryn Calloway.

Available now at most online booksellers!

~

Also stay tuned for - Riley and Leah's story in **COLD FEAR!**

ABOUT SUSAN

SUSAN SLEEMAN is a bestselling and award-winning author of more than 30 inspirational/Christian and clean read romantic suspense books. In addition to writing, Susan also hosts the website, TheSuspenseZone.com.

Susan currently lives in Oregon, but has had the pleasure of living in nine states. Her husband is a retired church music director and they have two beautiful daughters, a very special son-in-law, and an adorable grandson.

For more information visit:
www.susansleeman.com

Made in the USA
Columbia, SC
17 July 2018